MYSTERY
BY THE SEA

BOOKS BY VERITY BRIGHT

MYSTERY
BY THE SEA

VERITY BRIGHT

bookouture

Published by Bookouture in 2021

An imprint of Storyfire Ltd.
Carmelite House
50 Victoria Embankment
London EC4Y 0DZ

www.bookouture.com

ISBN: 978-1-80019-394-9
eBook ISBN: 978-1-80019-393-2

To Mike, for reading, and liking, the Lady Swift books even though he really shouldn't.

'Happiness consists of living each day as if it were the first day of your honeymoon and the last day of your vacation.' – LEO TOLSTOY

CHAPTER 1

''Tis terrible bad luck.'

Lady Eleanor Swift smiled. 'Really, Polly, whatever do you mean? You've no need to back up whenever we happen to meet each other. You could fit six people across the width of each stair with ease.'

'Mustn't cross on the stairs, your ladyship,' her young maid whispered. 'Begging your pardon for saying so, but 'tis terrible bad luck.'

'Ah, I see!' Eleanor frowned. 'Well, we definitely don't need any more of that!' She tucked some of her wilder red curls behind her ear. 'Perhaps we had better coordinate our ups and downs this morning then, Polly? Otherwise' – she peered over the polished oak bannisters at Clifford, her impeccably turned out butler, who was consulting a meticulously handwritten list in the hall below – 'we might both be in trouble.'

Her young maid swallowed hard and fiddled with the lace at the top of her apron. 'Oh lummy, Mr Clifford will be spitting feathers if things get late.'

Eleanor smiled at the image this conjured up. 'Don't worry, he's just keen to make sure everything goes to schedule because we're all going… on holiday!'

Polly squealed, then clapped her hand to her mouth. Clifford peered up at them disapprovingly. He pulled a fob watch from his pocket, consulted it with a sniff, and then shut the case with a resounding snap that echoed round the marble entrance hall.

'Oops!' Eleanor whispered, gesturing to Polly that they had better both get moving.

In the doorway of her bedroom, she paused, wincing at the tangled mountain of clothes on her bed and the straggle of shoes that littered the floor.

Oh botheration, why is it so hard to choose what to take, Ellie? It's only a week by the seaside. A flashback to her days cycling abroad brought a wistful smile to her lips. *You learned the art of travelling light then.* She looked at the clothes on the bed again and groaned. She'd crossed the world with less luggage. But this was 1921, England, and she was lady of the manor now, and was expected to look, and behave, like a lady. She sighed. *The trouble is, Ellie, you really don't feel like one!*

Mind you, it had only been a few months ago that she'd found out her uncle, Lord Byron Henley, from whom she'd inherited Henley Hall the year before, had been murdered. And only a few months ago that she'd broken off a – for her – long-running romance with a dashing young lord.

She shook her head. *Let the holiday decide what's next, Ellie. Kick up your heels, relax and have fun.*

'Right, best start packing then,' she said aloud.

A discreet cough interrupted her. She spun round to see Clifford in the doorway, his eyes averted so as not to be looking into her bedroom. Eleanor, having been brought up by bohemian parents abroad for much of her life, smiled at his propriety.

'Oh step in, Clifford, do. We can't talk if we aren't actually in the same part of the house, for goodness' sake.'

'My lady.' He turned to face her but remained on the other side of the threshold. 'I came to ask if your cases were ready for me to remove to the Rolls.'

'Ah! Not quite.'

'Not quite?'

'Alright, not at all. I confess my brain has gone to mush. I can't think of what I might need or want. I mean, it's the Grand Hotel in Brighton, and yet it's also the English seaside in March. How does one balance the height of glamour with possible drizzle and gusty winds?'

'Perhaps if you had prepared a list yesterday, or the day before that, as I suggested?'

She laughed. 'Oh dash it, I've been too excited that's the problem. After all that nasty business at Christmas, you, the staff and I deserve a break. Especially as it will also be my birthday while we're away.' Even though Clifford was her butler, she never really thought of him as 'staff'.

'And Master Gladstone?' Clifford added at the sound of crashing coming from Eleanor's adjoining bathroom. 'Although it seems he may already be occupied with some mischief of his own as usual.'

Gladstone was the elderly, but wilful, bulldog she'd inherited from her uncle along with the Hall, and, as she was finding out, its secrets.

'Gladstone?' she called out.

A grunt came in reply as he appeared, a soggy leather slipper covered in face cream hanging from his mouth.

Eleanor wagged her finger at him, trying not to smile. 'Naughty boy, you are going to make us late!' She stole a sideways peek at Clifford, who rolled his eyes.

'Something that is already late, cannot be made late, only later, my lady.'

Eleanor did her best to look serious. 'I shall be ready in ten minutes. Not a moment more.'

'Then, I shall see you in a *lady's* ten minutes.' His coat-tails swung round the door frame as he swept off silently down the corridor.

'A lady's ten minutes! The cheek! He means half an hour. Come on, Gladstone.' Eleanor clapped her hands. 'We'll show him. Ten minutes it will be, even if I arrive in Brighton woefully unprepared.'

She pulled her late uncle's fob watch from her skirt pocket and laid it on the bed. It was a precious memento of one of the few times she'd shared with him. Grabbing the nearest case, she began flinging clothes in.

'Underthings,' she said to the bulldog, who now sat on the bedroom rug with the cream-covered slipper. 'Mustn't forget underthings.' With both arms, she scooped everything from the second drawer in her walnut dresser and threw those on top of the muddle in the case. Adding three sets of shoes, she consulted the pocket watch. 'Ha! Still time for toiletries.'

Thus she came whizzing down the stairs nine and a half minutes later, red-faced and breathless but glowing in triumph. She jumped down the last step, landing next to Clifford's highly polished shoes.

'Ten minutes exactly!'

'Most impressive, my lady.' He gave his customary half bow. 'Will you take a coffee while Mrs Butters attends to your cases?'

Eleanor had inherited Mrs Butters, her motherly housekeeper, along with her other staff, on her uncle's death. Why Clifford would expect her to lug the cases out to the car, however, she couldn't fathom.

'May I ask why, Clifford?'

'To re-pack for you, my lady.'

She slapped the carved oak newel post and then shook her hand at the pain that shot up her wrist.

'Look here, I shall hit thirty years of age during this wonderful holiday of ours. I know you mean well, but I'm not actually the irritating nine-year-old you remember from the last time I was here.'

'If you say so, my lady.' His eyes gave a rare twinkle as he gestured towards the bright sitting room in the left-hand tower that flanked the front entrance. As well as being her late uncle's valet, Clifford had been his wingman and confidante for more years than she had been alive. And, despite his sometimes stiff manner, their relationship was developing along similar lines. 'Shall we?'

Only an hour and a quarter later than Clifford's schedule had demanded, a smart row of cases stood in the hallway ready for loading into the Rolls.

Gladstone had been bribed to behave with a bone he was now burying in the garden, and the ladies were assembled in a neat line at the bottom of the stairs. Eleanor smiled at them in the reflection in the gold-framed mirror above the telephone table as she pinned her hat.

'Ladies, we're ready, at last.' She turned round. 'Are you sure you'll be alright with bringing the other luggage down by train tomorrow?'

The plan was for Eleanor, Clifford and Gladstone to go by car, and the rest of the staff to join them the following day. The ladies would stay around the corner in a guest house run by an old friend of Mrs Butters.

Her housekeeper stepped forward, her wide smile and gentle demeanour giving her the air of the favourite aunt Eleanor had never had. 'My lady, we'll be right as a bucket of ninepences. We're all so excited to be coming as well. But without you, Mr Clifford and Master Gladstone here, we can scrub Henley Hall from top to bottom so you come home to the shiniest new pin you ever saw.'

Eleanor smiled. With her previous somewhat erratic and nomadic life, she had never envisaged Henley Hall feeling like home, but in the space of a short, crazy year, it was beginning to. She looked round at the four faces, thinking for the umpteenth time how lucky she was that she'd inherited such wonderful staff. That they had also become her new family brought a lump to her throat.

'I do wish you'd just take the day off though. To relax and pack and whatever.' All three of the ladies shook their heads vigorously. 'I also wish that we could have persuaded Joseph to join us. And Silas.'

Mrs Butters clucked her tongue. 'You'll never get old muddy boots to go on holiday with us women. The very thought would send him off hiding in that shed of his. Especially since you had that stove installed in there.'

Joseph had been the gardener at the Hall for more years that anyone could remember and felt more comfortable around plants than people.

Eleanor nodded. 'I know. But Silas?'

Silas was one of the Hall's, and her deceased uncle's, many secrets. She'd still never seen the elusive gamekeeper and had come to realise he was more of a security guard with perhaps some questionable methods and a past to match. But he had done an admirable job since her arrival, especially as she had been caught up in a startling number of murder cases in her short time there.

Clifford shook his head. 'Silas has sent his apologies, and his gratitude at your invitation, my lady, but he is not quite the man for donkey rides and ice cream. He will ensure the house is safe during our absence.'

Polly clapped her hands, her eyes wide at the description of their upcoming week away at the seaside.

Mrs Trotman, Eleanor's warm-hearted but no-nonsense cook, stepped forward with a large wicker hamper. 'I hope you find the picnic to your liking, my lady.'

'Picnic?' Clifford pursed his lips.

Eleanor fixed him with a good-humoured, but steely gaze. 'Yes, a picnic, Clifford. This is a holiday. Picnics are my most favourite thing in the world and as we are so behind with our schedule' – she ignored his pointed look – 'we shan't have time to pull into every eating establishment en route. Anyway, you would only sniff and declare each place unsuitable to dine in for a lady of my position.' She turned to her cook. 'Thank you, Mrs Trotman. Whatever you have prepared will be delicious, as always. I shall have to restrain myself from starting in on it before we have cleared the driveway.'

Clifford hastily picked up two of the cases. 'My lady, perhaps you would like to depart now?' He set them down again to pull open the double front doors. In doing so, he revealed the postman walking up the steps.

'Post, Mr Clifford,' he said unnecessarily as he held out a bundle of letters. He raised his cap to Eleanor. 'Good morning, Lady Swift. Enjoy your holiday.'

'Thank you, I fully intend to.' Being lady of the manor in a small village nestled in the Chiltern Hills meant that everyone knew your business, often before you did. 'I'll take the letters, Clifford. Would you mind carrying on with the cases?'

'Very good, my lady.'

Alone in the hall for a few moments, she shuffled through the post.

Ooh, that looks like an invitation, Ellie. She ran her finger over the embossed envelope. *Hopefully nothing too stuffy.* The second letter bore the stamp of South Africa. Undoubtedly, Thomas Walker, her old boss, imploring her again to return to her old job heading up the exploration of new destinations for his famous travel company. She looked up at a portrait of her late Uncle Byron and shook her head. 'No, thank you, Mr Walker, certainly not at the moment. I feel I have unfinished business here.'

Well, it ought to be attending to your love life, Ellie. It would be shambolic if it wasn't non-existent. Pulling herself together, she turned the next envelope up the right way and frowned. The writing was familiar, but then again, perhaps not? It bore a Brighton postmark.

Maybe it was the hotel confirming their reservation, as it had been a rather sudden decision to go.

'My lady.' Clifford's voice cut into her thoughts. 'Forgive my insistence, but if you start opening your post, we shall be fortunate to make Brighton before dark. Especially,' – he nodded at the wicker hamper he had picked up – 'if we are to stop for a picnic.'

'Picnics,' Eleanor corrected. 'In the plural, please, Clifford. Brighton is almost eighty miles away, I shall be ravenous more than once.'

He gave a discreet cough.

'Alright, out with it,' she said resignedly, shoving the letters into her handbag.

'The Grand Hotel is actually one hundred and twenty-three miles from Henley Hall. At an average speed of twenty-five miles an hour, it will take us just under five hours, not allowing for traffic or picnics.'

'Aha, watch and learn.' She pulled on her leather driving gloves and flexed her fingers. 'I shall simply drive faster.'

Although she knew him not to be of a religious persuasion, she was sure she saw him cross himself.

CHAPTER 2

Negotiating the heavy Rolls around the many tight bends of the country lanes was giving Eleanor a headache. Determined to prove she had mastered the car, she ignored Clifford's discreet, but constant, flinching as they missed stone walls and other vehicles by mere inches.

'Lucky you did such a thorough job of teaching me to drive, Clifford.'

'Thank you, my lady, but if you recall our lessons were somewhat interrupted at the regrettable discovery of a dead body.'

'Gosh, don't remind me.' She shuddered. 'It was a good thing in one way. Any more lessons and I fear you would have developed a nervous twitch.'

'Would have?' he muttered. At normal volume, he added, 'If you will forgive my observation, Master Gladstone is looking a little pale around his gills.'

She craned her neck to glimpse the dejected bulldog on the back seat in her rear-view mirror. As the car swung around the s-bends, he leaned first one way, and then the other, like a canine metronome.

'Nonsense, he's sulking because you won't let him sit in your footwell.'

'That is on account of there being insufficient space, given the length of my legs.'

She called out to the bulldog on the back seat, 'That, and he's worried you'll crease his trousers terribly, Gladstone!'

'Pheasants! Brake!' Clifford said sharply as a procession of the stately birds stepped out of the hedgerow. She stamped on the brakes and grimaced as the car came to a juddering stop.

He ran a gloved finger along his collar. 'It seems those birds are doubly blessed. They have not only escaped the perils of the car but also the gun. The shooting season finished only four weeks ago.'

She watched the birds step leisurely up the opposite bank and disappear into the tangled blackthorn hedge, the buds of its early white flowers brushing their long, striped tail feathers. 'Buckinghamshire is such a beautiful county, Clifford. In its own way, it's every bit as magical as some of the so-called exotic places I cycled through. Look at the Chilterns and Cotswolds so verdant, ever rising and falling, every skyline fringed with trees. And spring has such an exciting air about it, don't you find?'

Clifford turned in his seat to face her. 'Indeed, my lady. However, the Rolls is still stopped at an angle in the middle of the road.'

'Ah, so it is.'

'Perhaps you might wish to swap seats?'

Half an hour later Eleanor conceded that enjoying the picnic while Clifford drove was, in fact, a sound idea. With Gladstone's front paws on her lap, his tail wagged ever more furiously with each waxed paper parcel she opened. 'Gracious, Mrs Trotman has done us proud. Ham and egg pie, three types of sandwiches, those divine mini cheese-and-chive twists she makes and a Thermos of piping hot coffee.'

Clifford reached behind the passenger seat and retrieved an oval leather case, which he held out to her.

'Aha, and a small toast to kick the holiday off to a splendid start. Sherry, is it?'

'A particularly fine Oloroso, my lady. His lordship's favourite and his firm tradition on this very journey to the Grand Hotel, Brighton.'

'Thank you, Clifford.' She ran her finger along the little silver buckle of the case. 'I wish he could be with us. Especially on my birthday.'

'As do I, my lady. But he would heartily support your decision to take a rest at the seaside.'

'A rest,' she mused. 'Now I do like the sound of that. No nasty business. No sleepless nights trying to work through a notebook's worth of impossible clues. And definitely no heartache over a certain gentleman.'

Clifford cleared his throat.

'Over two certain gentlemen,' she admitted, catching his eye and hastily looking away. 'Anyway, I have decided I shall be a donkey ride and scandalous amounts of ice cream sort of girl for the duration of our little sojourn.'

'That is heartening news, my lady.'

They drove on in amiable silence save for Eleanor's exclamations as she savoured yet another delicious mouthful and Gladstone's soft whine for another titbit. Clifford peppered the journey with facts about the many sights they passed, her butler's encyclopaedic knowledge never ceasing to amaze her.

As the sleepy lanes of Buckinghamshire gave way to the more densely populated villages of Oxfordshire's flint cottages, Eleanor delighted in imagining the families who inhabited them, their lives and loves. Then, in the outer reaches of Berkshire, Eleanor asked Clifford to slow as they came to a lane lined with giant rhododendrons, sporting pink, purple and deep-blue flowers.

'Look at those, Clifford. They are so beautiful.'

Clifford seemed unmoved by their beauty. 'This lane borders Stratfield Saye House, my lady, once the home of His Grace, the Duke of Wellington.'

'And he found time to organise his gardeners to create this wondrous display? Amazing.'

'Perhaps you will find the next instalment of your sightseeing tour even more amazing, my lady.' Clifford turned left onto a long, straight road lined on both sides with eighty-foot-high sequoia trees. 'Planted as a memorial to His Grace.'

'Wow!' was all she could manage as she stared up at the hundred strong giant redwood trees. They reminded her of how much her late uncle had loved America, particularly the cowboys. He'd even gone so far as to ask Clifford to call him 'Tex' when it was just the two of them. She smiled. Uncle Byron really had been a proper English eccentric.

Two hours further on, Eleanor was feeling contented but stiff and fatigued from lack of movement as the steep hills of Surrey ceded into the chalk downs of Sussex. As the Rolls crested the last white-scarred escarpment, she slapped the dashboard. 'I win!'

Clifford pulled the Rolls to a stop to let her drink in the view. Despite the weakness of the March sunshine, the distant green-grey sea shimmered like mermaid's scales.

'Congratulations, my lady. You did indeed see the sea first.'

'And now I'm overcome by the urge to run down to the sea waving a bucket and spade. How peculiar.'

'Perhaps arriving in elegant style at the Grand Hotel might be more appropriate? I can discreetly secure you the requisite sandcastle-making equipment later if you wish?'

She laughed. 'Under the guise of there being a fictitious niece or nephew lurking in the offing, no doubt. You know, I shall reach the ripe old age of thirty this week and, until now, I have never spent a holiday at the English seaside.'

'I know, and I hope this one will create an album's worth of happy memories to make up for all those you missed. But that won't happen if we do not actually reach our journey's end. With your permission?'

As they finished descending the long hill into the main town, Brighton's four-mile parade didn't disappoint Eleanor's expectations. With the sea to their right and the long run of exquisitely built Regency townhouses to their left, she felt she had been transported back in time to the 1820s. Punctuated only by a few narrow roads joining the parade, the elegant line of crisp, pale-stuccoed buildings looked wonderfully regal. On each floor, decorative bay windows and doors gave on to intricate scrollwork balconies with commanding views of the sea. The architectural era's signature columns rose beside each smartly painted black or red front door. Many of them were entwined in climbing plants that would soon burst forth in fragrant flower, albeit several weeks after Eleanor and her staff were due to be back home.

'This is the Grand, my lady.' Clifford swung the Rolls into the long horseshoe entrance of the ten-storey palatial building.

She looked around and then up. Above her soared a towering monolith of cream stone, a row of ornate balconies gracing the floor-to-ceiling windows of each room. The columned arches of the elegantly imposing square tower at each end of the roofline added even more grandeur.

'Perfectly beautiful.' She clapped her hands in excitement. 'Now I suddenly feel about nine years old.'

He turned to peer at her. 'Perhaps that feeling might be contained until you are safely ensconced alone in your suite?'

'So I can burn up some of my excitement by jumping up and down on the bed, you mean? I seriously doubt it.' She noticed a frown on his face as he alighted from the car and came round to open her door. 'What's wrong, Clifford?'

He pursed his lips as she stepped out. 'Oh, I see what you mean.' She didn't mind opening her own door. After all, she'd done everything for herself before inheriting her uncle's fortune.

However, even she knew at a hotel as, well, grand as the Grand, a doorman would normally do so.

Clifford's frown deepened as they climbed the entrance steps and reached the red-carpeted ornate glass porch that ran the full width of the hotel.

'No concierge either?' Eleanor tutted. 'Not quite the service I expected.'

'Nor one you will be left to accept, my lady,' Clifford said with a sniff as he held the door open for her and followed her inside.

In the lobby, Eleanor paused. A disconcerting hush permeated the building. Stepping past the grand piano adorned with a lavish floral display, her heels made no sound as the thick mulberry design Wilton carpet made it seem as if she were walking on air. The cream walls and white ceiling roses shone with the soft golden glow from the many rococo chandeliers. She caught Clifford's eye and whispered, 'Something feels very odd.'

'Indubitably, my lady!' He slapped the palm of his hand on the top of the brass bell on the lobby desk. Scowling at the lack of response, he pursed his lips. Eleanor glanced around the lobby. *Where on earth was the staff?*

In one corner, a wiry, suntanned man with stained teeth perused the display of newspapers. Halfway down the scrollwork staircase, a curvaceous woman in a demure black-and-silver beaded dress with the deepest blue eyes Eleanor had ever seen paused with her hand on the polished oak rail.

A curl of smoke rising up from one of the red velvet wingback chairs by the enormous fireplace caught Eleanor's eye. With one impeccably tailored trouser leg slung casually over the other, a strong-jawed athletic man in a cream silk shirt and indigo tie held her gaze with a disconcerting un-English intensity.

At the glass display cases of jewellery and silver giftware, an incongruous pair in belted overcoats seemed deep in a whispered argument. One towered over the other, scowling hard enough to make the other step back a few paces, revealing a pronounced limp.

She shook her head. They were obviously all guests, not staff. Feeling decidedly uneasy, she looked down the corridor, only for her unease to increase. Four policemen were marching in her direction, two of them carrying something she couldn't quite make out but that made her feel even more unsettled.

Her attention was distracted as a rotund man in a striped suit flustered out of the door marked 'Manager's Office'. Clifford buttonholed him and told him in clipped tones what he thought of the lack of staff at their arrival.

The manager apologised profusely. 'The staff have been, er, detained unexpectedly to answer… to, er, attend to an unexpected matter. I will fetch…'

Who, or what, the manager was going to fetch was lost on Eleanor as the four policemen drew level with her. With a start she recognised what two of them were carrying: a stretcher. And on the stretcher lay a body covered with a white sheet.

A cold wash of sadness swept over her as she remembered attending to so many men during her time as a nurse during the war. Looking at the nearest policeman, she blanched at the green hue to his far too young face.

As the leading stretcher-bearer passed her, he stumbled, causing the sheet to slip off the body.

Eleanor automatically went to replace the sheet, but stopped in horror at the cold, dead eyes staring back at her. Light-headed, she tried to fight a rising tide of nausea. A strange buzzing filled her ears.

And then she knew no more.

CHAPTER 3

'Cold. So very cold,' Eleanor heard a disembodied voice mutter. It took a second to realise it had come from her own lips.

She became aware of thick soft wool being tucked round her shoulders. Forcing her eyelids to open, she blinked repeatedly in the hope that everything would stop revolving. Distracted by another wave of nausea, she shuffled into a more upright position. She looked down at the thickly padded scrolling arm of a settee. *Someone must have picked you up when you fainted and carried you here, Ellie.*

Thankfully, she could also make out the welcome sight of her butler standing at the other end, looking very concerned, and her bulldog curled up asleep by her feet.

'Clifford, where am I?' She drew her knees up to her chin and hung her head over them.

'In one of the private sitting rooms at the hotel, my lady. You had a most perturbing and regrettable experience.'

She felt her heart begin to pound and another icy wave engulfed her. She sat motionless, unable to process what her brain was telling her she'd seen.

'A warm brandy, my lady.' Clifford was immediately at her side and pressed a glass into her hand.

Numb, she felt the hardness of the glass against her chattering teeth as she took a sip. As the fiery warmth trickled down her throat, she became aware of a man perched on the edge of a deeply buttoned mulberry armchair. He wore a nondescript grey suit, his bald crown illuminated by the ornate cream wall sconce above his head. With beady eyes set under heavy brows, his pencil moustache added to his already deeply mistrusting air.

'Who are you?' she asked, thinking he didn't look like the fleeting glimpse she'd caught of the hotel's manager.

He reached into his jacket pocket and pulled out a badge, which he flashed at her. 'Detective Inspector Grimsdale, Brighton Criminal Investigation Division.'

Eleanor felt a frisson of dread run up her spine.

'Something in your manner is suggesting you are not here to check on my wellbeing.'

He held up a small leather notebook. 'Lady Swift, I have some questions for you relating to our enquiries. Are you feeling sufficiently recovered to answer questions regarding your involvement?'

She sat up straighter, confusion in her eyes. 'Involvement? I haven't done anything other than arrive for a much-needed holiday only to receive the shock of my life. What do you mean "involvement"?'

The inspector studied her face closely. 'Just before you fainted, one of my constables distinctly heard you say…' He looked down at his notebook. '"Hilary. It can't be you!"' He looked up sharply. 'What did you mean by this? Who is this Hilary?'

She stared at him. 'Why, the… dead man, of course!'

His eyebrows rose. 'And how would you know the dead man's name? Your butler here' – he nodded in Clifford's direction – 'told me that you only just arrived at the hotel, and that you know no one here.'

Eleanor swallowed hard. 'That's true… and yet… it would appear not.' She shook her head in confusion.

The inspector snorted in exasperation. 'Lady Swift, do you know the deceased or not?'

She caught Clifford looking at her with a puzzled expression. *Of course, he doesn't know either, Ellie.* She sighed deeply. 'Yes, I do. His name is Hilary Montgomery Eden. He is… was… my husband.'

The look of surprise on her butler's normally inscrutable face would have made her laugh in any other circumstances. Laughing, however, was the last thing on her mind. It seemed the inspector felt the same way as he looked up from his notebook. 'Eden?'

'Yes. Eden. Why is that surprising?'

'Because the man my men will have now removed from the hotel while we have been talking was a Mr Geoffrey Painshill.'

Eleanor shook her head vehemently. 'That was Hilary. You can't imagine for a moment I would be confused in recognising my husband?'

'As you wish, but it might interest you to know that his passport matched the identity under which he checked in. So, obviously you are either wrong, or he had a fake passport. Perhaps you would like to reconsider your statement that he was your husband? I can arrange another viewing of the body?'

'No, thank you. I would not like to reconsider, nor' – she shuddered – 'to see him again.'

The inspector grunted. 'So if he was your husband, his surname was, according to you, Eden. Why then do you go under another name, Lady Swift? Am I to deduce you were estranged?'

'Very estranged.' She shook her head in disbelief. *This must be a nightmare, Ellie. You'll wake up soon.*

The inspector's voice cut into her thoughts. 'And yet, I am supposed to believe it pure coincidence that you both arrived at this hotel within forty-eight hours of each other?' He pulled a grey handkerchief from his jacket pocket and blew his nose. 'Call me cynical but I am not a great believer of coincidences, Lady Swift. And, in this case, I find it improbable in the extreme.'

Eleanor leaned forward. 'Then you might not believe this either. But the reason I was so shocked to see Hilary's… body…' Aware of the wobble in her voice and the pounding in her chest, she accepted the small brandy top up Clifford held out to her.

The inspector looked up from his notebook. 'I'm listening, Lady Swift.'

She took a sip of brandy, closed her eyes and swallowed. Opening her eyes, she fixed them on the inspector. 'The reason I was so shocked to see his body is because my husband died six years ago.'

He held her gaze as he slowly put down his notebook and folded his arms. 'I think you'd better start from the beginning, if you would be so kind? When, and where, did you first meet Mr Eden?' His tone made it clear this was not optional.

She took a long breath and swung her legs over the settee so that she was sitting up fully and facing the inspector. 'I met him in South Africa, in Cape Town. I was working for Mr Thomas Walker at the time.'

He nodded. Everyone had heard of Thomas Walker and his pioneering agency that arranged tours to exotic places for the rich and adventurous.

'And this was when?'

'1914, a few months before war broke out. He told me he was an officer in the South African Army. And… well, suffice to say we enjoyed a whirlwind romance and married shortly afterwards.'

'And then?'

Eleanor rubbed her hands over her cheeks at the recollection of that awful day. 'He disappeared. Only a few weeks later.' She bit her lip. 'My husband turned out not to be an officer at all, but someone the South African Military Police were interested in… speaking to.'

'Really? And what makes you think he died six years ago?'

She took a sip of her brandy and swallowed hard. 'Because he was arrested and shot for selling arms to the enemy shortly afterwards.'

The inspector shook his head. 'And yet the dead man I myself examined in room 204 less than an hour ago, you still claim to be your husband?'

She nodded wearily. 'I cannot even begin to account for that. It's like living out an inexplicable nightmare.'

He picked up his notebook and wrote for a moment. Without looking up, he addressed her. 'So, there you were in South Africa, having received the news that your husband was a traitor—'

'Inspector!' Clifford stepped forward.

Unmoved, the inspector continued. 'What did you do then?'

Clifford handed Eleanor a pristine handkerchief. Discreetly wiping away the trickle of tears that had fallen down her cheeks, she regained her composure. 'War broke out shortly afterwards and even though there was no actual fighting in South Africa, they were short of nurses in West Africa and elsewhere. I'd looked after myself during my travels and had some rudimentary medical knowledge, so I volunteered. I also changed my name back to my maiden name as it was... easier than using my dead husband's. So I joined the South African Military Nursing Service for the remainder of the war.'

'You stayed in South Africa?' His tone was disbelieving.

'Not that I see it is relevant to whatever picture you are trying to create, but I was brought up abroad by parents often considered, well, rather bohemian in their outlook. South Africa felt much more like home than England, so, yes, I did. However, by a twist of fate, most of us were sent to Abbeville in France. Then, after the truce, I returned to South Africa and went back to working for Mr Walker. But life had changed and my heart was no longer in it. To cut to the end of my story, just over twelve months ago I received a letter saying my uncle had passed away and left me his estate so

I set off for England to see if that was where my heart might lie.'
She drained the last of the brandy, feeling totally wrung out.

The inspector tapped his pencil against his notebook page. 'And
you last heard from your husband when?'

'The day before he left, six years ago.'

'And not a word since? Really? Surely you must have expected
at least a note?'

'Why would I have expected to receive word from a man whom
I thought dead?'

'Hmm. If you truly believed him to be dead, why was it you
planned to join your husband here at the Grand?'

She closed her eyes and took a deep breath. 'As I already told
you, I did not. I could not possibly have imagined he was here.'

The inspector shrugged. 'It does sound very hard to believe.
The man my men have just removed from the hotel, covered in a
sheet, borne on a stretcher' – he paused at Eleanor's sharp intake
of breath – 'checked in on the evening before last. He then left the
hotel before breakfast the following morning. Only to return that
evening and, except for a trip out around nine thirty, stayed in his
room. The maid alerted the manager at nine o'clock this morning
that the gentleman had not vacated his room in time for it to be
cleaned and as no amount of knocking could rouse a response,
the manager used his pass key to enter the room, only to find that
the man was—'

'Dead,' Eleanor finished for him. She ran her hand over the soft
plum upholstery of the settee. 'I know, I saw him, remember? That
is the precise reason I awoke from an unladylike faint, swathed in a
blanket in this very room, although I have no idea how I got here.'
She looked questioningly at Clifford who bowed. 'I have to say
I am surprised, given my distressed reaction to witnessing my…
my husband's body being carried through the hotel, that more
compassion might have been shown.'

'Would you?' He gave her a thin smile. 'Lady Swift, there will be time for compassion to be shown later, if it is due, of course. Now, you stand by your statement that you did not know your husband was here at the hotel?'

'Of course I do.' She shook her head. 'I believed him already… dead, as I said.'

Clifford coughed. 'Inspector, perhaps Lady Swift might be able to rest now? This has been a most upsetting experience.'

'Perhaps it has.' The inspector rose. 'I have to warn you, Lady Swift, that your arrival at the hotel today is extremely suspicious. You may retire to your room now but must stay within the town's limits and remain available for questioning.'

She stood up. 'Before I leave, I have a question for you.' She clasped her hands to try and hide how hard they were trembling. 'How did my husband die?'

The inspector looked her in the eye. 'Well, Lady Swift, you yourself told me that he was shot for siding with the enemy six years ago on the other side of the world. If, however, you are referring to the man found dead in his hotel room this very morning…'

She nodded. *Stay calm, Ellie.*

'Then that man… was murdered.'

CHAPTER 4

The sting of the cold sea breeze whipped through Eleanor's tousled red curls and tugged at her cashmere scarf. She didn't care. For the first time since the distressing scene she'd witnessed in the hotel lobby, she could breathe freely. Having finally checked in, she had found her chest tightening even further as she'd entered her suite. Hurriedly turning around, she'd asked Clifford to accompany her on a walk anywhere away from the hotel.

Outdoors had always been her haven and nothing soothed her frazzled nerves more than walking and talking, usually to herself, or, since moving to the Hall, Gladstone. Now, however, she walked in silence along Brighton's raised promenade with the roar of waves to her left and Clifford's calming presence to her right. She tried to focus on the gulls fishing for crabs in the foamy shallows of the receding tide. But even staring at the hypnotic patterns their feet made on the wet grey sand couldn't quieten the troubling thoughts running around her head. Finally, Clifford spoke.

'Are you alright, my lady?' His normally inscrutable face was etched with concern.

'Alright… enough.' She turned to him. 'Thank you for being here, Clifford. It would be so much harder to deal with this on my own.'

He scanned her face. 'I would not countenance being anywhere else until all of this is over.' Her late uncle, on his deathbed, had made Clifford swear he would look after Eleanor's welfare, and he'd lived up to his word ever since.

'Thank you.' She paused and clung to the cold iron railing, running her gloved finger along the surface pitted by decades of salty sea spray. 'How is it possible that Hilary died this morning? That policeman, Grimsdale, said he'd… he'd been murdered. Stabbed in the back. But it was an army captain who came to tell me six years ago that… that Hilary had been sent before the firing squad.'

Saying those words aloud made her clutch her throat. Even though he'd deceived her and then left her, she had innocently loved him with all of her heart. With the overwhelming wave of grief that washed over her, she realised with a jolt that a part of her still did.

Clifford stayed silent, giving her jumbled thoughts and emotions room to spill out.

A rush of anger bubbled over her.

'Blast him! He called Hilary a traitor, but what does he know? I was Hilary's wife and I have no idea what the truth is. Oh dash it, Clifford, we've joked about my hapless affairs of the heart, but Hilary was… different.' She bit her lip as a particular memory swam before her tear-filled eyes. 'The day we married, I truly believed we both wanted to see the world together, to… raise a family together… to grow old together. What a fool I was.' Her head fell to her chest, the wind whipping the end of her scarf against the rail.

Clifford cleared his throat. 'My lady, it is not my place I know, but it pains me greatly to see you like this.' He stared out to sea. 'I have learned that the scars of lost love can be healed, and one can learn to love again.'

She gasped. 'Clifford! You too?' She peered at his face, which bore only his usual enigmatic expression. 'Gracious, I'm sorry. I didn't mean to pry.' She mentally slapped herself for momentarily forgetting how fiercely private he was. 'My apologies,' she repeated.

'There is nothing to apologise for, my lady, I believe I spoke out of turn. And to answer, Voltaire said, "Is there anyone so wise as to learn by the experience of others?"' Gesturing further along the promenade, he hastily added, 'Shall we?'

Eleanor noticed very few of the tiny kiosks or the ornate black street lamps and matching scrollwork benches which followed the sweeping curve of Brighton's seafront. Even the squawking of the seagulls and the clinking of the halyards on the myriad small sailboats rising and falling together in the swell of the waves failed to disturb her thoughts. Brighton was still out of season and only a few hardy souls were strolling the promenade, while many of the stalls dotted along the walkway were yet to open.

Still wrestling with a thousand questions, she realised Clifford had ducked under one of the few wind-blown, green-and-white striped kiosk awnings. He pulled some coins from his pocket, tipped his bowler hat to the warmly wrapped woman inside, and returned with two sticks of bright-pink rock. She smiled as she took the one he offered her.

'Thank you. I definitely feel nine years old now.' One of her most treasured memories filtered into her mind. Her mother tucking her up in bed after an upsetting experience and whispering, 'Sleep well, darling girl. All will be fine, I promise, because tomorrow doesn't know what happened today.' Her tears dried. She stared down at her stick of rock and then smiled up at Clifford.

'I do apologise. So much for your holiday. It's only been a few hours and you've already had to gallantly rescue me from a faint and suffer my uncharacteristically emotional tirade. But worst of all' – she pointed at his head – 'accept that the damp sea air has permeated the brim of your usually impeccably stiff bowler hat.'

He glanced up. 'That is no problem, my lady, I have brought a spare. And I thought we had agreed we would be confirmed donkey ride and ice cream types whilst in Brighton? A stiff bowler is not needed for either of these diversions, I fear.'

That drew a snort of a laugh from deep in her tired chest. 'I promise I shan't actually expect you to join me on a donkey ride.'

'There is some good news left today in that case.' He looked suspiciously at his lurid coloured stick of rock and pursed his lips.

'When in Rome?'

'On three. One, two, three.'

They both popped the top of the sweets into their mouths.

'Oh, do you know, it's quite good,' she said a moment later.

Clifford sniffed. 'With nothing else in line for a compliment at this precise minute, this'– he held the rock away from him – 'confectionery may be declared passable. That is, if one has no regard for retaining one's teeth.'

She laughed. 'High praise, indeed.'

They walked on as her racing thoughts settled into a less chaotic jumble.

'Clifford, why on earth do you imagine Hilary was here? I suppose what I really mean is, how could he have been alive all these years?' She sighed. 'And why… why didn't he contact me?'

Clifford smoothly dropped his stick of rock into a bin and coughed. 'Perhaps to spare you further distress, my lady? Even men with a chequered past can be capable of deep and honourable feelings.'

She stared up at the clouds scudding across the darkening afternoon sky. 'Do you suppose then there is any chance he came to England because he was looking for me?'

'That is a possibility.'

Her next words stuck in her throat. 'But someone murdered him, Clifford.' She shook her head sadly. 'It is so clear to me now that everything I thought I knew about him was false.'

He nodded. 'That may be so, my lady, but, at the risk of causing you further anxiety, I was significantly disquieted by Inspector Grimsdale's inferences that he finds your presence here suspicious.'

'Hmm. I was most unnerved by that too. It doesn't look good on my side though, does it? Estranged for six years, with no word from Hilary. Then he mysteriously appears in England and I arrive at the scene of his murder a few hours later.'

'I admit, my lady, on paper, that is an unfortunate set of circumstances.'

She groaned. 'And ones likely to lead that bullish Grimsdale to jump to all the wrong conclusions. He struck me as being a most cold-hearted and unsympathetic individual.'

Clifford arched one brow.

'What?'

'Forgive my observation but I vaguely recall a few similar conversations over another detective inspector, of whom one's opinion may now be significantly different. A gentleman much closer to home,' he said conspiratorially.

'Seldon, you mean?' Warmth surged through her chest. She'd met the gruff Detective Chief Inspector Seldon when she'd first arrived at Henley Hall and become embroiled in a murder. To begin with she'd found him insufferable, but as time went on she'd fallen for him. So much so, that on New Year's Eve she'd broken off her relationship with the son of a local lord, and promised herself she'd see where DCI Seldon would take her.

Clifford adjusted his cuffs. 'Unfortunately, Detective Chief Inspector Seldon's "patch", as I believe it is called, does not extend to Brighton. Nevertheless, in the past, we have proven that we are quite the team at unearthing the truth. And, against my better judgement, I confess I feel we have no choice but to investigate the tragic event at the Grand regarding your husband. However,

I insist on adding one caveat. Only if you are confident that you are robust enough to weather the consequences.'

She laughed grimly. 'No need to skip around the bush, Clifford, I know you mean I may not like the truth about Hilary and why he married me.'

He sniffed. 'Fortunately, I am not in the habit of skipping, my lady. I find it most unbecoming.'

She resumed walking. Now the tide had receded, she stared out on a large expanse of soggy sand to the horizon. She felt an unexpected surge of comfort from the timeless body of water acting out its daily routine regardless of human tragedies, large or small. Clifford fell in step behind in his customary manner.

'I will be fine,' she said with certainty. 'However, I apologise in advance as I fear you may be subjected to a few more emotional tirades and cold, wet walks as I need to gather my thoughts. But, in exchange, on our return to Henley Hall, I will purchase you the perfect new bowler hat so you still have a spare.'

'A most generous arrangement, my lady. One from which I shall unquestionably profit the most.'

Suddenly, he lunged forward and grabbed the collar of a grubby young boy who had dashed up to Eleanor.

'I'm not picking pockets, mister, honest,' the boy wheezed. 'Got a message for the lady.' He held up a folded square of paper. 'Look, see.'

'Who gave it to you?' Eleanor said, taking it.

The boy shook his head, wide-eyed. Deftly, he wriggled out of Clifford's grasp and disappeared down a side alley.

Frowning, Eleanor unfolded the paper and read aloud. 'If you want to find out who killed your husband, be at the end of West Pier at five past ten tonight. No police. Nothing clever.' She gasped. 'Clifford!'

He narrowed his eyes. 'It appears the first step in our plan may have been arranged for us.'

She looked at the message again. Then at his face. 'You think we shouldn't go, don't you?'

He inclined his head. 'I think it is far too risky, yes.'

'A trap, perhaps?'

'Possibly. I also think, however, as you doubtlessly intend to go anyway, we should at least be prepared.' He gave her a resigned smile.

At precisely ten o'clock, as they reached the bandstand halfway along West Pier, the electric street lamps that had replaced the gaslights only that year snapped off. Darkness engulfed them, only the feeble light of the waning moon showing the boards beneath their feet.

Eleanor, still wrung out from the emotion of the afternoon, shivered in the bitter March evening air. Clifford had repeatedly tried to persuade her to stay behind at the hotel, but she'd reasoned that the note had been written to her specifically and whoever had sent it was unlikely to take kindly to Clifford taking her place.

'Ready?' he asked.

'Not a bit. So let's go,' she whispered back.

From nowhere, Clifford produced a long black torch and clicked it on, casting eerie shadows along the length of the pier's wooden boards.

'Turn it off!' a voice growled to their right.

Clifford shone the light where the voice came from.

'OFF!' the voice barked.

The torch clicked off. The vague outline of a man was visible in the darkness.

'Lady Swift, I wasn't sure you'd show up.' The figure stepped closer. 'Hilary got one thing right. You're spirited.'

Eleanor swallowed hard. 'I didn't come here to talk about me. Neither do I care for your opinion. After all, we haven't even been introduced. Who are you?'

'Me?' A set of stained and broken teeth grinned in the dark as the shadowy form lit a cigarette from a pocket lighter. 'I'm the man who killed your husband.'

CHAPTER 5

Eleanor stiffened as she heard a pistol cock and then relaxed, as Clifford swung the gun into view.

Where on earth did he produce that from?

She addressed the ghostly form. 'Whoever you are, we're going to take you straight to the police.'

A scoff rang through the air. 'For what?'

Eleanor tried to keep the tremble from her voice. 'For murdering my husband in the hotel, what else?'

The shadowy shape stepped forward. Eleanor took in his fair hair, long nose and hollow leathered cheeks. It was the man who'd been in the hotel lobby apparently perusing the newspapers when she'd first arrived. He grinned.

'I wouldn't be doing that, if I were you.' The man's voice was gravelly, with a coarse London accent overlaid with an inflexion she couldn't place.

'And why not?' Clifford said, keeping the gun trained on him.

The man shrugged. ''Cos I never killed her husband, that's why.'

Eleanor frowned. 'You'd better stop playing games. You admitted to killing him a moment ago.'

'I didn't.' The stranger reached forward and coolly pushed the barrel of the gun away. 'I admitted to killing him six years ago.'

Eleanor felt all the air leave her body. 'You were part of the... the firing squad in South Africa?'

He shook his head. 'Nah, not part of it. I was in charge of it.'

His words ran around Eleanor's head. She imagined, as she'd done a thousand times before, her husband, hands tied, blindfolded, a line of armed men lining him up through their rifle sights. And then…

'Why?'

'You know why,' he said curtly. 'He was running guns to the other side.'

'No,' she snapped. 'I don't know. I'm fed up with lies and not knowing. Tell me what really happened in South Africa six years ago.'

The man nodded. 'And in exchange you tell me what really happened last night at the hotel between you and your husband, Lady Swift.'

Eleanor frowned. 'You seem to think that Hilary and I kept in touch, but you're sorely mistaken.'

'Perhaps. Perhaps not. Right?'

'Look, Mister whatever your name is. Answer my questions, and I'll answer yours. Deal?'

The man ran his tongue down the inside of his cheek. 'Deal.'

Eleanor glanced at Clifford, who nodded discreetly to her, lowering the gun.

'How was it that Hilary was still alive until… last night, if you were in charge of his execution all those years ago?' she asked.

He grinned, his stained teeth making her shudder. 'Ah. I expected some soldiers in the line to guess but I knew they wouldn't speak up, they'd learned long before to keep their mouths shut. But it went off so dandily, no one even suspected. All credit, Hilary played the dying man like a pro.'

Eleanor felt her stomach tighten. 'What do you mean?'

'I mean, I switched the bullets for blanks in all the guns. Strapped some bags of pig's blood to his chest. Job was a good one. Neat, huh?'

'You saved Hilary's life,' she whispered.

'Mmm.' He pulled out a pack of cigarettes and lit another one, inhaling slowly. The smoke swirled upwards and vanished into the darkness as he spoke. 'Wish I never had. If I'd known what a double-crossing fake he was, I'd have grabbed a rifle loaded with the real thing myself and finished him off there and then. And it would have been a pleasure. I risked everything, and he knew that.'

Clifford cleared his throat. 'It must have been quite the carrot he offered you to disobey orders so comprehensively.'

This brought a huge grin to the man's lips. 'It was the biggest, best carrot ever! Your husband called me to the door of his cell the night before he was due to face the firing squad. Said he'd been framed.' He scoffed again. 'Like I believed that. Or cared. But he also told me he would give me something in exchange for saving his life.'

'What did he promise to give you?' Eleanor said.

The man cocked his head at her. 'See, now. I'd tell you, but you already know, don't you? I'm thinking maybe you're every bit as good at acting as he was when he fell to the dust, his chest covered in blood, groaning his last.'

'Well, by your own admission, you're not always the best judge of character,' she said boldly, despite her pounding heart.

'You too, girl.' He ran his tongue over his bottom lip. 'If you really had no idea what your husband was up to, that is.'

'You believed he actually had whatever it was he promised you?' Clifford asked.

'Why wouldn't I? He showed me a taster. And it was a beauty, alright.' He threw the remains of his cigarette to the pier floor and left it smouldering. 'Weren't my idea. He suggested the deal. I was just an honest soldier looking forward to a pauper's pension and nowhere to call home like most soldiers once their country's got no use for them anymore. That wasn't a future, that was a prison sentence.'

Eleanor's initial anger became tinged with pity. She'd seen, first in South Africa, and then in England, how swathes of soldiers returning from the war had been left to fend for themselves. But she still needed answers. It was obvious he wasn't going to tell them what it was her husband had promised him in exchange for saving his life, so she switched tack.

'But how did you get Hilary out after he pretended to have been shot?'

'I helped my men load him on the meat wagon and stowed it in the usual lock-up. No one suspected anything. I returned at midnight, as arranged, for us to escape and finish our deal, but the swine had already made his own way out and scarpered.' The man's face blackened. 'I swore that night I'd get what was rightfully mine. No one cheats me out of a deal. No one!'

Eleanor instinctively took a step backwards. 'So you're saying you tracked him for six years and eventually traced him to the Grand Hotel in Brighton and then you killed him?'

The man sighed in exasperation. 'I already told you I didn't. Sure I went to his room that night about eleven thirty, maybe five-and-twenty to twelve, but he was already dead, stabbed in the back.' He looked at Eleanor and smiled evilly. 'If I had killed him, mind, I'd have stabbed him in the back as well. After all, that's what he did to me, the cheating swine! I searched the room, but with no luck.' He pulled out another cigarette. 'Anyway, lady detective, if it was me that killed him, why would I still be here?'

Because you never got what you came for. That must be it, Ellie!

The man's tone became more menacing. 'So now it's your turn. Because when I found him dead, the room had already been searched. Good and proper too. I gave it another go, but what was mine, wasn't there.' He lit the cigarette and chewed on the end. 'Maybe you killed him and took it? Stop playing around. Where is it?'

'I really have no idea,' Eleanor said coldly. 'Hilary left me without a word. I was told he'd been shot and believed he was dead until I saw him on the stretcher when I arrived at the hotel. That's the truth.'

'Not very convincing. Unlike that faint you pulled.' He shrugged. 'Like it or not, Lady Swift-Eden, we both want the same thing.'

She held his stare. 'I doubt that very much. I want justice for my dead husband and you… you want to rob him!'

He threw the cigarette down and ground it out with his heel. 'Whatever you want to call it, if anyone crosses me and I don't get what I want, there's going to be another murder.' He stepped backwards and was swallowed up by the darkness.

CHAPTER 6

After a fitful night's sleep and an even more fitful attempt at break-fasting, Eleanor was relieved to head to the train station to meet the ladies coming from Henley Hall. A vast arched glass canopy rose close to seventy feet above the bustle of the platforms. The clipped accents of first-class passengers in smart suits and dresses mingled with the coarse tones of third-class passengers dressed in their simple Sunday best.

Despite clouds of steam engulfing the platform as the express from London pulled in, she and Clifford soon spotted the ladies hanging out of the windows, shouting excitedly. Gladstone, recognising their voices, woofed and spun in wobbly circles on the end of his lead.

'Oh, my lady. What a trip we've enjoyed,' Mrs Butters called out as she walked gingerly down the carriage steps. 'It's a good thing you didn't have to witness Trotters being a total rascal, chattering on with the handsome gentleman in the seat opposite. Wouldn't take no for an answer, neither.'

Mrs Trotman appeared at the housekeeper's elbow. 'A man needs a bit of meat on him,' she said, a mischievous grin on her face. 'Can't abide a man who's all skin and bones.' She beckoned to Polly who skipped over to join them, a small wicker basket in each hand.

Clifford cleared his throat. 'I do apologise, my lady. It appears our ladies have been abducted en route and replaced with a troublesome pack of schoolgirls. Shall I have them sent straight back to the Hall?'

Eleanor smiled and shook her head. 'Take no notice, ladies. I promised you all a holiday, and that is precisely what you shall have! Besides, I've already won our bet. Clifford has eaten a stick of rock – well, he almost ate it – *and* he's agreed to ride a donkey!'

Mrs Trotman chuckled. 'Well, blow me down, that will be a sight, alright. If I'd known, my lady, I'd have asked your permission to bring your late uncle's camera so we might capture it to remember on the long winter nights.'

Clifford shook his head, but his eyes were twinkling as the corners of his lips twitched. 'In hindsight, my lady, I shall personally write to the railway board on your behalf, apologising for the behaviour of three of their passengers this afternoon. Goodness knows what the other passengers have had to put up with.'

Eleanor smiled at her staff. They were the perfect antidote to all the unpleasant business regarding her husband. In fact, she and Clifford had agreed they would keep the news from the ladies so as not to spoil their well-deserved holiday. The hotel manager had also requested the police keep the news quiet to preserve the establishment's reputation. Even the unsympathetic Inspector Grimsdale had let slip that the Mayor of Brighton had made it very clear nothing was to jeopardise the start of the Easter season, which started in three weeks' time.

Eleanor gave her maid a questioning look as the young girl stood excitedly opening and closing her mouth. 'What is it, Polly?'

She looked to Clifford for permission to speak. He nodded.

'I've never been on holiday afore, your ladyship. Nor been on a train. 'Tis so exciting, I could burst! Thank you so much, your ladyship.'

'It is my absolute pleasure, Polly.' And she meant it. The fifteen-year-old was more than just a maid to Eleanor. Her uncle had taken on Polly when she was a twelve-year-old orphan, long before Eleanor came to the Hall. After Eleanor and Clifford had solved a series of murders the year before and sent the guilty party to the insane asylum, she'd learned the culprit was in fact Polly's real mother. Even though there was nothing else she could have done, from then on, Eleanor felt a special responsibility for the girl's welfare.

She turned to take in all of her staff. 'And not just you, Polly. It's a pleasure to have all of you here. I mean it wholeheartedly when I say that you are all a very welcome sight for my sore eyes.'

The last sentence came out with more force than Eleanor had intended. Mrs Butters looked at her askance, but Polly saved Eleanor from having to answer any awkward questions.

'That'll be the salt in the sea, your ladyship. Mrs Trotman said we're all to be sure to swish our eyes several times a day to save them from getting sore.'

Eleanor wished with all her heart it was appropriate to draw this sweet young girl into a hug. Instead she nodded and smiled. 'Silly me. Thank you for the reminder, Polly.'

Eleanor looked down at the baskets in the young girl's hands. 'Oh gracious though, perhaps we'd better change our plans? Clifford and I thought you might like to start your holiday with proper seaside fish and chips in the café opposite the entrance to the pier. But you're probably full from your picnic?'

Polly clapped her hands as her cook and housekeeper both vigorously shook their heads.

Eleanor pointed in the direction of the pier. 'Fish and chips ahoy then!'

Eleanor and the ladies were soon settled into a table in the simple, but sparklingly clean, café. Clifford joined them a few minutes later after having arranged for Eleanor's extra luggage to be sent to the Grand and the rest of the bags to the ladies' boarding house a few streets away.

As the easy chatter flowed, Eleanor felt the stress from yesterday die away. Even Gladstone behaved himself, as least as much as could be expected for a dog who had long ago decided he was too old to be told off. Satisfied with a few chips under the table, he slipped into a deep doze and began to snore loudly under the red-and-white gingham tablecloth.

The freshly caught haddock in golden batter and the accompanying hand-chipped potatoes were soon devoured. Mrs Trotman surveyed Eleanor's empty plate.

'Seeing as how you enjoyed it so much, my lady, perhaps I should add this to the monthly menu?'

She nodded enthusiastically. 'Absolutely, Mrs Trotman, but you shouldn't be thinking of work, you're on holiday.' She looked from her cook to her housekeeper. 'What have you all got planned for this afternoon?'

'Whatever you need first, my lady,' Mrs Butters said, scanning Eleanor's face.

'Ah!' She paused so the waiters could clear their empty plates and replace them with treacle sponge pudding and custard. 'Then your afternoon begins as soon as you have eaten up because I am completely need free, thank you.'

Dessert was followed by pots of tea. While Clifford settled the bill at the counter and Mrs Trotman and Polly excused themselves, Mrs Butters slid up to Eleanor.

'My lady, I fear something is bothering you. And 'tis no good shaking your head, your face always gives you away to me.'

Eleanor patted her housekeeper's hand. 'Really, I'm fine, thank you. There have just been a lot of events in recent... weeks.'

'Tell you what,' Mrs Butters said lifting the tablecloth. 'How about the three of us take Mr Wilful under here with us? That'd leave you and Mr Clifford free to do as you please. And' – she nodded towards Polly who was now staring excitedly out of the window – 'we'll never drag young Polly off the beach afore nightfall, she's been talking about nothing else but playing in the sand and watching the Punch and Judy show.'

Eleanor smiled. 'That would be perfect, thank you. We will come and collect him from the boarding house later, if that will be alright?'

'Oh, don't you bother about when. My friend who runs it can't wait to meet him, having heard all my tales about his naughtiness. And besides' – she cast a concerned look over Eleanor again – 'I have a feeling, my lady, you might have other things on your mind.'

CHAPTER 7

Outside, Eleanor waved off the ladies and then turned to Clifford. 'Please do also go and indulge in whatever Brighton has to offer. I could meet you later for dinner, perhaps?'

He gave his customary half bow. 'Thank you, my lady. I rather fancied browsing through that famous part of Brighton known as "The Lanes" where several silk scarf shops are known to reside.'

Silk scarves were one of Eleanor's weaknesses. She owned far too many, but couldn't stop buying more.

'Fibber. I can't think of anything you'd probably enjoy less. So thank you for such a generous offer, but I will be fine.'

'And I will be too, if I know you are safe, my lady. We met a most untrustworthy character last night who may be responsible for the unfortunate death at the Grand, despite his protestations.'

She shook her head. 'I've said it before, and I'll say it again, I used to think I was the most stubborn person imaginable, but I think you might actually trump me. And, thank you, but if you are to accompany me, and discuss the events at the hotel, let's agree you call my husband Mr Eden? "That man" or "the body" sounds so… cold.'

He nodded. 'Agreed, my lady.'

As they strolled towards Brighton's maze of quaint, cobbled shopping lanes, Eleanor considered the conversation they'd had with the man on the pier.

'Neither of us were very sure what to think last night, were we?' she asked, hoping Clifford had received some magic insight overnight.

'Regrettably not. Any fabrication on his part was seamlessly delivered, I felt.' He glanced at her. 'He did mention that Mr Eden had spoken of you? Perhaps that brought you a modicum of comfort?'

She'd had that exact thought run round her brain all night. 'A little, although I'm sure the man on the pier would have said anything to get what he wanted. All we really learned for certain was that Hilary has been alive and well somewhere all these years, but he never contacted me.'

'True, but we have been living through troublesome times. With so many displaced, and worse, during and after the war, tracing anyone is an almost impossible task.'

She nodded, something tugging at her brain. The fog of churning emotions in her head, however, refused to clear into anything she could make sense of.

Clifford coughed softly. 'Closure sometimes arrives in an unexpected form, my lady. If you have changed your mind, we can abandon our efforts to find the truth and hope Inspector Grimsdale catches the culprit.'

She stopped and turned to him. 'And if he doesn't? Besides, you're right. Hilary was an adult and made his choices. I know you doubt it sometimes, but I'm an adult too. I can make my choices, just as he did.' She started walking again. 'And I choose to find out the truth once and for all.'

'Spoken like your late uncle, if I may say so.'

That meant a lot to her. Heartened, she continued, 'Let's assume for a moment that the man on the pier wasn't lying, and he didn't kill Hilary and Hilary really did double-cross him. It would seem highly likely in that case that Hilary repeated his less than honourable behaviour with someone else and that person murdered him?'

'My summation also, my lady, if you will forgive my character assassination of Mr Eden without ever having had the opportunity to meet him?'

As they turned under an arch into the first of the back streets, Eleanor had a strange feeling. 'I have the distinct impression that—'

They both flattened themselves against the arch's brickwork as a car screeched alongside. A tall man in a black mask jumped out, waving a pistol.

'Get in!' he snarled, grabbing Eleanor's arm.

She stared at Clifford, who nodded.

Eleanor didn't resist as she was shoved into the front seat, where she came face to face with the unexpected sight of a masked driver perched on a cushion. The first man bundled Clifford into the back seat.

'Go! GO!'

The car lurched forward and then stalled. The driver cursed. Clifford cleared his throat.

'Three things strike me as peculiar in your most unexpected offer of a lift.'

'Yeah, well, something else'll strike you between the eyes if you don't pipe down,' the man with the gun growled.

'One question though?' Clifford persisted.

'Shut it.'

'Two men in masks?'

'Are you deaf?' the man shouted. 'Keep quiet or else.' He leaned forward to the driver. 'What the hell are you doing? Get going!'

The driver threw his hands up. 'You nicked it. I told you I'd never driven one like this.' He graunched it into gear, and the car lurched forward again.

Eleanor swallowed hard and braced herself, hoping she had understood Clifford's hastily coded message.

'But I fear we need to alight,' Clifford continued in his measured tone, 'at number… THREE!'

Eleanor elbowed the driver in the jaw, smacking his head against the window. From the back seat she heard a crunch of nose against glass. The car hit the pavement and stopped.

Quickly, she gave the man next to her another elbow punch with all her strength and then tumbled out of the door. 'Run!' she heard Clifford shout.

Go, Ellie! He's made it out too. She sprinted into a long narrow passageway, hoping that the prick of light she could see filtering around the corner was daylight. Breathing too hard to know if there were footsteps pounding after her, she ran on until she reached the end of the tunnel.

A form stepped in front of her and smartly sidestepped her instinctive kick.

'Clifford, it's you!'

'Yes, my lady.'

She spoke while taking deep breaths to calm her heart. 'Sorry… about trying to kick you, but… but how did you get to the end of this passageway before me?'

'These passageways are in fact drainage tunnels, my lady, designed to swiftly channel the water away from the grand buildings along the front in case the sea wall ever collapses. I took the next parallel passageway and have nothing more than the extra length of my legs to explain my earlier arrival.'

She ran her hand through her curls and glanced behind her. 'They don't seem to have followed us, but that was too close. In fact, if it hadn't been for your quick thinking with the number thing, goodness knows what would have happened.'

'Actually, my lady, we have his lordship to thank for that. He used it once to extract us from a rather similar situation in Algiers.'

'Perhaps he was looking out for us just then?'

'Possibly, my lady.' He frowned. 'It seems we are safe. For now. But I am greatly concerned by the turn and speed of events since our arrival.'

She smiled ruefully and shook her head. 'None of this was on my holiday to-do list, that's for sure. Maybe we should postpone our shopping trip and return to the hotel, avoiding anywhere deserted on the way?'

'Agreed.'

As they walked, it was Eleanor's turn to frown. 'Why do you suppose they tried to kidnap us?'

'Likely because they were the ruffians who killed Mr Eden and ransacked his room. On failing to find the item they were looking for, they assumed, as did our man on the pier, that Mr Eden passed it on to you.'

She groaned. 'So now we have no choice but to find out what this wretched item is that was worth killing Hilary for. And we can't go to Grimsdale because he already disbelieves everything I've said.' She checked the street on her left wasn't deserted before turning into it. 'If we could just get hold of this troublesome object, we'd have the best chance of finding out why Hilary was killed for it. Then we might be closer to finding out who killed him.'

Clifford nodded. 'Indeed, my lady, I am getting the distinct feeling that were we to possess this item, every criminal in Brighton would come knocking at our door, Mr Eden's killer included.'

CHAPTER 8

'Perhaps we will try shopping in The Lanes tomorrow?' Clifford said as they safely reached the red-carpeted entrance steps of the Grand Hotel.

'Well, we need to shop elsewhere first,' Eleanor said as she stepped inside, rubbing her bruised elbow. 'For disguises. And excellent ones at that!'

'Strange that a lady would need a disguise on holiday?' came an unwelcome voice from behind an enormous Grecian urn.

Eleanor rolled her eyes. 'Inspector, good afternoon.'

Grimsdale's bald crown appeared between the fronds of gladioli and arum lilies as he rose. 'Lady Swift, finally you return. I have been waiting for you.'

'Most fortuitous timing then because here I am.'

His mouth set in a thin line. 'I need to ask you some more questions. But not here. Please follow me. We can talk in room 204.'

Out of the corner of her eye, she saw Clifford stiffen. She swallowed hard, aware that Grimsdale was watching her carefully. 'I think I recall you saying that was my late husband's room?'

'You have an excellent memory, Lady Swift. Or perhaps you have been in there?'

Keep calm, Ellie. 'No, I have never been in… that room.'

'But you may choose to? Assuming you are found to have no involvement in the death of Mr Eden – or Painshill – as the widow, I thought you might like to record any items you wish to keep. These can then be sent on to you later, after the investigation is closed.'

The inspector seemed to have another motive, however. 'Also, despite your self-professed distance, as the closest person to your late husband, there is a chance that you may notice something pertinent that my men missed?'

Including whatever got him killed? She bit her lip. 'Fine, Inspector. Lead the way.'

The excitement of riding in the hotel's innovative hydraulically powered lift passed her by as she fought to control her rushing emotions. As the attendant stopped the lift on the second floor, she felt Clifford press a clean handkerchief into her hand from behind. Her fingers closed tightly around it.

As she stepped out of the lift, the tall man she'd seen in the lobby wearing an overcoat when she'd first arrived passed her. He kept his eyes fixed forwards, but she was uncomfortably aware that he was looking at her, nonetheless. Following the inspector along the thick plum-carpeted corridor, her mouth was dry, her throat tight.

At the door, Grimsdale raised a hand. 'I may have forgotten to mention whoever killed Mr Eden also ransacked the place.'

The room was less luxurious than her suite, but still beautifully appointed. Striped Wedgwood blue-and-silver wallpaper, peppered with a small walnut writing desk, a matching dressing table, chest of drawers and a single wardrobe. A sumptuous leather chesterfield armchair facing the window looked out over the promenade to the sea.

The chaos of clothes and belongings strewn across the floor, however, destroyed the room's elegance. In the centre of the room, two suitcases had been stripped of their inner linings, their tattered edges waving as Grimsdale strode past them.

Eleanor's first impression was that Hilary had been travelling light as, despite the mess, there were few personal effects to be seen. Three pairs of suit trousers, six shirts, two tailored jackets and a leather belt were all the clothing. But then she glimpsed a flash of blue silk.

Hilary's favourite scarf! *The one he tied into a temporary sling for you, Ellie, that day you were thrown from the horse.* She looked up to see Grimsdale staring at her, his pencil moving across his notepad. She cleared her throat. 'Where… where exactly was he killed?'

He nodded to the walnut writing desk facing the far window. 'He was found slumped over the desk with a knife sticking out of his back.'

She closed her eyes and swallowed hard at the image. Sensing Clifford was reassuringly only half a pace behind her, she opened her eyes and tried to regain her composure.

'I assume you have checked what is left of the suitcases?'

Grimsdale nodded and nudged open the door of the en suite bathroom. 'And the remains of his toiletries case.' She peeped past him and caught her breath at the tumble of shaving gear and the smashed cologne bottle that littered the floor. The sight of his familiar tan leather washbag having been slashed from end to end with a knife made her feel light-headed. Scrutinising the rest of the room, she ruled out any hiding places the killer might have missed, for the entire place was tiled with a scrolling wave motif. With the clawfoot bath standing as the centrepiece, there were no concealed nooks or opportunities for loose wainscotting.

Back in the sitting room, the inspector appeared to be losing patience. 'Do you see anything unusual, Lady Swift?'

She shook her head slowly. 'I assume his leather satchel bag is in the bedroom area?'

He inclined his head. 'Satchel bag?'

'He never travelled without it. But perhaps he had changed his habits.'

'Apparently not.' He slid a Chinese screen to one side.

She stepped towards the bed as if in a daze. Her fingers ran along the mattress and onto the strap of the satchel Hilary had always had with him wherever he went. That it was now shredded like the rest of his luggage made the fact of his death seem more final than all the other decimation around her.

He'd even produced her surprise honeymoon present of the most beautiful emerald necklace she'd ever seen from that very satchel. That was after he'd carried her over the threshold of the romantic wilderness lodge he had booked for them. That her present had been stolen before the end of their trip had saddened her at the time. But now, standing amid the disarray of the last moments of the man she realised she knew little about, she admitted to herself that the theft might have been just one more lie.

She forced herself to speak. 'I can't see anything that might help you find the monster who did this.'

'What about his watch?'

'His watch?'

'Yes. I've never known a man travel without the aid of some kind of timepiece, have you?'

She shrugged but stepped automatically over to the left-hand bedpost and reached for the slim length of leather cord she knew would be there. Turning it round, she stared sadly at the empty end of the loop. 'The killer took his watch.'

'No. I did, Lady Swift. You see, we in the police force are fully capable of conducting a thorough search. But I wanted to see how well you knew the man you still profess was your husband.'

'A mean trick,' she muttered.

'Murder is a mean business, Lady Swift. Enlighten me, please. Why did he hang his watch behind his bedpost?'

She closed her eyes and spoke through her fingers. 'His father died of a stroke in bed when Hilary was six, I think it was. His mother woke him and walked him to the grandfather clock in the hallway and made him stop the pendulum as a mark of respect, which broke his heart. From the first day he owned a watch, he swore to always hang it out of sight at night. He told me if he ever died in his sleep, no one would find it and be asked to stop it for his death.' A stream of tears ran down her cheeks, which she failed to stem with Clifford's handkerchief.

'I see, I had no inkling of the significance,' Grimsdale said without feeling. 'Shall I add it to the list of effects you wish to keep?'

Clifford gave an uncharacteristic snort and stepped in front of the policeman. 'When you have quite finished with *all* the gentleman's effects, you will have someone neatly package every one, regardless of their condition. You will then dispatch them to Henley Hall.' He pulled a card from his waistcoat pocket and thrust it into the inspector's hand. 'Here is the address.'

'There is one more thing I wish her to look at,' Eleanor heard the inspector say.

'It's alright, Clifford, thank you.' She turned to Grimsdale. 'Where is it?'

'In the manager's office.'

She followed him, glad to escape the room.

The manager's office was a rather grandiose version of the hotel itself. Swathes of green flock fabric hung in perfect pleats the full length of one wall. Two chairs, upholstered in the same colour, sat either side of an imposing mahogany desk with a green leather writing inlay. Aside from a large bookcase of neatly labelled files and two plain standard lamps illuminating the somewhat gloomy space, there were no other items of furniture.

The inspector took the chair behind the desk and waved Eleanor into the other.

She reluctantly complied. 'Inspector, I would appreciate it if we could make this as quick as possible. I really have been through enough emotional turmoil for one day.'

For once, Grimsdale gave her the impression that he believed her. Unlocking the top desk drawer, he pulled out a wallet and passed it to her.

'Do you recognise this?'

She nodded. 'Yes. I believe it is Hilary's. Does it bear an embossed bird on the other side?'

'You can look for yourself. The only fingerprints on it were his.'

She turned it over. 'I imagine you found this on the bedside table?' she said without thinking.

'We did. Peculiar, wouldn't you say?'

She shrugged. 'I don't know what to think. It seems whoever killed my husband wasn't after his money.'

'No, clearly, despite the room being searched, it wasn't a case of robbery. Please look inside, perhaps something will strike you.'

There appeared to be little inside. The main pocket contained several bank notes she recognised as being marked from the South African Reserve Bank. There was also the stub of a second-class Blue Line ship's passenger ticket from Natal to the Port of London, which had been scheduled to dock four days previously. She ran her fingers along each of the other pockets but found nothing more and handed it back.

'Missing anything?'

'How would I know? When we were together, I was not in the habit of searching Hilary's wallet.'

Grimsdale skimmed a rectangular photograph face down across the desk to her.

'I thought you might have been looking for that when you went through his wallet, that's all.'

Trying to stop her fingers trembling, she ignored the few faint ink markings on the back and picked it up.

Please don't let it be Hilary with another woman.

She turned it over and sighed in relief. It was a photograph of Hilary, looking like the happiest man alive. Impeccably dressed in a dinner suit, he stood smiling at the camera, incongruous with the dirt floor of the lean-to shelter adorned in flowers he stood under.

Then realisation dawned. It was over. All her years of wondering, of hoping. Now she knew.

'Thank you,' she said matter-of-factly. She held the inspector's questioning gaze. 'Perhaps this will convince you once and for all that Hilary and myself were unquestionably estranged.'

She skimmed the photograph back to him. 'That is the picture taken on our wedding day. And as you can plainly see, Hilary cut me out of it. A long time ago, if the condition of the cut edge is anything to go by. Good day.'

CHAPTER 9

'Where can I take you, my lady?' Clifford said gently as he pulled the door of the manager's office shut behind her.

'Anywhere away from here.'

'Follow me.'

As Clifford led the way she spotted the short man she'd first seen in conversation with the taller man. He was lounging on the far side of the lobby where he had an unobstructed view of the door into the manager's office. Unless it was her imagination, he too was surreptitiously taking a keen interest in her. In the furthest corner of the hotel's glass-covered terrace, she absently accepted the lap blanket the suited waiter offered and let Clifford order for her. As lunchtime had passed, they were alone, save for two elderly ladies and the dapper man she'd also noted in the lobby when she'd first arrived. He was seated apart from the ladies at the opposite end of the long chandelier-lit extension.

'Leave the tray, I'll pour, thank you, Thomas,' Clifford said.

Eleanor looked up to see the waiter hesitating over the unorthodox request.

'It's fine really, thank you,' she managed with a weak smile.

As the waiter walked away, she turned to Clifford. 'Thomas?'

'As a guest's servant here at the Grand, my room is on the same floor as many of the staff, all of whom have proved to be most genial. Thomas usually works on the front desk but as the hotel is understaffed at the moment he also helps out in the dining room.

We discovered that we both enjoy Tolstoy and were delighted to swap books for the week.'

She smiled. 'I can't imagine any situation you could be dropped into where you wouldn't instantly be welcomed. Be that the king's court or the pirate's tavern in the most treacherous end of nowhere.'

He bowed and placed a steaming cup of tea in front of her. Leaning across, he then added a generous measure of what she assumed was brandy from a miniature crystal decanter. 'Your sangfroid has remained admirably intact, my lady, but perhaps a little extra fortification would not go amiss?'

'Thank you. Did I really think a holiday by the sea would be a good idea?'

'I heartily wish that I had suggested booking anywhere but the Grand, my lady. All of this unpleasantness would have passed you by had we booked into any other hotel.'

'Do you really think so? Honestly, I'm not so sure. Whoever it is that's after what Hilary had seems horribly determined. Somehow I get the feeling I would have been sought out at some point, seeing as several dubious types already seem to think I have it in my possession.' She stirred her tea thoughtfully. 'Mind you, I suppose, as you said, given the chaotic state of things after the war, I doubt if anyone would even have known Hilary and I were ever married.'

She groaned. 'That was a bit of a punch in the stomach, though, seeing our wedding photograph... cut like that.' She kept her eyes on her tea. 'I don't understand why he would do that. I mean, even if I meant nothing to him, why go to all the trouble of cutting me out and then still carrying the other half around? It wasn't as if we fought, or parted on bad terms. The last time we spent together was wonderful.' She blushed as the full memory of their last night flooded back.

Clifford's tone was non-committal. 'It is a puzzle, my lady.'

'Clifford.' She looked up at him. 'You mean well I know, but there can be no other explanation and I should just accept it. He cut me out of his life and I suppose cutting me out of the photograph probably just reinforced his relief it was over.'

'Supposing is good, but finding out is better.' He paused. 'Mark Twain,' he added. 'If you are resolved in thinking that Mr Eden felt the need to move on from your marriage, then that is fine. You are now at peace with that idea. So would there be any harm in pursuing the rest of the story? You said you wanted to find out the truth, no matter what.'

'Go on,' she said quietly.

'If what we discover proves you were right, you will not be subjected to any more upset because you have, as I said, already made peace with the idea. But if we reveal a more positive reason for his actions, might you not then move on through life eminently lighter of heart?'

She nodded glumly. Aware that her despondency was adding to the gloomy pall over the afternoon, she tried to lighten the mood. 'Thank you for wading in with Grimsdale by the way, much appreciated.'

'Perhaps we might omit him from our conversation, with your permission, of course. I confess to finding it hard to control my temper when his name is mentioned.'

She tilted her head. 'Do you actually have a temper, Clifford? I find it difficult to imagine.'

He adjusted his perfectly aligned tie. 'If the situation dictates.'

She managed a small chuckle. 'You know, you have a wonderful knack of knowing what to do and say to make me feel better in even the trickiest of situations. But I suppose you had years of practice with Uncle Byron.'

She choked on her tea as he laughed out loud, only the second time she'd heard him do so since she had come to live at Henley Hall.

'What? What did I say?' She was a little bemused.

'Please accept my sincere apologies, my lady, that was unforgivable but also, regrettably, uncontainable.'

'What exactly did I say that was so amusing?'

'Merely the notion that any of the twenty plus years I enjoyed in his lordship's service could ever have prepared me for the unprecedented situations I have found myself in since you arrived.' He shook his head. 'It has been quite the extraordinary ride.'

She winced. 'Sorry.'

'But not in any way an unpleasant one,' he added. 'Interesting. Surprising. Deeply concerning in regard to your safety on too many occasions. Perhaps *unpredictable*, even on a daily basis, would be the best description.'

'Yet you've taken everything perfectly in your stride. You've never flapped or faltered once.'

'I am a butler, my lady.'

She nodded and raised an eyebrow. 'Oh, of course, the conclusive answer.' She knew better than to rib him on that score. Her mind drifted back to the manager's office. 'After what our friend told us on the pier last night, I suppose I shouldn't have been surprised that Hilary's room had been ransacked. I wish we knew something about the item his killer was looking for, though.'

'We do, my lady.'

She looked at him quizzically. 'Do we?' She thought hard, but drew a blank. 'What?'

'That whatever Mr Eden's killer was seeking is too large to fit into a gentleman's wallet, but not too large to be concealed in his satchel.'

She slapped her forehead. 'Of course, you clever bean! The murderer didn't even open Hilary's wallet, but slashed his beloved satchel.' She frowned and shook her head. Something was nagging at her memory again. 'The desk!'

Clifford arched an eyebrow. 'I'm sorry, my lady?'

She jumped up. 'Grimsdale said Hilary was found stabbed in the back at the writing desk! Come on!'

She rushed out of the terrace, followed by her confused butler, ignoring the two old ladies' remarks about 'the youth of today'.

'My lady, I cannot.' Clifford shook his head and stayed resolutely in the corridor outside her suite.

'Oh for goodness' sake, Clifford! We can't afford to be overheard, this is too important.' She tipped out her handbag onto an exquisite inlaid table and pawed through the contents. 'Look!' She held up the envelope he had interrupted her in opening as he'd chivvied her to start their journey to Brighton. 'I knew I recognised the writing.' She showed him the handwritten address. 'It's Hilary's,' she whispered.

Clifford glanced up and down the corridor before stepping inside and closing the door behind him.

She gestured to him impatiently. 'Come over here.'

Again, he shook his head, his back pressed to the door. She had never seen him look so uncomfortable.

What is his problem, Ellie? We're not in my bedroom, only the sitting room, it's no different to the sitting room downstairs. She shook her head.

'Okay, Mr Etiquette, stay where you are and I'll be quick. Thank you for always being the gentleman and protecting the lady's reputation, but I'm sure propriety allows a lady's butler to attend to her in the sitting room of her suite.' She grabbed the hotel letter opener before joining him. 'I can't believe I've had this all along and didn't realise it. I forgot all about it until Grimsdale mentioned Hilary being killed at his desk. Obviously he can't have been writing this letter at the time as I wouldn't have received it, but it finally jogged my memory.'

'You have had rather a lot going on, my lady.'

She nodded. 'I just couldn't remember at the Hall why the handwriting was familiar.' She peered at the envelope and let out a long breath. 'Here goes.'

'Are you sufficiently prepared for whatever it might contain?'

'Not even a tiny bit. Good job you fortified my tea.' With a trembling hand, she ran the letter opener carefully along the top of the envelope. 'Empty! Look.' She held it open for him to see. 'But it can't be,' she muttered. 'Oh, Hilary, talk to me, please.' She put her fingers inside and ran them along the back. She gasped. 'There's something glued inside.' She pulled it out, ripping the envelope as she did so. 'Oh, gracious! Clifford, it's' – she held it up – 'the other half of our wedding photograph!'

CHAPTER 10

Outside on the top step of the hotel's majestic staircase, Eleanor felt her head was finally beginning to stop spinning. There was still a biting sea breeze, but the sun shone in a sky speckled with fluffy white clouds lazily sauntering along as if they were the ones on holiday.

'Sorry, Clifford,' she mumbled. 'I thought I'd been down the steepest part of this wretched emotional helter-skelter.'

'No need at all to apologise, my lady. However, perhaps a break from all of it would help? An engaging distraction, as it were?'

'Yes, it certainly would. Let's see if we can find the ladies.'

'Eminently doable.'

'But they won't want me tagging along. They'll only feel they have to behave.'

'At the seaside on holiday? I sincerely doubt it. And even if they intend to, I am confident they won't manage it.'

How he had deduced that the ladies would have visited the bright lights of the entertainment halls and now be at the Palace Pier, she could not fathom. But the sight of the three of them arm in arm, laughing as they walked along, brought her the sense of grounding she craved.

Even in her short time at Henley Hall, there had been some significant squabbles between Mrs Trotman and Mrs Butters. And she knew that Polly's clumsy forgetfulness drove them both to distraction. Clifford, too. And he sometimes found the ladies a challenge to oversee, but it had never been more clear that the four of them were a team. One bound by more than just being thrown together through their employment. Behind all the respectful adherence to the rules of the staff hierarchy, they were friends.

And she was part of it too, she realised, as the three of them spied her and ran over calling out, Gladstone trotting alongside barking excitedly. *Make that the perfect six, Ellie.*

'My lady? Hooray!'

Gathered in front of her, Mrs Butters nudged Polly, whose cheeks coloured. 'Go on, my girl.'

Polly reached into her coat pocket and pulled out a small tissue-wrapped package. 'We bought you a present, your ladyship.' She bit her lip. 'I hope 'tis not against the rules.'

Eleanor took the package from the young girl's outstretched hand. 'Gracious, thank you. But the envelopes I asked Clifford to give each of you were for you to spend entirely on yourselves on your holiday.'

Mrs Butters waved her hand. ''Tis only little.'

Pulling open the tissue paper, Eleanor caught her breath. 'Ladies, it is absolutely beautiful.' She lifted up the darling plaited bracelet of starched green ribbons of every shade. 'Green is so my favourite colour.' Below hung four shiny tin charms.

'I chose the seagull,' Polly said. 'Because she made me think of you flying along on all your magical travels.'

Mrs Butters chuckled. 'And I picked the dog because we all know how much you love Mr Wilful here.'

'Beggin' your pardon, my lady, but I chose the little knife and fork because you're always so complimentary and enthusiastic about my cooking,' Mrs Trotman said.

'And the delightful little clock?' Eleanor asked with a sideways glance at Clifford.

The ladies looked at each other. 'We chose that in Mr Clifford's absence because we know how much you enjoy following his schedules,' Mrs Butters said through a fit of giggles which set them all off.

'Ladies, sincerely it is the most wonderful present I have ever received.' She laid it over her wrist, Mrs Butters looping the delicate chain clasp closed.

'Have you both a little while to join us? 'Twould be such a treat.'

Fearing her voice would give her away, Eleanor simply nodded.

It was a perfect afternoon. The sea breeze died down from biting to nipping and occasionally the warmth of the early spring sun reminded one that summer, not winter, was around the corner. Eleanor and the ladies explored the esplanade and piers, giggling at the risqué postcards and pointing out everything that caught their eye. The milder temperature had enticed more people outside, giving the long parade something of a fashion-show air. Ladies in colourful silk dresses and fur coats held tight to the arms of smartly suited gentlemen, most sensibly still carrying umbrellas knowing how fickle seaside weather could be.

Eleanor was captivated by the elegant window displays of the many shoe shops, while Mrs Butters cooed over the rainbow array of delicate fabrics in the haberdashers and Polly drank in the rows of feathered, fringed and netted hats and fascinators in the milliners. Among the rather wind-blown stalls set up on many of the wider street corners, they idled over the collections of artwork, chatting with the artists. It was fascinating to learn the history of many of the buildings and boats included in the seascapes.

At one street corner, Eleanor stood quietly as she watched Clifford in animated discussion with the painter of a scene of the nearby Beachy Head Lighthouse being constructed twenty years earlier.

The engineers had built a cable car purely to transport the building materials from the cliffs to the lighthouse, spanning the five hundred feet out from the cliffs, the sea approach being too dangerous. It obviously appealed to Clifford's love of engineering and science. As he moved on, she discreetly paid for the painting and asked for it to be delivered to his room at the Grand.

Fortified by a stop off in a sweet little café in one of the quirky boutique-filled lanes, the five of them hurried off to the beach and a Punch and Judy show. Despite the lack of tourists elsewhere, a size-able crowd had gathered in front of the narrow stage, which stood about eight feet above the sand. The gold-painted sign declared this to be *Professor Willoughby's Royal Show*. Framed by an ornate wooden cut out of a theatre's decorative arch, the sides and back of the pop-up theatre were made of red-and-yellow striped calico pulled taut to hide the puppeteer inside at work.

Clifford made sure Polly had a good view of the hook-nosed puppets and soon she and the other ladies were tired from laughing at the crocodile repeatedly stealing Punch's sausages and Punch fighting with the doctor who had come to examine him. Hoarse from shouting at naughty Mister Punch, they finally set off to find another café where they revived themselves by devouring cockles and whelks, prawns and candyfloss.

As they wandered back along towards the pier, Clifford paused to tie his shoelace. The ladies, meanwhile, dissolved into fits of giggles in front of the ornate fronted 'Miniature Picture Palace'. Polly clapped her hands over her mouth and stared wide-eyed at Mrs Butters, who had shuffled in front of one of the posters in the window.

'What is it?' Eleanor said.

'Oh, apologies, my lady, it must be the sea air affecting our sense of humour.'

'Come on, let me in on the joke.'

With a mischievous grin, Mrs Trotman pushed Mrs Butters aside to reveal the poster. It depicted a coin-operated free-standing viewing machine and written inside the outline of a keyhole the words 'What the Butler Saw! Only 2d.'

The ladies stared at Eleanor apprehensively until she exploded into laughter. 'Can you imagine if Clifford even catches us looking at the poster? The poor man will blush from his impossibly shiny shoes to the tips of his ears.'

'Quick, he's coming,' Mrs Trotman hissed.

Feeling guilty, they spun round and slapped on their best innocent expressions. Eyeing each of them in turn like naughty children, Clifford shook his head. 'I see it is not just the staff who are flouting the rules of propriety.'

As they moved on, a man in a tightly belted overcoat and fedora approached them carrying a camera on a wooden tripod. 'Good afternoon, folks, excuse me interrupting. I wonder if you would care for a photographic memento of your trip to almost sunny Brighton?'

Eleanor nodded. 'We would absolutely love that.'

'Price includes developing and sending to any address in the country by post.' The photographer was obviously delighted at what was probably his first piece of business all day, given the less-than-sparkly weather and the lack of tourists.

With the group pose sorted and Gladstone finally persuaded to sit still, the photographer disappeared under a dark cloth and called, 'Let's see beautiful smiles all round, folks!'

Just as the photograph was taken, Gladstone decided that the seagull he'd been eyeing on the beach needed chasing and shot off after it.

'No, boy. Come back!' Eleanor called after him as he lumbered down the short flight of steps. Clifford was quickly on his trail, his long strides making swift progress in closing the gap. But the seagull had got the measure of the panting bulldog and came to rest ten feet from the shore, bobbing on the heaving waves. Oblivious to the swell of the sea, Gladstone barrelled in after it and then came to a stunned halt as he was lifted up and thrown about by the choppy water.

Eleanor ran to the sea's edge, but by then Clifford had ripped off his shoes and socks. Rolling up his trouser legs, he waded in to catch the struggling bulldog. Re-emerging soaked from the waist down he put the dog gently on the sand and ruffled his ears. 'Not without a life jacket, Master Gladstone. You're not built for swimming, remember?'

'Oh, Clifford,' Eleanor said, dropping to her knees and nuzzling Gladstone's soggy nose. 'Thank you.' But then she failed to hold back the giggle that broke out of her at the sight of her usually impeccable butler dripping onto the beach. With his sodden trousers turned up at different lengths and his feet covered in sand, he looked too comical. Recovering, she tried to sound concerned. 'You must be so cold. I bet the sea is absolutely freezing, isn't it?'

'I believe "bracing" is the official seaside term, my lady.'

As Clifford bent to put his shoes on, the photographer appeared at Eleanor's side and said in a low voice, 'The image of such a smart gentleman wading into the sea in March after a mischievous dog was too funny, madam. I couldn't resist it.' He patted his camera. 'But that one will be developed and sent to you on me, just for him having made my day.' With another chortle he set off across the sand, whistling.

Back at the Grand, Clifford slid in via the staff entrance, given his disordered appearance, taking Gladstone with him. Eleanor pulled out her pocket watch. She was at a bit of a loose end for the hour until they had arranged to meet back up. When they did, they would need to find a restaurant where they could eat together. Society certainly didn't condone butlers dining with their employers, so they needed to find one well away from the Grand. Eleanor sighed, wishing, not for the first time, that she had been born in the future, when society would surely be based on a more equitable footing.

But then she realised all that sea air had made her quite ravenous. Putting campaigning for social justice on temporary hold, she went in search of a pre-dinner snack.

CHAPTER 11

Back in her room, relaxed from her afternoon with her staff, Eleanor looked around with renewed interest. Since arriving at the Grand, she'd simply been too caught up in the dreadful events of the last twenty-four hours to notice her surroundings. Across the sumptuous cream carpet, separated by an exquisite marble and onyx coffee table, sat two sky-blue and silver velvet settees, their bold geometric print echoed in the wallpaper. One wall of the room was occupied entirely by floor-to-ceiling windows, shrouded by the sheerest of pleated silver voile. Taking the turned glass rod, which served as a decorative curtain pull, she pulled the shimmering fabric aside and stared out at the restless sea.

Hilary crossed that, Ellie. Likely thirty days aboard, sailing the South Atlantic and the North, too. Could it have been all with the intention of seeing you? What other explanation could there be for sending you the other half of our wedding photograph? And for keeping it all those years? Maybe in his wallet, close to his heart? And yet before you realised he had kept the other half of the photograph, you were sure your marriage meant nothing to him!

Fearing she would explode with her conflicting emotions, as well as the events, of the last twenty-four hours, she decided a bath and a change of clothes would at least distract her burning brain.

In her adjoining cream-and-gold bedroom, silk wallpaper depicting exotic birds filled the wall opposite her queen-sized bed. She smiled at the pretty dish of Turkish delight on her pillow and the vase of fresh flowers left by the cleaning staff. At least if life was going to veer off the rails, it had happened somewhere luxurious. Even the bathroom was worthy of a sultan's palace. One wall depicted Botticelli's 'Birth of Venus', artfully edited in the modesty stakes by the careful placement of two wall sconces. The remaining walls were decorated with embossed shell-motif tiles. An indulgent deep, gold, claw-footed bath along with twin gold-tapped washbasins occupied this end of the bathroom. Choosing from an array of bath oils, she slid into the hot water and let the steam melt her angst away.

An hour or so later, Eleanor looked around at the bright silk wall hangings and the ornate lamps which shone through the latticed stonework of the tiny galleried landing above her table. Clifford, true to form, had found just the kind of restaurant she loved.

'Is this a suggestion of Thomas'?'

'Actually, your uncle and I used to dine here when the need arose, my lady. A Punjabi dining room, authentic to its Indian roots. It is also a discreet setting, being off the main thoroughfare.'

'Well, it all smells far too delicious for me to even begin looking at the menu.'

A smiling waiter appeared at their table.

'May I?' Clifford asked.

She nodded, but her jaw slackened as Clifford launched into what she assumed was near-fluent Punjabi. The waiter's face lit up, and he was soon eagerly pointing out particular dishes on the menu.

Once Clifford had finished ordering, and the waiter gone, she gave him an enquiring glance.

'Did you pack any more surprises in your case, Clifford?'

'That we will only discover as events dictate. But as to my knowing a smattering of Punjabi, his late lordship and I while in the army spent several years in Northern India, as you know. We both developed a great respect for the local people wherever we found ourselves to be lodging. In fact, there is a considerable population of Indian soldiers who remained in Brighton after the war.'

'Really? I never knew that.'

He poured her a tall glass of water with fragrant mint leaves. 'Are you feeling somewhat restored after our afternoon among the rabble that are masquerading as your respectful staff?'

That made her laugh. 'Yes, thank you. It is such a treat to see them enjoying themselves. And they are hilarious. When they're allowed to be,' she said carefully, wanting to make sure he didn't think she was criticising his way of handling them on a daily basis.

He nodded. 'Agreed, but one cannot always be on holiday. The eminent Irish playwright, Mr George Bernard Shaw noted, "A perpetual holiday is a good working definition of hell."'

She laughed. 'I know what he means. Mind you, I've never really been one for too many rules and what I love about holidays is there are none.' She shrugged at his mock look of horror. 'I guess my parents gave me so much freedom, I never really learned how to obey rules.'

'Something I learned quickly, my lady. From your very first visit to Henley Hall as a child I realised I would have to be extra resourceful.'

'I suppose in some ways, I was spoiled. Or neglected, depending on your viewpoint.'

'Or given the freedom to find your own way, perhaps?'

She smiled at him, remembering the quote from Oscar Wilde he'd hidden in one of her shoes when she'd first inherited the Hall. 'Be yourself, everyone else is already taken.'

He smiled back. 'I am pleased to see you are feeling somewhat better, my lady.'

'Much, thank you. So much so actually, would it spoil your meal if we talked a little about the photograph Hilary sent me? You're such a good sounding board because I know you'll make sure the conversation will be drowning in logic and reason.'

He arched a brow. 'Is there any other way to converse?'

She reached into her handbag and pulled out the half of her wedding photograph, running her finger down the frayed cut edge.

'It looks like you had an idyllic setting,' Clifford said, clearly hoping to help her begin.

'We did. And it felt so right on the day and until… until he disappeared. I keep vacillating between believing he did care for me and then hitting the ground with a painful bump as my thoughts whisper not to be so stupid, he couldn't possibly have.'

'Would it be inappropriate to suggest Mr Eden might have wanted to return to you, but was thwarted in some way?'

'Who knows? As we've said before, we have all been through extraordinary times, times I hope we never repeat. It is possible he simply couldn't return. Or even find me.'

Clifford cleared his throat. 'And it does appear that he was caught up in some… complicated business matters.'

'It's alright, we both know you mean questionable, dangerous and almost certainly highly illegal. None of the roguish types we've encountered so far would be candidates for a gentleman of the year award, would they?'

'Indeed not.'

They paused as the waiter returned bearing an enormous tray stacked with a raft of clay dishes, each bubbling and wafting delicious aromas.

'Wow! What a stunning spread.'

'A whistle-stop tour of the incredible culinary traditions of the Punjab region, my lady. But I know you cycled that way when you crossed the Himalayas, so I believe it is already familiar to you?'

She nodded. She'd cycled around the world before she'd taken Thomas Walker up on his offer of a job in South Africa. Most people she spoke to expressed disbelief that a woman could have undertaken such a journey. She invariably pointed out to them, however, that she certainly wasn't the first. Annie Londonderry, a Latvian immigrant in the US, had taken that accolade way back in 1895.

'Wonderful cuisine though it is, Clifford, it really wasn't quite the perfect food for cycling. Now, however, I shall be able to do it justice!'

With their plates sizzling and their palates tingling, they continued their previous discussion.

'I know we've gone over this, Clifford, but why do you suppose Hilary was here?'

He held her gaze. 'In truth, I have only two theories at this point. One, that he was here to conclude whatever… business he was involved in. Which means there must be some reason he chose Brighton as opposed to any other town, but what that reason is eludes me.'

'And the other?'

'That he returned to England to see you, my lady. Although, again, why was he in Brighton? The South African ships dock at London.'

She turned her fork in her hand. 'Wouldn't that be the ultimate tragedy? I mean, after all those years, if he had decided to contact me, even if only to explain where he'd been and why he let me believe that he had died. But then that he was murdered before he could tell me in the very hotel I was booked into the following day.'

'Undoubtably. But there is still the possibility, remote I admit, that whatever the reason Mr Eden was killed, it is not related to either of those scenarios.'

'I suppose so.' She held the photograph up to the light.

'And the inscription?' Clifford pointed to the reverse side. 'I noted a similar set of faded markings on the half the inspector showed you.'

'Golly, I missed those.' She gave a wan smile. 'I've just been staring at the picture itself, wishing he was still standing next to me.' She turned the photograph over and peered at it, struggling to make out the faint lettering. Clifford moved one of the lamps nearer so they could read each of the incomplete lines.

> Lady Eleanor
> Captain Hilary
> Married on
> At the Hotel
> Something old
> Something borrowed
> And a sixpence

Her hand went to her throat as she read the last line.

> Till death do

'That's Hilary's handwriting, Clifford. And I remember this photograph, of course, but it never had this writing on the back. He must have written this after he disappeared.' A frisson of something she couldn't name ran down her spine and back up through her chest to her heart. 'Clifford, what was that Mark Twain quote you said this morning?'

'"Supposing is good, but finding out is better."'

'And how right he was!' She turned the photograph over and stared at the image of herself in her bridal gown. How happy she looked in the simple ivory silk dress, smiling up at her new husband. *Ex-husband now, Ellie, you saw his body. He's not coming back this time.*

She looked up at her butler with an expression that brooked no disagreement. 'Clifford, I don't care what Hilary was mixed up in; I owe it to him to find his killer if the police don't. And I owe it to myself to find out why he still had our wedding photograph six years after he left me. And why he sent me the half he did. And…'

'And, my lady?'

'And if he really loved me.' She laid the photograph down a little sadly. 'Or not.'

CHAPTER 12

Despite Clifford's insistence that Eleanor jam a chair under the door handle into her suite the night before, she slept only fitfully. However, she felt surprisingly restored the following morning. A generous plateful from the hotel's extensive breakfast definitely helped, as did the sun streaming in through the floor-to-ceiling windows. As the waiter offered her more coffee to finish, she inhaled the delicious aroma but shook her head and groaned. 'No, thank you. I'm afraid I have failed to show sufficient restraint to leave room. My compliments to your chef, but I shall need to purchase an entire new, and larger-sized wardrobe if he keeps this up.'

'I'll pass on your compliments, Lady Swift.'

She looked around the almost empty breakfast room. 'Is it always this quiet in March?'

'This year is, in fact, exceptionally so, Lady Swift.'

He left her to deal with the other guests, only four, dotted about the exotic palm-filled room. Three tables away sat the strong-jawed man she had noticed smoking in the hotel's lobby on the day they first arrived. Immaculately dressed in a tailored steel-grey suit, the unusual amethyst purple of his tie caught her eye. She'd learned from Clifford his name was Willem de Meyer. He selected a cream bloom with purple edging from the crystal vase on his table and slid it into his lapel buttonhole.

At another table, the two elderly ladies were twittering over their smoked kippers. As they talked, they repeatedly knocked their walking canes from the arms of their chairs with their velvet-jacketed elbows. But it was the other guest who was making her feel uncomfortable. The curvaceous woman with the deep-blue eyes who Eleanor had first seen on the staircase in the lobby kept staring in Eleanor's direction despite the woman's pretence of reading the book in front of her. The waiter had called her Miss Summers. Her dress – a decorous navy twinset and two strands of pearls – failed to convince Eleanor that Miss Summers was as modest as she was trying to appear. Even with her blonde hair twisted into a demure chignon, the heavy use of blush and kohl gave her the air of someone aware that her charms could be extremely useful.

Clifford appeared with Gladstone and she joined them, motioning towards the French doors out to the hotel's small ornamental garden. 'A little constitutional after a hearty breakfast is always a good idea, I feel, Clifford.'

As he closed the door behind her, she tightened the belt of her jade-green wool jacket against the cool air and lowered her voice. 'I do wish you had gone and had breakfast yourself instead of watching me like a hawk. Though I appreciate your concern, I'm sure I shan't come to any harm in full view of the other guests. Although I may be in significant danger of overeating from devouring sausages, salmon and a delicious stack of pancakes.'

'Perhaps, my lady. But perhaps not.'

'Let me guess, you've been awake most of the night too, only you managed to arrive at some cogent conclusions?'

'Hopefully. Although in between I did manage to lose myself in the exceptional detail of the marvellous lighthouse painting, for which, again I thank you most sincerely. And yourself?'

'Oh you know, bouts of nightmares. Being on the *Titanic* with Hilary as it went down, interspersed with visions of you riding into the hotel pond on a donkey to rescue Gladstone from the ornamental goldfish.'

'Ah. Then I suppose we should be thankful for the restorative effects of a mountain of sausages and pancakes.'

They followed Gladstone as he trotted down the stone steps, past the beds of early spring guelder roses, irises and lily of the valley. At the end of the herringbone brick path stood a conservatory, a glass pagoda housing a mosaic-topped table surrounded by four white, wicker, wingback chairs, each nestling a plump peacock-feather print cushion. Once inside, she pulled out a slim tissue-wrapped parcel from her pocket and wafted it under Gladstone's nose, smiling as he spun in a lopsided circle with a deep woof.

'I thought you might be missing Mrs Trotman's special breakfast treat, old chum.' She passed him the sausage she'd been unable to finish.

From the inside of his jacket, Clifford produced a long slim flask that he set on the table before pulling a chair out for her.

'The warming coffee you didn't manage with your breakfast,' he said by way of explanation as he poured her a steaming cup of richly roasted coffee.

She smiled at his thoughtfulness. 'Because you knew I wouldn't be able to resist the incredible array of breakfast items. Very kind and disturbingly astute. I guess I have Thomas to thank for filling your Thermos?'

'Actually, yes. He was particularly keen to oblige my request.' Clifford cleared his throat. 'He is rather a fan of yours.'

She frowned. 'Why? I wasn't even aware I had fans.' She glanced down at Gladstone, who, having devoured the sausage, was now resting his head on her lap in the hope of more. 'Unless you count greedy bulldogs, that is.'

Clifford's eyes twinkled. 'It seems Thomas has somehow formed the unshakeable belief that you are the famous American actress Gloria Swanson, checked in under an assumed name for anonymity purposes.'

Eleanor tried to surreptitiously wipe away with her sleeve the coffee that she had snorted through her nose at this news. Realising she'd failed, she took the handkerchief Clifford offered her. 'Where on earth did he get that impression?'

'Perhaps from an overactive imagination and a heartfelt longing to meet the lady in question?'

'But that's ridiculous. I should probably know, but do I even look like this woman?'

'From certain angles. But, if you will forgive my observation, mostly in the area of deportment. Miss Swanson is considered to be Hollywood's most elegant star.'

She shook her head. 'He obviously didn't see me yesterday then, sprawled on my knees in the sand, cuddling Mr Wilful here after you rescued him from the waves.'

'Very likely he did, my lady. Miss Swanson is known to be a devoted dog lover and often takes one with her when she travels. It is also unusual for a guest of the Grand to have such a large entourage to accompany them around the town as you did yesterday with myself and the ladies.'

She cocked her head. 'But you didn't see fit to put him straight on who I really am?'

'Disgracefully, no.' He held up a hand as she went to speak. 'For two reasons. First, the other hotel staff have delighted in fuelling his notion. It has become something of a game between them, and, as the interloper they have kindly welcomed into their midst, it was far from my place to interfere.'

'Hmm. And the second?'

'I thought his fixation with the idea would come in useful, should we need to call on his assistance during our investigations.'

She laughed. 'Clifford, beneath your flawless demeanour, I detect the hint of a scallywag. But if needs be, I shall play along and try and pull off the Hollywood heroine persona.'

'Then let us hope that does not result in diminishing Miss Swanson's reputation to that of also being a scallywag. However' – his demeanour became serious – 'are you still resolved in the decision you made last night at dinner?'

'Even more so, having woken to the sight of the cut photograph propped against the lamp on my bedside table this morning.'

'Then, at the risk of causing you further anxiety, might I share a thought with you?'

She nodded tentatively.

'As we know from Detective Inspector Grimsdale the timeframe within which Mr Eden died—'

'We do?'

'Indeed. You may have tuned out when the inspector shared the details of Mr Eden's death. You were in shock. It seems—'

'Wait a minute, I need—'

Clifford passed her a notebook and her uncle's favourite fountain pen.

She opened her mouth to say something, then shook her head with a fond smile. Turning to a clean page, she wrote the two words:

HILARY'S MURDER

She looked at Clifford and shook her head again.

'I never expected on my thirtieth birthday to be trying to solve the case of a man who died twice!'

CHAPTER 13

'Are you alright, my lady?'

Clifford's voice broke into her thoughts. She shook her head. 'Perfectly, thank you. Now, what did Grimsdale say?'

Clifford looked unconvinced, but dutifully cleared his throat. 'Mr Eden checked in around five-and-ten to eleven on the evening of Saturday, the fifth. He then left the hotel before breakfast the following morning around seven, only to return that evening at six and, except for a trip out around nine thirty, stayed in his room. The maid alerted the manager at nine o'clock the next morning after breakfast, as Mr Eden had not vacated his room in time for it to be cleaned. And as no amount of knocking could rouse a response, the manager used his pass key to enter the room, only to find Mr Eden—'

'Dead.' She pictured him at the writing desk, but with an effort shook the image out of her head. 'You really do have an amazing memory, Clifford.'

'Thank you, my lady. Thomas told Detective Inspector Grimsdale that on Sunday night, Mr Eden entered the hotel at ten forty-five and proceeded straight upstairs. Thomas assumed to his room. And that was the last sighting of him alive.'

She jotted down a summary as he spoke.

Clifford waited until she had finished and then continued. 'The body – sorry, my lady – Mr Eden was found the following morning by the manager at nine fifteen. The coroner examined the, er… deceased around an hour and a quarter later. He estimated the regrettable incident had occurred a maximum of twelve hours and a minimum of four hours before he carried out his examination. He cautioned, however, that Detective Inspector Grimsdale should allow a certain amount of leeway between these two times.'

She wrote again, then tapped the page with the pen. 'But as we know from the man on the pier – *if* we believe him and what choice do we have? – Hilary was dead when he searched his room at eleven thirty. So, if that's the case he must have died between… ten forty-five and… eleven thirty.' She returned to the top of the page and added the line so it now looked like this:

Saturday, 5th
10.45 p.m. – Hilary checked in

Sunday, 6th
7 a.m. – Left hotel in morning
6 p.m. – Returned in evening
9.30 p.m. – Left hotel again
10.45 p.m. – Thomas (desk clerk) sees Hilary enter hotel and go upstairs (to his room?)
11.30 p.m. – man on pier searches room. Hilary dead.

Monday, 7th
9.15 a.m. – Hotel manager and maid find Hilary dead in his room
10.30 a.m. – Coroner examines Hilary – puts time of death around 10.30 p.m. to 6.30 a.m.

She went to suck the pen and then changed her mind. 'So, the desk clerk, Thomas, saw Hilary alive at ten forty-five and the night porter locks the door at eleven. So if Hilary was murdered sometime between ten forty-five and eleven thirty, then it must have been a member of the staff? Or a guest?'

Clifford nodded slowly. 'Detective Inspector Grimsdale mentioned that there was no sign of a break-in and Johnson, the night porter, is usually in the lobby, I'm told, twenty minutes or so before his shift starts. So unless one of the staff let the murderer in, I think we can presume your conjecture is correct.'

'And, given that we are pretty sure the murderer ransacked Hilary's room, but failed to find what he was looking for—'

'We can assume the murderer is still at the hotel as no one has checked out.'

'Exactly.'

Clifford cleared his throat. 'We may be able to narrow down our suspects a little further, my lady. As you know, my room is on the same floor as many of the staff and there has been little talk of anything else except Mr Eden's demise and the subsequent interrogation of the staff by the police.'

She nodded. 'I'm sure it has been no fun for them.'

'Indeed not. However neither has it been too taxing. Given the lateness of the hour, most of the staff were already in their quarters, and as they share a minimum of two to a room, they were all able to substantiate each other's alibi. The few exceptions, such as Thomas, who, as we know, was on the front desk, and the manager, were also able to verify their alibis. Johnson, the night porter, confirmed Thomas' alibi from around ten forty-five until Thomas went off shift at eleven, and then his roommate confirmed his alibi for the rest of the night. The manager apparently similarly had witnesses to verify his alibi, although the staff weren't privy as to who the witnesses were.'

She pursed her lips. 'Mmm, one of the staff could still have waited until their roommate was sleeping and then crept down and into Hilary's room.'

He nodded. 'That is not beyond the realms of possibility, but given the location of the staff quarters and the layout of the rooms themselves, it would have been very tricky to leave and return with no one knowing, as I am well aware.'

She let out a long breath. 'Okay, so we'll concentrate on the guests, but we should at least ask the manager if any staff were taken on recently. Or we could ask Thomas, actually.'

He held up a cautionary finger. 'But that would assume Thomas could not be a suspect.'

'Good point. But that goes for the manager too, but I suppose we have to start somewhere. I'll employ my artful questioning technique.'

Clifford let this hang in the air for a moment. 'Perhaps I should be the one to ask Thomas if Mr Eden had booked ahead?'

'While I dazzle him with my Hollywood-worthy winning smile.'

'What could possibly go wrong, my lady.'

As they made their way to the hotel lobby, the manager stopped them just inside the main entrance. He ran his hands down the line of strained buttons on his striped grey waistcoat. 'Please can I offer my sincere apologies, Lady Swift, for the, erm... inconvenience of the disturbing event you witnessed on your arrival. I would be delighted if you would consider the dining room at your disposal for the rest of your stay, on the owners' account, of course.'

Eleanor smiled, appreciating the gesture but wondering how on earth free meals, however sumptuous, could be compensation for the sight she witnessed on their arrival. 'A kind and generous thought, but not necessary, thank you.'

She glimpsed Clifford's lips twitching, but continued on. 'In fact, I congratulate you on how the situation has been handled. It cannot be easy dealing with such an incident whilst running a hotel of this size and distinguished reputation. I understand most hotels struggle with a very high turnover of staff, that alone must be very time consuming for you.'

The manager's flaccid chin wobbled as he shook his head vehemently. 'Gracious no, not here at the Grand. I insist on a most rigorous system of hiring staff, but also one for ensuring their retention as well. Our staff are very happy and understand the privilege which working here affords them.'

Clifford nodded. 'That has certainly been my experience.'

'I'm very pleased. In fact, the last time a member of staff left us was because they married and followed their new husband back to his native Scotland.'

'A September wedding? I hope it wasn't as chilly as it is now,' Eleanor said.

'September? Did I say that? No, no, it was bitterly cold being as it was in December.' With a click of his heels, he nodded and walked away, disappearing into the lift.

Eleanor eyed Clifford's expression. 'You would have preferred me to take up his offer of working my way through the entire menu without incurring the cost?'

'I was merely thinking of the benefit to the household accounts, my lady.'

She tutted. 'Clifford, I'm really not that rapacious. I'm not a greedy bulldog, unlike some amongst us.' She ruffled Gladstone's ears and then noted Clifford's arched brow. 'Well, not away from Mrs Trotman's fine fayre, anyway.'

'However, if I might in fact offer my admiration for you declining his offer. It brought him considerable relief and eased the conversation significantly. And the question of any new staff was, as you promised, artfully woven in.'

She nodded. 'So it seems that no one was taken on recently. That may not mean they had no part in Hilary's murder, but if he didn't make a reservation, then it's certainly less likely. I mean, we can assume none of them would even have known he was coming to the hotel when they were taken on.'

Clifford nodded back. 'And as Mr Eden came from abroad, unlikely they would have known him previously. Although, I believe you told me he was originally from this country?'

She nodded. 'Sydenham in South East London. Ah! There's Thomas.'

Eleanor sashayed over to the fitted cases of jewellery and silver giftware, flashing the desk clerk a beaming smile as she did so. He ran a hand over his neat side parting and swallowed hard. Clifford approached the desk.

'Err, how can I help, Mr Clifford?' The clerk's eyes strayed back to Eleanor, who wandered over to one of the wingback chairs and arranged herself elegantly, making a show of adjusting the pleats of her sage silk skirt. Yesterday afternoon she had bought an oversized pair of sunglasses, which were rapidly becoming the de rigueur accessory for all Hollywood stars. Now she slipped them on and gave Thomas her best wave as if she were Gloria Swanson herself acknowledging her legions of fans as opposed to one lone desk clerk.

Clifford cleared his throat loudly in an effort to regain the clerk's attention. 'Thomas, I wonder if the gentleman from 204 who was unfortunately... "permanently indisposed" on Monday morning had called ahead to make a reservation?'

The clerk frowned. 'A strange question.'

'If I can rely on your discretion?' Clifford paused until Thomas nodded. 'The lady' – he indicated Eleanor – 'is worried about any adverse publicity. She is here incognito, as it were, and would be most grateful to anyone who helped her avoid the unwanted attention of the press.'

What connection this had with Clifford's question didn't seem to bother the clerk. He leapt at the opportunity for the film star he was besotted with to be in his debt.

'Ah! In that case, no. I was on duty the evening the gentleman, Mr Painshill, checked in but he simply arrived and asked for a room. As the season doesn't start until Easter weekend, it is not that uncommon for guests to arrive without a reservation.'

Eleanor frowned to herself until she remembered that Hilary had booked himself in as Geoffrey Painshill. She busied herself admiring her nails as she heard Clifford add, 'The lady will be most grateful to hear that. And to you too.'

'To me?' Thomas said in delight.

'For your discretion in not mentioning this conversation to anyone. As I said, she does not wish to draw attention to her presence.'

'Oh absolutely. Please assure the lady I shan't breathe a word.'

Tapping the lobby desk with the flat of his hand, Clifford turned to meet Eleanor who threw the clerk a finger wave before gliding on half a step ahead. As they passed the grand piano, she whispered, 'My turn to applaud. Your performance was far more award-worthy than mine.'

'With apologies, I beg to disagree, my lady. I feared I might need to proffer a handkerchief, given how close he was to drooling.'

CHAPTER 14

Pleased with the news that the ladies had planned a fun day trip to the nearby historic town of Lewes, Eleanor was delighted with Clifford's suggestion to visit the Grand's main rival, the Metropole.

'Unless, that is, you are still too replete from breakfast, my lady?' Clifford said.

She scoffed. 'That was ages ago now. I bet the Metropole has cake worth risking indigestion for.'

'His lordship always said exactly that.'

'Which is why you suggested it, of course.'

Taking advantage of the Grand's dog-sitting service, they left Gladstone in the care of the concierge, and headed out into the morning sun in search of early elevenses.

In contrast to the set back, palatial vision of stuccoed cream stone that the Grand cut, the Metropole loomed imposingly over the main street. Its red-brick and terracotta frontage felt more formal and austere to Eleanor. Inside, however, the tea room was a haven of serenity. It seemed a hundred miles away from the unpleasantness she felt she had been living and breathing at the Grand. She paused in awe at the double-height floor-to-ceiling windows, each one over twenty feet wide and separated with an ornate mirror set behind a low-hanging chandelier.

'I feel like a princess,' she murmured as she took the seat the waiter pulled out for her.

'As you should.' Clifford gave her a conspiratorial look. 'As my ward, out to be spoiled as part of your birthday tea.'

'I had no idea we would need to pull the wool over so many people's eyes on this holiday,' she said once the waiter had left them. 'But as it is the only way you and I can talk over tea in public without causing a scandal, I'm game.'

Clifford adjusted his tie. 'However, please forgive my reduced formality whilst we engage in the charade, my lady.'

She waved a dismissive hand. 'Doesn't the stifling etiquette of it all strike you as being as ridiculous as I find it, Clifford?'

'I really couldn't say.'

'You could, you know.'

He gave a rare smile. 'I know who I am and who I may be if I choose.'

'Really? I have no idea who I am at this point in my life.'

'It is a quote.' His eyes twinkled. 'I confess to enjoying a revisit to Cervantes' *Don Quixote* for a wander through the fantasy of "what if" on occasions. However, we each have our station in life, which it is easier to accept and be sincerely grateful for than forever rail against.'

'Although my station has changed significantly, several times actually, but most notably so since Uncle Byron left me Henley Hall. I think that's what makes it so frustrating. Now, as the supposed lady of the manor, I've got even more blasted restrictions society insists I conform to.'

'And yet, many of those restrictions are intended to safeguard both the lady and her reputation. Whilst I wholeheartedly do not appreciate the many constraints placed on ladies purely because of their gender, I do fear a world where they are not treated with respect and solicitude. I could never consider a man a gentleman should he loosen his grip on gallantry, whatever society might permit in future years.'

She smiled. 'Ever the chivalrous knight. Anyway, this place was the perfect suggestion. My head feels clearer just being away from the Grand. And just look at the cake stands!'

Once tea and cake had been served and they were alone again, Clifford passed Eleanor her pen and notebook. Turning to a clean page, she tapped her chin thoughtfully.

'Shall we ignore the staff initially? They all have witnesses to back up their alibis and, as we said earlier, if there have been no new appointments in four months, it would be a particularly involved plot to take a post all that time ago. I mean, why? In the hope that Hilary would conveniently book in? And how would any of the staff have known about this mysterious item Hilary had, which, if we are right, he was murdered for?'

Clifford nodded. 'Agreed, given the police have, it seems, come to a similar conclusion. And furthermore, given the late hour Mr Eden retired on the fateful evening, we can assume not only that the murderer was most likely a guest, but that he was already in the hotel. It would have been very conspicuous for the killer to have roused the night porter, though we obviously need to check with him.'

'Unless the murderer bribed the night porter to let him in without recording it? Anyway, let's both see what we can deduce on that score later.' She jotted a reminder to do so on the next page. Then she frowned. 'But surely Grimsdale will already have taken the details of all the guests?'

'And insisted none of them leave Brighton. We are all under surveillance in that regard.'

'So, again as we thought, it is most likely that the murderer is still here. Because if he had fled the inspector would be focusing on him alone. Besides, we think he wants Hilary's mysterious item.'

'Quite so. Whoever it is, they are particularly confident it seems. To commit a murder and then calmly stay put rather than fleeing shows a strong degree of self-possession.'

'Hmm, that and a callous disregard for human life. And why was that woman staring at me at breakfast?'

Clifford furrowed his brow. 'I assume this has nothing to do with the present conversation?'

She shrugged. 'For some reason it reminded me of it. She was in the hotel when we first arrived and at breakfast this morning she was definitely scrutinising me.'

'What was the lady wearing, might I ask?'

'Navy-blue cardigan, matching short-sleeved V-neck jumper and calf-length pleated skirt of the same colour. Two strings of pearls, a tortoiseshell hair clip around her chignon and brocade T-strap shoes, better suited to the dance floor than the breakfast room. And rather liberal on the make-up front.'

'A most comprehensive description. Is there a sliver of a chance she might have been returning the scrutiny she felt herself to be under?'

'She started it,' Eleanor huffed, then tasted the slice of strawberry and sherry-infused cream chocolate cake. 'Oh, too divine.'

Clifford raised his teacup. 'If we could put aside the lady in question, and the cake, for a moment, we need to work through each of the guests.'

She reluctantly put down her fork. 'Exactly. Because either the murderer followed Hilary here, was tipped off by someone already at the hotel, or Hilary himself volunteered the details of where he was to his killer. He might have arranged to meet the very person who murdered him.' She shivered. 'Luckily it's out of season and there are few guests, but how do we narrow down the few there are?'

'Perhaps by finding out who they are. If you will excuse me for a moment.'

She watched him step over and speak to their waiter, who led the way out of the tea room. Intrigued, she decided laying waste to a fair proportion of the cakes would save her curiosity eating her up.

On his return, Clifford eyed the layers of the two china cake stands, now relieved of many of the petits fours.

He took his seat. 'And your favourite among the selection?'

'Too hard to choose. The cream eclairs are sublime. The sour fruit tartlets just too heavenly. Those marzipan and fondant icing fellows kept calling my name.' She dabbed her mouth with her napkin. 'But the blueberry meringues have completely turned my head.'

'At least we have managed to sweeten a morsel of the unpleasantness of recent events.'

'And what fiendishly clever ruse have you just been on?'

'Merely telephoning your number one fan for a little more information.'

She groaned. 'I shall feel terrible if Thomas finds out the truth about who I really am.'

'I see no reason why he will. And it is making his month to believe he is helping your well-deserved break between films more restful. To the point that he was happy to confirm several key things for us.'

She leaned across the table eagerly. 'Go on.'

'Elbows off the table please, my dear,' he chided for the benefit of an expensively dressed middle-aged couple watching them as they passed.

'In other circumstances, this would be great fun, you know,' she whispered. 'I shall sit properly and you can tell me everything while I make notes.'

He nodded. 'Firstly, we have it confirmed that no one visited or left a message for Mr Eden. Thomas also asked the girl on the hotel exchange. Mr Eden did not use the telephone in his room to call beyond the hotel.'

'Excellent. Is there more?'

He nodded. 'Perhaps the part you might be most interested in. The other desk clerk mentioned to Thomas that Mr Eden asked for a letter to be posted for him.'

'The photograph he sent me, do you suppose?'

'I imagine so because' – he scanned her face – 'apparently he seemed very secretive about it. He repeatedly looked over his shoulder and stressed the importance of the letter reaching the intended recipient as quickly as possible.'

'But that could still have been another letter?'

'How many people do you suppose Mr Eden knew in Little Buckford, Buckinghamshire?'

'The clerk noticed the address?'

'He did, my lady. In our stay here, I have been consistently reminded that hotel staff are invariably fascinated by the private lives of the guests. Especially in such a luxurious establishment where the class divide is so pronounced.'

'Gracious, so Hilary really wanted me to receive the photograph.'

Clifford nodded. 'Also, in answering the clerk's polite conversational question of whether the letter would be a surprise, Mr Eden answered that' – he softened his voice – 'yes, he supposed it would be.'

As she took a large gulp of her tea, he moved swiftly on.

'Perhaps most in our favour, however, is the good news about the guests.'

'Aside from the fact that one of them may very well be a murderer?'

'Indeed. However, if Mr Eden made no reservation and his death occurred after the night porter locked the hotel door—'

'—we need to talk to the night porter of course.'

'As we said before, my lady, yes. But assuming the night porter was not bribed to admit the murderer, then it seems the murderer must have followed Mr Eden here, or been tipped off that he had booked in. Either way—'

'—it means the murderer booked in at the same time as Hilary, or no later than…' She examined her notebook. 'Than?'

Clifford coughed. 'The man on the pier said Mr Eden was dead at eleven thirty and though we doubt the man's character, we have agreed in the absence of other information to go with his version of events for now. Therefore the murderer must already have checked in to the Grand by Sunday night.'

'Exactly what I was going to say, sort of. I mean, it's much more likely that the killer followed Hilary here and then posed as a normal guest, rather than the killer being a long-standing member of staff who randomly decided to murder a guest after an unblemished work record. So all we need to do is find out—' She looked up at him from her notebook. 'Go on, you've already asked, haven't you?'

He nodded. 'Thomas confirmed that between eight on Saturday evening, the evening Mr Eden checked in, and eleven on Sunday evening, the time the night porter locked the door, only five guests checked in, all of whom are still in residence.'

Eleanor smiled grimly. 'Let me guess? The man we talked to on the pier who saved Hilary's life from the firing squad?' She wrinkled her nose and doodled two fists in her notebook. 'That man has all the hallmarks of being a street fighter turned soldier. Since we spoke to him I've only seen him in the hotel once, and he studiously ignored me.'

Clifford nodded. 'His name is Mr Rex Franklin, assuming that he is not using a false name like Mr Eden. And can you guess any of the other four?'

She nodded back. 'The unlikely couple? You know, the tall chap and his exceptionally short sidekick who have also studiously avoided us... since they – I'm assuming it was them – tried to kidnap us. I've a good mind to have it out with them, but I'm sure they'll only deny it.'

He nodded. 'Mr Noel Longley and Mr Bert Blunt, assuming – again – anyone is using their real names. And I agree, I think little will be gained by confronting them at this juncture, although is it rather discomforting to be under the same roof. Any more?'

Her eyes narrowed. 'The woman with the curvaceous figure. A Miss Summers I believe.'

He nodded. 'A Miss *Grace* Summers.'

She wrote down the four suspects on a new page:

<u>Suspects/Guests</u>
Rex Franklin – man on West Pier
Noel Longley – tall man who tried to kidnap us?
Bert Blunt – short man with limp – driver in car that tried to kidnap us?
Grace Summers – seems very interested in me?

'And the last of the five?' she asked.

'I believe you have already mentioned him to me once?'

'Ah! Mr Willem de Meyer? Tailored Savile Row worthy suit, impeccable taste and a jaw that could take a hundred punches without so much as a flinch?'

'That sounds like the gentleman.'

She added his name to the list and sat back.

'So now all we have to do is find out which one is the murderer. I think this calls for more tea.'

CHAPTER 15

Back at the Grand, Eleanor let out a quiet whistle as they drew near the tall glass doors that led through to the bar. The tall man, Noel Longley, who she was sure had tried to kidnap her with his short companion, Bert Blunt, was perched on a stool reading a newspaper.

'Look who's whiling away the afternoon, drinking alone.'

'Most fortuitous. Perhaps it is time we tackled him, my lady?'

The thick red-and-gold fleur-de-lis-patterned carpet muffled their footsteps as they approached the man reading a newspaper at the bar.

'Good afternoon, Mr Longley, if that is your name.' She took in the long scar that ran along his cheek and the blueish-purple bruise that covered the bottom half of his hawkish nose.

He eyed her suspiciously. 'Almost gave me a heart attack, the pair of you sneaking up like that.'

'Much as you and your partner did to us, so I guess that makes us even.' She gestured to Clifford, who spoke to the burgundy-waistcoated barman. She turned back to Longley. 'Allow me to show you a more effective way you might ask a lady to talk to you.'

The barman placed a cut-crystal glass of gin and tonic in front of her and a whisky-filled tumbler next to Longley's fingers, which were drumming the bar testily.

'There,' Eleanor said, raising her glass. 'You could simply have asked me to join you for a drink. So much easier than waving a gun and bundling us into your car, don't you think?'

Longley ran his tongue down the inside of his cheek and then took a swig of his whisky. 'No idea what you're talking about, dear lady. You seem to have me muddled with some other chap.'

There was something about the man that shouted 'fake' to Eleanor. His suit was expensive, but it didn't sit on him well, as if it had been tailor-made for someone else. And his accent was too plummy, too rounded. Behind it, she detected a hint of the wrong side of London.

'Except that I haven't. You and your partner are quite distinctive, you realise.' She lowered her voice. 'Even in masks.'

He turned around and leaned against the bar while taking another sip of his drink. 'Now, if you're going to stand about wasting my afternoon, you'll need a different topic of conversation, my dear, because this one is going nowhere, if you know what I mean? Whoever you think I am, you're sadly mistaken.'

'As you wish.' She smiled sweetly. 'Where's your partner today then?'

He stared at her over his glass. 'You mean Bert?' He chuckled. 'He isn't my partner, he's my cousin. And I must say' – he glanced at Clifford and then back at Eleanor – 'you two are mighty nosey, whoever you are.'

'I prefer curious,' Eleanor said. 'So much more ladylike. Which is why I'm curious to know where you both were the night the man in room 204 died.'

It was Longley's turn to look at her scathingly. 'Now why would a lady like your good self be interested in such a scandalous occurrence as a man being murdered?'

Eleanor shuddered involuntarily at the malevolent glee with which he said the last word. She could sense Clifford's anger at the man's callous attitude and waved a calming hand as she blinked back the hot tears that pricked her eyelids.

'He was my husband, but somehow I think you already knew that. Now, you haven't said where you both were when he died.'

Longley swigged back the last of his drink. 'No, I haven't, and I'm not going to. If you want to find out, ask that inspector chap. My cousin and I both gave him our statements.' He waved the glass at the barman and gave her a wink. 'Good game this, huh?'

Eleanor gritted her teeth. 'I've no idea. I'm not playing.'

The man rubbed his chin, staring at her as if she was an amusing child. 'I tell you what, I've changed my mind. Out of the goodness of my heart, I'll tell you where we were. Not that it's any of your business, but I always like to help widows when I can.'

It took all of Eleanor's self-control not to kick him in his plummy accent. Instead, she waited for him to continue.

'As it happens, my cousin Bert and I were enjoying a game of cards in my room. Gin rummy, actually. What can I say, I'm a chancer, cards have always been my thing.'

Eleanor leaned forward. 'I hope you lost. A lot.'

She swigged down the last of her gin as Clifford did the same with his drink. As she turned to go, she paused. 'One last question, Mr Longley. Why are you here? Really?'

Longley shrugged. 'My cousin and I are down here on our holidays, like everyone else.'

She folded her arms. 'Do you and your cousin normally try to kidnap ladies on your holiday?'

He shook his head and gestured round the bar. 'There really aren't many ladies here to kidnap, are there?' He gave his forehead an exaggerated slap. 'Of course there is that one I saw slipping into your husband's room around half-past nine the night before they found him dead.' He held his hands out in mock apology. 'Don't shoot the messenger!'

It took every fibre of Eleanor's self-control again not to lay her hands on him. Instead, she casually shook out her red curls and then wiggled her ringless wedding-ring finger at him. 'Sorry to disappoint, if you're trying to shock me. My husband was free to do as he wished. Besides, I'm sure there was a perfectly plausible reason for her being there.'

He ran his tongue over his bottom lip. 'A woman like that is like a black widow spider, if you know what I mean.'

Eleanor shook her head. 'See now, you've added besmirching a lady's reputation to your dubious list of holiday activities. I'm pleased for her that she isn't here to hear you.'

He laughed and raised his voice as the woman Eleanor now knew was called Grace Summers sashayed by the bar. 'Oh, but she is.' He followed her with his eyes until she rounded the corner and then picked up his newspaper. 'See what I mean? Deadly. No one's husband is safe from the likes of her.'

CHAPTER 16

Much later that evening, Eleanor still hadn't shifted the possessive feeling that had overtaken her at the news that Grace Summers had been in Hilary's room. The distinct path in the luxurious cream carpet of her suite, from the door over to the windows and back, was testament to how deeply it had unsettled her. A long-emptied box of chocolates sat forlornly on the coffee table, next to a pile of room-service plates, as she hadn't been able to face dining downstairs.

She flopped down onto the velvet settee facing the tempestuous sea view, an unopened book beside her. The wind had got up and in the moonlight she could see it whipping the waves into a frenzy of foam. Even the sight of Gladstone curled in his basket, his wrinkled jowls flapping as he snored, failed to improve her mood. She threw her head back over the top of the settee and let out a groan.

In her upside-down position, she saw a folded piece of paper slide between the legs of the chair jammed under her door handle. She checked the time: ten past midnight.

What the?

She stayed still, listening for footsteps, but the thick hotel carpet muffled any sound. She jumped up, grabbed the note and flipped it open.

Dear Hollywood Star, your number one fan and the other staff have gone off duty. Fancy grilling the night porter?

She smiled at Clifford's humorous invitation. *Do we ever, Ellie!* She quickly checked her clothes and make-up and hurried out. He was waiting at the end of the corridor.

'Good evening, my lady.'

'And the same to you, Clifford. Why the cloak and dagger with the note? You could just have knocked.'

'True, but I feared after such a long, and eventful, day, you might be asleep.'

'Very thoughtful but I wasn't, so what's the plan? I'm sure the night porter isn't allowed to hobnob with guests.'

He shook his head. 'Most definitely not. I fear he would worry about being reported to the manager for "hobnobbing" as you delicately put it.'

'And that wouldn't make him at his ease.'

'Exactly. Whereas, I am not a guest per se, merely the servant of a guest.'

'Okay, you have a cosy chat with him while I secrete myself in the near vicinity so you don't have to repeat everything he tells you to me afterwards.'

From the top of the stairs, Eleanor spied the canopied red leather porter's chair. A balding crown fringed with grey hair and a pair of round wire spectacles poked out. She could also make out the navy-and-gold epaulettes on the shoulders of the night porter's oversized uniform. She imagined, given his diminutive frame, that even the lightest of March sea breezes would surely carry him up into the sky like a child's lost balloon.

Clifford descended and stood in front of the chair, blocking the night porter's view. Eleanor, taking her cue, snuck down and circled round the entrance lobby until she reached a chair hidden from the night porter's sight by one of the giant Grecian urns.

In the event, it proved unnecessary as the porter was fast asleep. Clifford coughed gently. And then more loudly. The porter jerked awake and automatically went to stand.

Clifford waved him back down. 'It's only me, Mr Johnson.'

In the chair behind the Grecian urn, Eleanor shook her head marvelling again at how her butler seemed to know everyone's name and gain their confidence within moments of arriving, well, just about anywhere. She craned her neck to hear as Clifford continued talking to the now awake porter.

'It seems I am the only one who can't sleep. And they say sea air is supposed to help send you off to the world of nod!'

The porter's reedy voice answered. 'Good evening, Mr Clifford. I'm sorry to hear you can't sleep. Is there something I can do for you?'

'Indeed there is, Mr Johnson. I'm looking for someone to share ten minutes and' – Clifford pulled out a bottle of tawny port from inside his jacket – 'a glass or two of this with me.' He leaned in conspiratorially. 'Young Thomas mentioned that Mr Hargreaves is away this evening.'

So that's why he chose this time to interview him, Ellie. The manager's away. She risked peeping around the urn, a large potted plant still hiding her from the porter's view. She could now clearly see and hear the two men.

The porter's eyes lit up at the sight of the port. 'Lawks, that's mighty kind of you, Mr Clifford. Let me get us a couple of glasses.' Pausing only to heave one of the wingback chairs over for his unexpected guest, he shuffled off through the door to the bar.

Clifford stepped over to the newspaper racks and perused them until the porter returned balancing a tray. He set it down on the inlaid side table in the centre of the two chairs. 'Thought we might have some nuts to go with the port.'

'Perfect.' Clifford waited for him to take a seat and then settled into his chair before pouring them both a generous measure and then raising his glass. 'To the sea!'

The porter repeated the toast and then stared quizzically at Clifford. 'The sea, Mr Clifford? Are you a sailing man?'

Clifford shook his head. 'Not at all, although I've spent a fair amount of time on ships with my former employer, Lord Henley. I heard from young Thomas, however, that you are an old navy man?'

The porter nodded. 'All me life from a nipper. Well, from fourteen, like.'

Clifford nodded. 'You must miss it. The excitement. Maybe even the danger?'

'Can't say as I do. There was more time spent polishing brass, scrubbing decks and mending ropes than much excitement or danger, though I've weathered a fair few storms aboard.' He patted the arm of his plush, red seat. 'No. I prefer me chair here. It never threatens to tip me out over the arm never to be seen or heard of again. 'Cos when a fellow goes overboard it takes a fair while to turn around one of them ships even if it is noticed. And in a rough or icy sea, well…' He shrugged but then chuckled. 'I prefer hotels to ships. The Grand has never threatened to sink with all hands on board!'

From her hidden position, Eleanor smiled.

Clifford cleared his throat. 'And yet there was a man lost overboard only the other day, if you know what I mean? That poor fellow, Painshill, wasn't it? Brought through here on a stretcher. Did you have much to do with him?'

The porter stroked his chin. 'I barely saw the poor gentleman, actually. If I remember rightly he booked in Saturday night? Came in just as I was preparing for me shift. Didn't say much, I only noticed him because he seemed a tad worked up. He never even replied when I bid him goodnight, that distracted he was.'

Eleanor stole a sideways peep at Clifford and wasn't surprised to see he'd kept his expression neutral. 'Perhaps the gentleman was simply tired?'

The porter shook his head with a grim expression. 'I'm pretty sure it was something else. He fair shot up the stairs and that was the last I sees of him. Didn't clap eyes on him on Sunday night, but then I had a spot of trouble filling me Thermos for the night so I might have missed him if he came in before eleven. And then come Monday morning, well…' He shrugged.

Clifford refilled their glasses. 'Painshill aside, you must be privy to a few odd things in your job.' He lowered his voice. 'I always imagined in every hotel that any guest trying to sneak in a little worse for wear, or perhaps with an… extra companion, would try to befriend the night porter. You know, as a much-needed ally.'

The porter shook his head again, but failed to cover up the smile that sprang to his face. 'This is the Grand, Mr Clifford. I think the cost of the rooms is designed to keep out those who don't know how to behave.'

'What about the night Mr Painshill died in 204?'

'Never saw a soul.' His face clouded as his hand went to his inside pocket. 'Honest.'

CHAPTER 17

Thankful that the wild weather of the previous night had been replaced by another day of bright sunshine and relatively clear blue sky, Eleanor slipped off Gladstone's lead to let him scamper down the beach, which was dotted with driftwood and empty indigo razor clam shells caught in the long brown fingers of patches of waxy kelp. He lolloped along until a scent pulled him to a jerky stop, upon which he started digging frantically.

Stooping to pick up an irresistibly bright pebble of fine-grained red sandstone, she chuckled at his exuberance. 'If he's daft enough to chase another seagull into the waves, Clifford, it'll be my turn to wade in and rescue him. No arguments. You definitely earned your lifeguard badge the other day.'

'Fortunately for all his woolly-headed foibles, my lady, Master Gladstone has proven on occasions he is not entirely without sense. I believe the shock was a sufficiently sharp lesson not to repeat the folly of trying to outwit a creature designed to be at sea.'

Eleanor pointed to the bulldog's half-buried body, arcs of sand showering into a ridge along his back as he created a crater around him. 'Are you sure?'

At that moment Gladstone pulled his head out of the hole, triumphantly swinging a leather sports shoe by the soggy laces.

Clifford tutted. 'It appears I was indeed significantly over generous in my estimation, my lady.'

As they continued along the almost deserted beach, Eleanor shoved her hands in the pockets of her olive-green wool jacket and fell into deep thought. Too many muddled questions were running round her head for her to even begin to articulate. Snatches of the various conversations over the last few days jumbled in and out, raucously vying for her focus.

Surely something should have leapt out at you by now, Ellie? This is Hilary we're talking about. Your Hilary. You must be able to work this out. But what on earth was he doing here? More to the point, what was he mixed up in that was so bad it got him killed? Oh, Ellie, you'll never learn, you're still clinging to that vain hope he loved you. Yes, but might he have… once?

'You are already eating one, my lady?' Clifford's voice cut into her inner argument.

'What?' She looked down and took her hand from the paper bag of sweets he held. 'Oh sorry, I might have disappeared into my head for a moment.'

He nodded towards the esplanade. 'I suggest that we avail ourselves of one of those beach huts and make use of this.' He pulled her notebook from his inside coat pocket. 'If that meets with your approval, of course?'

Not surprisingly, given the still low temperature and dearth of tourists, the row of twenty wooden huts were as deserted as the beach itself. Eleanor climbed up the five short steps of the dark-blue hut, holding the smart white-painted rail.

'Aren't we supposed to pay someone to use these?'

He joined her. 'No doubt an attendant will appear in due course.'

'Ooh look, it's perfect, there's two deckchairs here against the wall.' She grabbed the nearest one and yanked on the wooden arms. 'Dash it, why are these things so complicated?'

Having helped Gladstone up the steps, Clifford took the chair and with a deft twist of his wrist, snapped it open. He pulled out a large white handkerchief and dusted it down before presenting the chair to Eleanor. She sat, well aware from the look on his face that whatever liberties he might be forced to take elsewhere, he would not sit with her in such public view.

'Right, let's begin with our chat with the night porter. Did you believe him when he said Hilary looked shaken in the lobby?'

'Absolutely. Perhaps it is not surprising that he observed some perturbation in Mr Eden's demeanour given—'

'He was then murdered?'

'Yes, my lady. But you would receive a different reply were you to ask me if I believed Mr Johnson when he told me no one else had come or gone that night.'

Eleanor looked up sharply from her notebook. 'Really? I didn't pick up on that. She tapped the pen on her chin. 'Interesting. Well, we'll have to find out more as soon as we can. As to who among our suspects might be the "ghost" that spooked poor Hilary? If the night porter didn't see who it was, I doubt we'll be able to discover more. My money's on Longley. As I said, I'm pretty sure he was the rogue who forced us into the car at gunpoint as well.'

'Despite the man's denial, I have also come to the same conclusion, my lady. The bruising on his nose seems to clinch it, although when we have the opportunity to see if his cousin's nose is also bruised, we can be more conclusive.'

'Good point.' She scribbled in her notebook. 'Longley certainly has a bad enough attitude.'

'I agree, my lady. To my mind, Mr Longley was also most unconvincing about why he and his companion are here in Brighton.'

'I know, all that rubbish about holidays and card playing. And equally so about them being cousins. I know family members can differ, but really such a height variation? Longley is easily a foot taller.'

'Malnutrition as a child. A congenital condition of the growth plates in the long bones. One parent of significantly reduced stature. All potential explanations.'

'We'll see. But if his nose is black and blue, I shan't care who he is. We should go to Grimsdale and tell him they tried to kidnap us.'

'And how shall we explain that we did not report the attempt at the time?' He scanned her face as he continued. 'And how shall we avoid further scrutiny which might result in your half of the photograph being taken away from you?'

She caught her breath. 'No, Clifford! That's all I have from Hilary. And it's not much of a memento as it is. My own wedding photograph sliced in two.'

'I wish I could say otherwise, my lady.' He ran his finger around his collar.

'Alright, Clifford, what is it?'

He coughed gently, and she groaned.

'I know, I know. Thank you for your discretion. However, we do indeed need to discuss Longley's assertion that Miss Summers was in Hilary's room the night he was murdered, which was a very unseemly time for her to be there.'

'Perhaps the lady knew Mr Eden in a perfectly innocent capacity, such as a business one?'

'Well, she certainly looks like she means business, don't you think?' Eleanor muttered uncharitably.

What Clifford thought she never discovered as his reply was interrupted by a piercing scream.

CHAPTER 18

Clifford stepped outside, and then hurriedly stepped back in.

Eleanor stared at her butler. 'Clifford, don't just stand there. Someone might need our help!'

Uncharacteristically, he stayed where he was. 'I am sorry, my lady, but I fear they are beyond help.'

Eleanor gasped. 'Whatever do you mean? Who is it?'

He pursed his lips. 'Regrettably, it is… the ladies.'

She gaped at him, then understanding dawned and her face broke into a smile. 'Oh, I see. Well let's go and say hello.' At his look of horror, she hissed, 'What?'

He swallowed hard. 'The three of them appear to be dressed only in… bathing suits.'

Eleanor leaned past him and peeped round the side of the hut. 'Oh, Clifford, they are having such fun!' She couldn't tear her eyes away from the sight of the three of them decked out in what was clearly the work of her housekeeper, who was an adept seamstress. In blue, green and pink gingham, their swimsuits sported sweetheart neck lines running down to a bibbed front and frilled shorts that finished mid thigh. She could see why Clifford refused to join them, as the ladies daringly also sported bare arms as well as legs.

Clifford winced as more ear-piercing screams rang out. He hung firmly on to Gladstone's collar, the bulldog straining to join the ladies on the beach. Mrs Butters' voice could be heard clearly above the screams of the other two.

'Trotters! This is positively the last time I ever enter into a bet with you!'

'I told you,' Mrs Trotman shouted back as she grabbed Polly's hand and gestured for her to do the same with Mrs Butters. ''Twas you who made us bathing suits when we were getting excited about coming here all those weeks ago! In truth, I think you just fancied parading your wares on the beach, Butters!'

'I only made them to humour you into thinking I would take up your silly bet, Trotters!' Mrs Butters yelled back as they reached the edge of the freezing March waves. Despite the sun, it would take many more months before the sea warmed up enough for any, except the foolhardy and brave, to risk its chilly waters.

Clifford coughed. 'My lady, I am exceedingly sorry but I am entirely unable to intervene given the state of… undress the ladies are in.'

'Good!' She snuck another peek at the ladies who were now knee-deep in the sea, their squeals louder than ever at the biting cold water. She turned back to him. 'From this point forward, you are under strict instructions to allow them to be as mischievous as they wish whilst they are down here in Brighton. This is their one chance to let their hair down.'

He sniffed. 'And their standards, it would seem.'

She tilted her head. 'I suggest we discreetly leave the ladies to their fabulously disgraceful behaviour and continue our conversation back at the hotel.'

As they stepped inside the lobby of the Grand, Eleanor nodded towards Miss Summers who was exiting the lift. 'I think I'd better deal with her first. It's eating me up to leave the question of what she was doing in Hilary's room unanswered any longer, assuming Longley was telling the truth about seeing her.' She lowered her voice. 'You have been far too gallant to mention the thought that I know has struck you too. Namely that if she was a paramour of Hilary's, she may have been carrying on with him before we married, and may be the very reason he left me.'

He nodded. 'If that proves to be the case, my lady, do not worry. I shall arrive at the police station with sufficient bail money.'

With her heart pounding and her cheeks flushed, Eleanor made a poor job of being discreet in trailing Miss Summers through the lobby. And an even worse job down the long richly carpeted corridor towards the Regent Room. Watching Miss Summers' rear view wiggle in pale-blue high heels, incongruous with the reserved black suit she wore, made Eleanor's blood pressure rise. *Keep it together, Ellie. You said it yourself, Hilary was free to do as he chose.* But her heart countered this instantly. *Not while you were married to him, he wasn't!*

At the door into the Regent Room, Eleanor paused, watching the woman thread her way through the mostly empty tables to the far end of the room. Having chosen a rather over-decorative cocktail, she wandered to the nearest table and sat down. Eleanor nodded to herself and strode over, gesturing to the barman that she would have the same.

'Well, fancy meeting you here, Miss Summers. Mind if I join you?' She sat down without waiting for a reply.

'Excuse me?' The other woman frowned. 'I don't remember us meeting.'

'Good memory, we haven't.'

'Then why did you say "fancy meeting you here"?'

'Because you were staring at me so insistently at breakfast the other day, I assumed we must have met.'

'I wasn't staring. I was… reading my book.'

For a moment, Eleanor was taken by surprise at the softness of the woman's voice. And the baby blue of her eyes. There was none of the hard edge she had expected to see in her features up close. Rather, she gave off an air of vulnerability. Despite this, Eleanor continued to stare unblinkingly at her.

'Ah, thank you.' Eleanor took her drink from the waiter.

After a minute, the woman shuffled in her seat. 'Alright, I was staring. I was admiring your Titian red curls if you must know. They're very striking,' she ended grudgingly.

Eleanor eyed her suspiciously, unsure how genuine the woman was. She mentally shook her head. *Who knows, Ellie? All you can do is put it out there and see what she says.* She leaned back in her chair. 'You know, I didn't have you down as the type of girl who dallied in gentleman's rooms at unseemly hours.'

The woman inhaled sharply. 'How dare you!' She glanced around the room. 'Do you usually latch onto some poor unsuspecting stranger without an invitation and then proceed to insult them?'

Eleanor looked up at the ceiling as if giving this deep consideration. 'Only when it is warranted. But my apologies, Miss Summers. Of course I wasn't trying to insult you. That was meant to be helpful advice.'

'I don't see how!'

Eleanor leaned in. 'Well, if the other guests are talking about your… indelicate behaviour, I just thought you'd like to know. It might help you be more discreet next time.'

Miss Summers pulled back and fiddled with her skirt. 'Well, it's rubbish. I haven't been anywhere near a man's room.'

Eleanor said nothing, letting the silence between them unnerve the woman even further.

'Not that it is any of your business if I had,' Miss Summers said snappily.

'Ah, but you see, Miss Summers, I do need to disagree with you there. Because the man in question was…' She paused and smiled sweetly at the woman. 'My husband.'

The other woman blinked several times as she stared down at the ivory linen tablecloth.

'And,' Eleanor continued, 'somebody made me a widow only a few hours before I arrived here.'

When she finally replied, the woman's voice was quieter, weaker. 'My condolences, of course. Losing someone special hurts more than you think you can bear, I know.' She looked up and held Eleanor's gaze. 'But I hope it eases your distress a little if I assure you that I was not acquainted with your husband. At all.'

Eleanor failed to keep the anger from her voice. 'And yet, Miss Summers, you were seen entering his room on the night he died!'

The woman looked shocked, but then regained her composure. She stared at Eleanor coldly. 'Whoever you've been speaking to must have muddled me with another female guest.'

Eleanor scoffed as she waved her arm around the room. 'You and I are the only female guests here, apart from those elderly sisters. And no one is going to mistake your curves for my lack of them.'

The woman shrugged her shoulders and rose to leave.

Eleanor rose too and blocked her path. 'Wait! Tell me, why are you here?'

The woman glared at her. 'If you must know, I am in Brighton to hawk myself round to prospective employers. I'm not one of the privileged ones. You see, no one left me a fortune and a country estate!'

With that, the woman strode around Eleanor and out of the bar.

As she left as well, Eleanor nodded to herself. *That woman may, or may not, have known Hilary. But, Ellie, she certainly knows a lot about you!*

CHAPTER 19

'Well, I couldn't find him anywhere all afternoon.' Eleanor pulled her emerald-green beaded shawl around her shoulders. Clifford nodded to the doorman and stepped back to let Eleanor pass through into the unseasonably warm lamp-lit evening.

'He certainly hasn't checked out, my lady. Thomas confirmed that when I made this evening's arrangements for Master Gladstone. The staff haven't seen the gentleman since he took an early lunch. Thomas also mentioned that Detective Inspector Grimsdale has given the manager strict instructions. If any of the guests who were here during Mr Eden's stay try to check out, they are to restrain them from leaving and call him immediately.'

'And yet we are all able to come and go around the town as we please, although I've noticed a number of policemen patrolling the promenade outside the hotel.' She tipped her head. 'Our murderer could easily have escaped by now.'

'True, but until one of them is in possession of the item they seek, it seems unlikely they will. Unless, of course, one of them already has the item but is afraid that leaving would definitely draw the police upon them.'

'Dash it, where have you gone, Mr de Meyer?' she muttered, looking for his telltale Savile Row suit. *He checked in after Hilary, Ellie, so he's a suspect until proven otherwise!* She gave up and shook her head. 'Let's forget Mr de Meyer for now, Clifford. Murder or no murder, this is still our holiday. The ladies will be waiting for us. And I can only imagine how excited they will be, so we keep to our promise – no hint that we're in the middle of any ugly business, agreed?'

'Agreed.'

Even before they reached the first of the ornate scrollwork arches of the long ice-cream-pink Hippodrome Theatre, they heard the ladies' voices trilling out along the pavement.

'There they are!' Mrs Butters waved, while Polly clapped her hands and Mrs Trotman beamed them a smile.

'Good evening, ladies. Have you behaved yourselves today?' Clifford asked, his deadpan face concealing the mischievousness of his question. Eleanor barely hid the grin that sprung up at the memory of them in their bathing suits.

The three of them stared wide-eyed at Clifford, shot each other a look and then nodded slowly.

'Excellent,' he said. 'But surprising. Shall we?'

Eleanor had to admit that even before they stepped inside, the theatre's glittering facade held all the promise of a special night to remember. As the looped garlands of brightly lit white bulbs swung in the light sea breeze, they cast a dancing light the full length of the walkway. They also illuminated the gallery of colourful posters lining the front of the building, each giving a tantalising glimpse of one of the vast array of variety acts on offer.

She watched Polly pause in front of the first, the maid's mouth hanging open.

'Excited?'

The young girl turned to her, eyes wide with wonder, and nodded dumbly.

From the inside pocket of his black chesterfield overcoat, Clifford produced five printed tickets. Stepping across to one of the young men in smart red waistcoats standing either side of the theatre's doors, he handed them over before saying something Eleanor couldn't catch. The doorman ripped four of the tickets in half and returned the other one to Clifford before gesturing for them to enter. Eleanor watched Clifford put the intact ticket into Polly's hand with a rare smile.

'To add to your souvenir collection.'

Polly put it carefully into her coat pocket with a shyly whispered, 'Thank you, Mr Clifford, sir. 'Tis perfect.'

Eleanor thought she had seen the inside of enough theatres to take this one in her stride, but she had come unprepared for the circus-worthy spectacle that greeted them. As they took their plush red seats, which matched the flock of the horseshoe-shaped walls, she stared up at the tent-inspired domed roof, supported on sixteen gilded pillars. Extravagant painted plaster reliefs curved out over the seats below, each one a stage set in itself. Either side of the enormous stage's ornate proscenium arch, a gold-curtained entrance harked back to the theatre's origins as the world's most lavish permanent circus.

Looking around, she was surprised to see how much the theatre was filling up given how quiet the streets and the beach had been most days. Seated on her right, Clifford handed her a programme and passed another along for Mrs Trotman to share with the others.

'Harry Randall, Ella Retford, Letty Lind, Wilkie Bard. Gosh, what a line-up!' Eleanor cheered.

'Plus Wee Georgie Wood and Arthur Roberts, my lady,' Clifford said as he pointed further down the list of names. 'Had we arrived in Brighton only a few months earlier, we could have seen Lillie Langtry perform. And we would have seen Charlie Chaplin delight the audience here again.'

She remembered Clifford telling her that Charlie Chaplin was her late uncle's favourite performer.

He lowered his voice. 'I believe, however, the ladies are in for a particular treat this evening. Among the many acts, a fair number are known for their ribald comedy.' His hand went to the Windsor knot of his tie. 'Hence my sitting on the end of our row.'

She cocked a questioning eyebrow at him.

'That, in line with your request, I may pretend I haven't seen them tittering at the more inappropriate lyrics and antics, my lady.'

She grinned. 'I so appreciate you allowing them to enjoy themselves unreservedly. But then you'll have to do me the same honour and pretend you haven't seen me laughing either.'

Within the first third of the three-hour show, they had been treated to a variety of acts – singers, a family of acrobatic jugglers, twin-sister ballet dancers and a skilled escape artist. But it was the contortionist's wiry fox terrier who stole Eleanor's heart every time he jumped up to balance on the top of the contortionist's head. With each new act, another artfully painted backdrop rolled down to fill the back of the stage.

By the halfway point, they had laughed, gasped in awe and clapped until their hands stung. Polly had also been through three of Mrs Butters' handkerchiefs, as the magic of each act seemed to bring on more tears of wonder. And then the pantomime element drew an eruption of cheering and whistling as a heavily made-up dame swanned on singing saucy lyrics in a giveaway baritone voice. Eleanor stole a peep at Clifford and had to stifle a giggle. Staring straight forward with his lips pursed, he sporadically shook his head and fiddled with his tie.

She nudged Mrs Trotman who had dissolved into hysterics and grinned at Mrs Butters who was busy wiping tears of laughter from her cheeks. This set the tone for the next half hour of the programme as artist after artist reduced the audience to louder and louder paroxysms of mirth. Even Clifford had trouble hanging on to his inscrutable butler's expression.

Then another backdrop change heralded a shift in mood as a beautiful young woman stepped from the wings and captivated the auditorium with angelic renditions of several popular songs. Before long, the entire audience was swaying and singing along. Then all too quickly, she was gone and the next act was being announced. Eleanor watched the ladies whispering excitedly and then Clifford nodding to himself as a magician completed trick after trick at lightning speed.

In the brief pause as the stage was cleared again, Clifford turned to Eleanor.

'Enjoying the show, my lady?'

'Enormously. I can't think of anywhere I would rather be. Or with any other people.'

'Most heartening to hear.'

It was the next act that really caught Eleanor's attention. 'Ooh, a quick-change artist! How on earth does she get through so many outfits so swiftly!'

'Perhaps, my lady, you could go to the stage door and ask the lady for a few pointers?'

'Don't be daft. She's not going to give her secrets away. Besides,' – she gave him a puzzled look – 'why would I want to be able to do that?'

'I really couldn't say.' His eyes twinkled. 'Although, such a talent might enable you to finally arrive on time for functions and perhaps meet the meal schedule at the Hall more effectively?'

She laughed, but shook her head. 'Nice try!'

CHAPTER 20

They spilled out onto the pavement at ten o'clock, with their ears still ringing from the raucous clapping and whistling as the final curtain had fallen. Despite the late hour, the still surprisingly mild evening air was the perfect complement to their high spirits. The other theatregoers adjusted their capes and coats and gradually dispersed, the couples arm in arm, leaving Eleanor and her staff still debating which act was their joint favourite.

Eleanor suddenly stiffened and tapped Clifford's elbow. 'Look!' she whispered, making sure the ladies couldn't hear. 'Over by the doorway of that public house.'

'Ah, Mr Longley and his partner in kidnapping, Mr Blunt, deep in a very animated conversation,' said Clifford.

'And, helpfully, Longley is hurrying off somewhere. Let's collar his vertically challenged friend while we can.' She slapped her forehead. 'But wait, we can't leave the ladies to walk back to the boarding house alone, it's far too late. Suppose Longley decides to include them in another kidnapping attempt?'

'Not a problem, my lady.' He strode over to a man in a thick coat and a peaked cap. 'Ladies, her ladyship has one last treat lined up for you this evening.' He gestured towards the man's small open hansom cab, which had seen better days but looked sound enough.

Mrs Trotman gasped. 'Us? Riding back in style?'

'Whatever will my friend at the boarding house say?' Mrs Butters said, clearly delighted with the idea. Polly's jaw fell to her chest as she gaped at the two women.

'Enjoy your ride, ladies,' Eleanor called.

Clifford pressed several coins into the man's hand. 'Escort these ladies to the actual door of their lodgings.' He held up another coin before adding it to the others. 'And do not leave until they are all inside.'

The ladies gone, Eleanor and Clifford crossed the street to where Bert Blunt was tightening the belt on his overcoat, despite the mild weather. 'Well, what a coincidence,' Eleanor said, stepping in his way. 'Did you enjoy the show?'

He stared at her, eyes wide. Then he looked to Clifford and swallowed hard. 'I, erm, wasn't in the theatre, miss.'

'Even more surprising then that we should have ended up on the same street tonight.'

'Is it?'

'Well, you probably know the answer to that better than I do.' She smiled innocently as his eyes repeatedly pulled away from her stare as she searched for signs of bruising from where she had elbowed the second kidnapper. Defeated by the shadows, she waited for him to reply.

'Erm, do I?' He ran his hand round the back of his neck. 'Well, I'd best be getting along.'

'My thoughts entirely. Seeing as we're fellow guests at the Grand, we've every reason to get along.'

'No, miss, I meant I ought to be on my way.'

She shook her head. 'You're not much like your friend, you know? He made conversation quite the chore, but you' – she stepped towards him making him shrink backwards – 'you are eminently easier to chat to. But then they say opposites attract, don't they?'

'We're not friends,' he said cautiously. 'No, no, we're, erm, cousins.' He gestured to his short stature. 'He took the height for both of us, as you can see, miss.'

'Well, how are you enjoying it?'

Blunt looked even more confused. 'Enjoying what, miss?'

'You know, your cousin said you were both here for the sea fishing?' *Is there such a thing in Brighton, Ellie?*

He shook his head vehemently. 'No, Noel and me, we're on our holidays, that's all we're here for. Get out of London for a bit, hole up at the seaside, like.'

Eleanor let out a laugh. 'Gracious, you said that so forcefully you made it sound as if you are running away from someone. Or perhaps you were running *after* someone?'

He shuffled his feet. 'Not doing any running. Got a problem with me leg, you see. Short, and I got a limp. Life's cruel like that.'

'Hmm. I never really thought of life as being cruel, more that it's people who can be. Like when you hear that someone took a man's life in our very hotel. Did you know him, by the way?'

'What? The bloke who died?' He shook his head again. 'Never met him. Don't, erm, even know which bloke it was.'

'Strange,' she said slowly, 'your cousin, Noel, did.'

His head jerked up to stare at her. 'You sure?'

'Yes. He knew that it was my husband. Still, luckily you weren't caught up in any of the nasty business seeing as you were busy all evening. Oh, I hope you won by the way.'

He looked over her shoulder as if hopeful for an escape route. Pausing, he cleared his throat before answering. 'No, Noel beat me. Always does.'

'Ah, poker takes a lot of dedication to master, I believe. It was poker you were playing, wasn't it?'

He nodded but pointed down the street. 'Poker it was. I ought to be shuffling on my way. Noel will be waiting for me.'

'Oh,' she said with well-hidden mock surprise as she looked around, 'I assumed you had arrived here together. You seem quite the inseparable pair.'

'No, no. I just, erm, popped down on my own to' – he gestured to the public house behind him – 'have a pint.'

Eleanor smiled and stepped aside. 'Then don't let me hold you up. We'll see you around the hotel. How long are you staying for?'

'Noel hasn't decided yet. Night to both of you.' And with that, he scurried off as fast as his limp would allow.

She watched him go and then turned to Clifford. 'It must have been a difficult series of card games, seeing as one was playing rummy and the other—'

'Poker. Well done, my lady.'

As they reached the entrance steps of the Metropole Hotel where they had taken tea the day before, she paused. 'Good call, Clifford. Their late bar will be open for ages. We can go through the muddle of information we've learned on the case so far. But, in hindsight, we probably should have picked up a hansom cab like the ladies. If our kidnappers had decided to have another go, we might not have been able to fool them so easily.'

Without replying, he handed her the collapsible umbrella he was carrying.

She was surprised at its weight until the penny dropped. 'Clifford, it's not just an umbrella, it's a cosh!'

'Correct, my lady. His lordship made some judicious modifications to turn it into a weapon.'

'Good old Uncle Byron,' she said fondly. Not only had he been somewhat of an eccentric, he'd also been an inveterate inventor. In fact, one of his inventions, a kind of plough cum battering ram that could be attached to the front of the Rolls had saved her life. Unfortunately, all his inventions hadn't been able to save his own. The piercing memory of her conversation with his murderer, who she and Clifford had finally caught not long ago, was etched forever in her thoughts.

Peering sideways at Clifford, she could see he was painfully reliving the same moment. 'We got justice for Uncle Byron,' she said softly.

He smiled at her with genuine warmth. 'Indeed, we did, my lady, and I am eternally grateful to you for the part you played in doing so. And rest assured, I shall do my utmost and beyond to achieve the same for Mr Eden.'

She smiled back at him. 'Thank you, Clifford. We might, however, achieve it more comfortably out of this biting wind?'

CHAPTER 21

As Clifford dealt with their coats, Eleanor concluded the Metropole's silver and mirrored chic bar to be a favourite of theatregoers. She chose a table where they wouldn't be overheard and slid onto the high-legged upholstered seat. Her nails drummed on the marble top as she waited for Clifford to join her.

'Refreshments are on their way,' he said and then lowered his voice. 'Again, my apologies for my reduced formality as we resume our pretence of my being your guardian.'

She smiled and accepted her notebook and fountain pen. A waiter appeared with a loaded tray of drinks and delicious-looking appetisers.

Clifford gestured to the mini plates of devilled eggs, potted cheese and crackers, bacon soufflé tartlets, dressed prawns and mixed olives. 'Despite the lateness of the hour, I have noted you often find fortification of great assistance when engaged in deep thinking.'

'Thank you.' She smiled as she dived in. 'They do look divine.' During a pause, she opened her notebook and groaned at the untidy jottings. 'I'm sure it's just a matter of time, Clifford, before your impeccable organisation and meticulous attention to detail insidiously work their way into my psyche, wouldn't you say?'

His eyes twinkled. 'Let us hope not, my lady. If influence transfers one way, it would surely also do so the other way.'

She chuckled. 'And the idea of your having to operate with my less structured way of working fills you with dread, doesn't it?'

'I should say it would be more accurately described as "horror",
were I to be truthful.' Quickly holding up a finger as an astonished
laugh burst from her, he continued. 'However, I would unquestionably be the better man if I could.' He picked up his glass. 'Perhaps
we should raise a toast to complementary attributes.'

Feeling cheered by his unwavering support, she raised her glass
in return and then spun her notebook round to face him. 'Then
please help my thoughts which are uncharacteristically scrambled
by emotion this time. Where do you suggest we start?'

'With a…' He blanched looking at the jumble of notes and
doodles. 'A new, slightly more ordered, apologies, I meant updated,
timeline of events?'

'Top-notch idea.' She turned to a new page and rewrote then
updated the list of their chief suspects.

> Rex Franklin – was in charge of firing squad – saved
> Hilary's life
> Noel Longley – denies knowing Hilary, but tried to kidnap
> me and Clifford
> Bert Blunt – definitely Longley's partner in crime, also
> denies knowing Hilary, also definitely second man who
> tried to kidnap me and Clifford
> Grace Summers – denies knowing Hilary, but knows a
> lot about me!
> Willem de Meyer – booked in after Hilary same as other
> suspects, but so far haven't managed to talk to him

'Right, so far we've learned—' Her pen scratched across the
paper as she added a new heading – 'Timeline' – which she
underscored twice. Then below it she wrote down everything
they had been told.

9.30 p.m. – Miss Grace Summers seen by Longley going into Hilary's room
10.45 p.m. – Desk clerk wishes Hilary good night
11.35 p.m. – Rex Franklin goes to Hilary's room – finds Hilary dead – searches room – finds nothing

She looked up and wrinkled her nose. 'It's not very detailed, is it?'
'Admittedly it is a trifle lacking in substance at the moment.'

'Dash it, Clifford! This doesn't constitute a timeline. It's only three entries long, and yet it covers almost two hours. The murderer seems to have covered their tracks too well. We need to seriously speed up our progress.'

'Perhaps. Although as the insightful Leo Tolstoy reminded me last night in *War and Peace*, "the two most powerful warriors are patience and time". Both must be maximised to be as effective as possible.'

She resisted the strong urge to roll her eyes. 'Well, I insist on being in charge of "time" and I say we need to work faster. You can have "patience", I've always found her intensely irritating.'

'I thought that was prudence?'

'Her too. Now, let's move on to the alibis our suspects have given us. Perhaps there's a clue in them we've missed, though the real problem is that suspects always lie.'

He nodded. 'It is an unbecoming trait.'

She turned to the page with a doodle of a pair of legs, which ended at the waistband and the diminutive male figure next to them. 'Let's start with the odd couple. Longley denied being half of the kidnapping team, but I didn't believe anything he said. Oh, Clifford!' She clapped her hand over her mouth as this came out loudly enough for the patrons of the bar to turn and stare at them. 'Oops! Why didn't I think of it before? When I was bundled into the passenger seat of the kidnappers' car, I noticed the driver was sitting on a cushion.'

'Hmm. To see better over the long bonnet of the vehicle, I conjecture.'

'Because he's so short! It's them, that clinches it.'

'No pun intended, of course,' Clifford said drily. She stared at him blankly until he explained. 'Clinch is a traditional Scottish word for a limp.'

She fought the smile this brought on. 'Right, moving on then, Noel and his companion of reduced stature are supposedly here on holiday, not!' she exclaimed in a low voice. Under their listing in her notebook, she wrote:

Noel Longley and Bert Blunt – almost certainly lying about playing cards in Noel's room around the time of Hilary's death – also vague about time went to bed – only each other to substantiate alibi

'Right, Miss Summers next,' said Eleanor.

Grace Summers – said she is here to find a job – denies Noel Longley's assertion that she was in Hilary's room around 9.30 p.m. on night of Hilary's death

'So, now Mr Franklin.' Her pen flew across the page under his description.

Rex Franklin – only one who admits to knowing Hilary – admitted to being in charge of Hilary's firing squad but helped him escape by switching bullets for blanks – claims Hilary already dead when he went to his room and searched it around 11.35 p.m. – also claims Hilary duped him out of something

She tapped the pen thoughtfully against her chin. 'What was it he said when you queried why he had believed Hilary ever had whatever it was?'

'That Mr Eden had shown him "a taster" and it was "a beauty".'

Eleanor sighed. 'Maybe Hilary really was gun running then? That just leaves Mr Willem de Meyer and he seems to have disappeared.' She cocked her head. 'Surely though, unless he is back tonight, the hotel manager will alert the police to the fact he's missing?'

'If the manager hasn't, we should take it upon ourselves to highlight his absence.'

She turned her notebook round to face him again. 'Please tell me your shrewd command of logic can see something I'm missing in all of this.'

'Yes,' he said slowly. 'The half of the photograph Mr Eden sent to you.'

Her cheeks coloured. 'I've come to the conclusion it was a bitter goodbye he couldn't resist because he knew something was going to happen to him.'

'So have I.'

Her jaw fell at his reply. 'What!?'

'Forgive me, I should have added "in part". To explain, we learned from Thomas, the desk clerk, that Mr Eden appeared most anxious that you should receive the envelope. In my experience, that is not the usual reaction for someone sending a malicious missive.'

'Go on.'

'It has occurred to me that Mr Eden most likely sent it to you because he needed you to receive it.'

Her eyes widened and her lip trembled. 'Because then I could have saved him?'

'Regrettably not. I think he knew a powerful enemy, or enemies, had him cornered and he anticipated he wouldn't leave Brighton alive. Now, if, and I do stress *if*, Miss Summers is or was associated with Mr Eden, it would seem that it was from him that she gained her knowledge concerning your inheritance of Henley Hall and your uncle's fortune.'

Eleanor slapped her forehead. 'Of course!'

'And therefore it would not seem too large a leap of imagination to assume Mr Eden also learned of your solving several murders. After all, you did make the local, and on one occasion, the national papers. I speculate that, trapped as he was, he needed a method of communicating with you that only you would understand or recognise. So, if it fell into the wrong hands, it would be all but meaningless.'

She gasped. 'So he sent me the photograph?'

Clifford nodded. 'I believe Mr Eden deduced that you would have worked out from the crest on the envelope that it came from the Grand Hotel, Brighton. Most hotels, as you know, my lady, have personalised writing paper and envelopes in guests' rooms. The only thing I cannot fathom is why he cut it in half and only sent you one half?'

She frowned. 'I've been wondering that too. Perhaps he intended to send me the other half.' She swallowed hard. 'But he ran out of time.'

Clifford nodded. 'Possibly, although that doesn't explain why he cut it in half. Unless… do you have it with you, perhaps?'

'I haven't been able to be separated from it, even though it hurts every time I stare at it.' She pulled it from her dress pocket and placed it on the table.

'If I may?' Clifford picked it up. 'And you believe this to be Mr Eden's writing on the reverse side?'

'Yes. I've been trying to draw a little comfort from seeing his writing again.'

'Hmm.' Clifford reached into his inside jacket pocket and took out a palm-sized, teardrop-shaped brass object. With a deft flick of his wrist, a glass circle popped out, fastened at the pointed end of the case. 'A powerful magnifying glass,' he said without meeting her questioning gaze. From another pocket he pulled a slim torch and clicked it on. He ran the magnifying glass slowly over the lettering, scrutinising every inch.

Eleanor frowned. 'What are you doing?'

'One moment, please.' He moved to poring over the cut edge of the photograph itself. 'Ah! As I suspected.'

Her curiosity got the better of her. 'Well? What have you discovered?'

He set down the magnifying glass and showed her the back of the photograph. 'Mr Eden did not write the words on the back of this soon after your wedding day, as you imagined. Neither did he cut it in half then. Both acts were committed only a matter of days ago, I am certain.'

Her words tumbled over themselves. 'But how? I mean, why… how can you be so sure?'

He handed her the photograph and the magnifying glass and held the torch for her. 'The ink has faded, yes?'

'Yes, with age.' She frowned. 'Ink does.'

'Not to this extent. Not since Mr William Perkin's most fortuitous discovery for ink production while trying to find a cure for malaria.'

'Surely it would have been better if he'd succeeded with a cure?'

'Unquestionably. However, in trying to produce a synthetic form of quinine, he created what he termed "mauveine", a type of synthetic dye. It revolutionised many industries, being used for everything from ink to hair dye.'

Eleanor's frown deepened. A wandering thought crept into her mind, but she ruthlessly stamped on it. *Concentrate, Ellie! If Clifford thinks this is important, it must be.* 'What does Mr Perkin's dye have to do with Hilary's writing?'

'Because Mr Eden watered down the ink. He diluted it to make it appear as if the ink had aged and faded. However, given the urgency of his situation, he did not have the opportunity to purchase distilled water. Instead, he was reduced to using impure water. From the tap in his adjoining bathroom, I suspect.'

She rubbed her eyes. 'Put me out of my misery and speed up the explanation, please.'

'Very good. Unlike distilled water, the minerals in ordinary water can interfere with the constitution of the mauveine dye in the ink, causing its elements to separate. Resulting in' – he shone the torch closer to the photographic paper – 'the sporadic distortion of colour and intensity you see here.'

'Although you can only see that under this magnifying glass,' she said in awe. 'And what about when he cut it in half?'

'Equally, there are signs that a hurried attempt was made to age the cut. The uneven edge has almost certainly seen the use of a gentleman's razor.' He pointed to the edge. 'It has been used to pull out many of the paper's fibres, creating the impression the edge has worn by being carried in a pocket—'

'Or in his wallet. That's where Grimsdale said he found it.'

Clifford nodded and clicked off the torch. 'But now we are facing a most difficult conundrum.'

She nodded back. 'I know, we need to match it with the other half to try and work out why Hilary cut it in half. But Grimsdale distrusts me and isn't going to allow me to see it again. And he certainly isn't going to let me take it away.'

'And at best, he would be highly displeased with you for having withheld your half of the photograph.'

'Yes, and he would definitely confiscate it as evidence. Dash it, Clifford, we need that other half. It might be the breakthrough we're waiting for.'

'I agree, although I confess at the moment how to obtain it eludes me.'

She took a deep breath as something stabbed at her brain. 'It doesn't elude me.' She spun round on her chair to stare at the enormous decorative silver clock that filled a large alcove between two doorways. She winced. 'Five to midnight. Fingers crossed, Clifford. This is one conversation that will definitely not wait until a more seemly hour. It's time to call in a favour.'

CHAPTER 22

The persistent cry of seagulls and the blustery wind whistling over the cliffs made Eleanor feel she was a hundred miles away from all the unpleasantness of the last few days. She picked her way along the uneven path, staring at the crashing waves below. Despite the wind, the air was warm for the time of year and the sun as bright as a June day. Only a handful of clouds dared intrude on the bluest sky she'd seen since arriving at the seaside, and even they kept away from the sun itself, as if embarrassed to be there.

Now and then she stole a sideways glance at her companion's chestnut curls blowing against the turned-up collar of his blue wool overcoat. And then she coloured as he looked at her, his deep-brown eyes holding hers questioningly.

'Quite the bracing walk,' she said awkwardly, her fingers straying to her emerald-green silk scarf.

Detective Chief Inspector Seldon nodded. 'Absolutely. But after the substantial late breakfast you insisted on treating me to, I fear this is the only way I shall stay awake long enough to help you get the other half of your wedding photograph.'

When she'd rung him last night, she'd been amazed at how readily he'd agreed to come down and speak to Grimsdale and obtain the other half of her wedding photograph for her, albeit in his usual gruff manner. But then again, it had been midnight.

She shoved her hands in her sage-green jacket pockets and continued at the fast pace needed to keep up with his long legs. 'It really is most frightfully kind of you, Inspector. Especially since you wasted half a day of your holiday kicking your heels with me at the Metropole for breakfast. Then the aquarium, and now up here on the cliffs. I can't believe Grimsdale has been called away for the morning so, on top of everything else, you need to wait to ask him in person.' She had no idea what reason he was going to give Grimsdale for needing the photograph. She assumed he would use his superior rank, but she just felt it best not to ask.

'It isn't a waste of any time at all. I was at a loose end, in truth.'

'Oh.' She tried to ignore the peculiar sense of disappointment his admission brought.

He glanced at her sharply. 'Work has been so busy in the last twelve months I haven't had a chance to think what I might do with my days off. I did need a break, however.'

She silently agreed with him. There was no denying his dashingly handsome features were showing the signs of too many late nights. The strain of being one of the few senior officers spread far too thin across London and Oxford was etched on his face. He'd also told her recently that there had been budget and staff cuts in his department.

'My apologies then. I've added three cases to your workload since I arrived at Henley Hall.'

'Four, actually. The last one occupying the entire Christmas period.'

Oh dear, Ellie, it sounds like you've been a right pain since you appeared and he's regretting coming down to help today!

She forced a laugh. 'Perhaps to make up for it, I could lend you Clifford. He'll have you sorted six months in advance of your holiday with a meticulous handwritten itinerary.'

'A delightful offer. Although it sounds more like a chance for you to cause mayhem with Henley Hall's meal schedules in his absence.'

'Dash it, you rumbled me.' She negotiated a particularly spiky bush growing in the middle of the path. 'He is absolutely wonderful, genuinely. Yet at least twice a day I want to boil his head.'

Seldon laughed out loud. A deep laugh that she found infectious.

As their laughter died down, she felt an awkward silence coming on and jumped in. 'Well, it's not surprising you find it hard to relax. I know how dedicated you are to your job, despite how stressful it must be.' She winced. 'And I've probably compounded that stress now and then. But I'm sure you don't remember that,' she added quickly.

Seldon's lips curled upwards, but he seemed to fight the smile. 'Lady Swift, I could hardly forget how many times you have deliberately gone against my advice. And my cautions and even' – he stared at her – 'my threats to arrest you for interfering in a case.'

She shrugged. 'I'm not the best at being told what to do. Too much time growing up alone, making up my own rules as I went along, I think. And, seeing as I'll be thirty tomorrow, there's probably little chance I'll change now.'

His face registered something she couldn't fathom, but as he didn't reply, his silence felt disapproving. His next question surprised her. 'And how is Master Gladstone, the sausage-stealing monster of Henley Hall?'

She laughed. 'Enjoying his seaside break enormously, thank you. As are the ladies.'

Seldon rubbed his forehead. 'You have brought your entire staff on holiday with you?'

She nodded. 'Of course. Oh, except Joseph and Si—' She stopped, not wanting him to ask her about Silas, her mysterious gamekeeper-cum-security guard she was now sure had a rather dubious past, given Clifford's cryptic answers to her questions about him.

Seldon's brows met. 'Strange then that I wasn't called down to Brighton earlier.'

'Whatever for?'

'Oh, you know, to escort England's most unorthodox lady of the manor and her rabblesome staff back to Buckinghamshire after too many rowdy celebrations running into the small hours. Only that,' he ended, looking out over the sea.

Is he making fun of you, Ellie? She had, in truth, had some rather exuberant, and late, evenings with her staff that had left her wondering how they managed to be so fresh-faced the following morning. Especially as her housekeeper and cook were a good twenty years older than her.

'Well, I've been very well behaved. It's the ladies who have been getting up to all sorts.'

Seldon shook his head. 'As I said, most unorthodox.'

'It's only fair. It's their holiday as well as mine. And as you yourself have found, holidays do not always pan out the way you planned.'

At that moment they rounded the headland and the full force of the wind hit them, catching the end of Eleanor's silk scarf. In a trice, it billowed out from round her neck and disappeared over the cliff. She ran as close to the edge as she dared and stared out in dismay at the sight of it floating off over the beach hundreds of feet below.

'Oh botheration!' she muttered.

'Was that precious?' Seldon's voice in her ear made her jump. 'I can take the next path down and try to retrieve it for you.'

'Very kind. It was my mother's, actually, but I do have a few others of hers. And I've put you to enough trouble already. I'll just turn up my collar for now.'

'Here.' He removed his blue wool scarf from his neck and offered it to her. 'I would feel terrible if you caught a chill on top of everything else.'

'That's very kind, but you're the one who's rundown from working all hours.'

'Well, we can't both wear it. And I don't need you being unwell on my conscience.' He held her gaze. 'Obstinacy can be dangerous for one's health, I've heard, especially in ladies who mistakenly believe they are invincible.' Awkwardly wrapping the scarf around her neck, he tucked the end in behind her right ear, catching one of her red curls, then took a hasty step back. He wrinkled his nose. 'You definitely look better in your customary green. Let's walk.'

Fearing the mix of emotions playing out on her face would give her away she buried it in the surprising softness of his scarf. The intoxicating scents of cedar, citrus and fresh soap made her tingle.

'By the way,' Seldon said. 'I almost forgot to mention. I made a call and checked out the details of those four men and one woman you asked about. It seems they all came across on the same boat from South Africa as Mr Painshill, sorry, Eden. Bit of a coincidence.'

She shook her head. 'Coincidence, my foot! What's Grimsdale doing about it?'

His brow furrowed. 'I'm sure Grimsdale's aware of the fact, but you can't just arrest someone because they came over on the same ship.'

She laughed and nodded. 'I know, you need that annoying little thing called "evidence".'

Further along, Seldon stopped by a wooden bench. 'Would you like a rest?'

'No, thank you, I'm fine. But I would like to drink in this incredible view for a moment.' She slid onto the end. He waited for her to get comfortable and then took the other end. They stared out over the green-grey sea, punctuated by the tiny white dots of seagulls bobbing on the rolling waves. She bent down and picked up a pink stone worn circular by the sand and wind. She held it in her palm. 'I do love the sea.'

He took the stone and turned it over in his hand. 'Did you spend a lot of time near it as a child?'

'Not so much near it, as on it. We sailed a lot, mostly between all the overseas postings my parents took.' She shuffled her feet. 'Looking back, I realise they didn't always trust the authorities and preferred to make their own way.'

'That explains some of it,' he mumbled. He caught her staring at him. 'To paraphrase yourself earlier, I've rubbed up against your own mistrust of authority too many times. It makes every conversation feel as though I am unwittingly engaged in a boxing match.'

He turned and stared at her hands. For a moment she thought he was going to reach out and take them, but he suddenly snapped his arms behind his back and cleared his throat. 'I am sorry, it must be very difficult for you since you arrived here. And my sincere condolences for being…'

She gave him a wan smile. 'Widowed? Twice, as well. To lose one husband may be regarded as a misfortune, to lose the same one twice looks like carelessness.'

He smiled ruefully. 'That sounds rather like something Clifford would say.'

She nodded. 'He did, well, apparently Oscar Wilde said it first about losing both your parents, something I've also successfully done.' She looked up at him and shook her head. 'Mr Wilde would consider me most dreadfully careless.'

'Careless is not a word I have tended to associate with you.'

'Really? What word do you associate with me? Infuriating? Like I might once have mentioned I found you?' She groaned inwardly. *Why did you say that, Ellie?*

What had seemed like such a good idea the previous night was now beginning to feel a hideous blunder. Here she was trying to cover up her bubbling emotions over Hilary's murder while discussing it with a man who Clifford determined was attracted to her. And, she could no longer deny, she him, despite their constant and heated quarrels.

To her surprise, Seldon shook his head. 'I think I would tend towards "impetuous", and sometimes "reckless".'

His words reminded her of a recent telephone call where he'd uncharacteristically told her he'd rather all the criminals in England went free rather than she place herself in danger. She blushed and then tried to cover it up. 'Now then, shall we continue our wonderful walk? I really do feel terribly bad at imposing on your holiday time. If there is anything I can do to repay you while you're here, please do say.'

He touched her elbow to make her turn back to him.

'Maybe there is one small thing.' He looked into her eyes. 'Call me Hugh.'

CHAPTER 23

After a deep sleep and a breakfast of sublime smoked salmon, poached eggs and mini pancakes topped with bacon, Eleanor felt ready to tackle a new day. Especially her birthday!

Back in her suite she ruffled her bulldog's ears. 'Sorry to break it to you, old chum, but your bowl isn't going to refill itself with more sausages.' She shook her head as he stiffened at the 's' word, his imploring eyes trying to weaken her resolve. 'Good try, but not cute enough for me to let you get fat, not even on my birthday. Now, come on, we've got a busy day.'

She pulled out her favourite green jacket from the exquisitely inlaid mahogany wardrobe, pausing to run her fingers down Seldon's blue scarf looped over the next hanger.

'Oh gracious, Gladstone, I quite forgot to give this back. I'll have to return it later.' She hesitated, but somehow her flushed cheeks were soon buried in the scarf and Seldon's comforting scent as she remembered his parting words.

'I told Grimsdale I needed to borrow the photograph in order to cross-reference it with another case that might have some bearing on his. I need to give it back tomorrow, but it's best we don't meet again until you've sorted out this business… and your heart. I could not intrude. Leave the photograph at the lobby desk in an envelope and tell them that someone will collect it in due course. I'll make sure it gets back to Grimsdale.'

With a nod, he'd shaken her hand, hanging on to it for a heartbeat, and then turned on his heel and left her wishing the world would stop spinning.

Feeling guilty, she jerked upright and stared at the photograph of Hilary on the table. *Oh, Ellie, why are you so hopeless with men! Hilary can never be with you now. And maybe he never was.*

The image of Grace Summers flashed in and out of her mind. She knelt and wrapped Gladstone in her arms, consoled by the kisses he bestowed upon her cheek. 'At least you still love me, even if it is only for the sausages.'

Down in the lobby, her dutiful butler was waiting for her.

'Morning, Clifford.' She dropped the bulldog's lead into his outstretched hand.

'Good morning, my lady. And happy birthday. The ladies are looking forward to our early celebratory luncheon.'

'Thank you. I believe celebrating stepping into my fourth decade over lunch with them and yourself will be just the tonic I need to regain my old form.'

It seemed that the weather knew it was Eleanor's birthday as the sun shone in a cloudless sky, and the normally chattering wind had dropped to a whispering zephyr. First, they headed to The Lanes to stroll among the myriad fashionable boutiques. Eleanor fell in love with the quirkier among them, their designs appealing to her love of vibrant colours and unusual designs. The staff, mostly women, were dressed in charming little outfits themselves and more than happy for Eleanor to peruse the rails and glass cabinets at her leisure.

She couldn't help colouring slightly at the many envious stares of the other elegantly turned out young and middle-aged women shopping as she instinctively picked out colours and styles that complimented her striking red hair and green eyes to perfection. Then, despite the many distractions on offer, she took pity on Clifford – who had shown the patience of a stoic – and set off to meet the ladies in the delightful little seafront eatery Clifford had booked.

With its spotless cream walls hung with photographs of happy
families playing on the beach and cheeky seagulls perched along
the Palace Pier, there was no denying the cosy holiday atmosphere
of the restaurant. Even the simple cotton napkins had a delicate
grey-and-pink shell motif, echoed in the starched tablecloths. The
addition of the low-hanging ship's-style lanterns over each table and
the glass-panelled wooden partitions provided a fun nautical theme.

Polly gasped in delight. 'Oh look, the napkin rings are in the
shape of little crabs and lobsters as well!'

'My lady,' Mrs Butters said. 'Happy birthday. We are all so
honoured you've chosen to spend your lunchtime with us. 'Tis the
highlight of our holiday.' Mrs Trotman and Polly nodded.

'Well, I hope not,' Eleanor said playfully. She leaned across to
the three of them and whispered loud enough for Clifford to hear,
'I hope you have plenty more mischief planned before we return
to Henley Hall.'

Mrs Trotman chuckled. 'Oh, my lady, have we ever!'

Even the corners of Clifford's lips twitched as the four of them
laughed at this.

'But only if we can drag young Polly along the streets faster,'
Mrs Butters said fondly. 'We've spent that much time waiting for
her to stop gawking at the Indian gentlemen we keep passing.'

Polly blushed. ''Tis their clothes, your ladyship. I've never seen
such beautiful material on gentlemen before. Even their umbrellas
are as decorated as a palace.'

'There is absolutely nothing wrong with appreciating someone
else's culture, Polly. You must enjoy all the sights Brighton has to
offer.' She clapped her hands. 'Now, let us lay waste to this delightful
restaurant's menu. Although, I confess, even after reading it from
end to end, I simply can't choose. It all sounds too delicious for
words. Clifford, help!'

'Very good, my lady.' He rose and strode to the smiling waiter
just emerging from the kitchen.

*

It was close to two hours later that Eleanor pushed her plate away. 'What a brilliant idea, Clifford. A pick and mix of most of the dishes on the menu for us all to share.'

'Perhaps "a buffet" might be a more grown-up term, my lady?'

'Perhaps, but where's the fun in growing up too soon?'

He arched a brow. 'Thirty years of age is too soon?'

'Definitely. I'll let you know when I'm ready to, though.' Eleanor winked at Mrs Butters. 'Right now I am full of the most delicious crab cakes, potato and chive fritters, and potted shrimps, whitebait and braised onion rissoles. Not to mention the marmalade pudding and apple pie. So there is only one thing that will end the perfect birthday lunch. Are we all game?'

The ladies nodded enthusiastically. Clifford sat poker straight, eyeing her sideways. 'And what would that be, my lady?'

'A donkey race on the beach. All five of us.'

Polly giggled but then clapped her hand over her mouth. Mrs Butters nudged her. 'We arranged the donkeys on the way here, just as you asked, my lady. Five sturdy fellows and one of them especially good for anyone with longer legs.' She winked at Eleanor.

'They have numbered bibs we can each wear too,' Mrs Trotman said. 'But the donkey man did say as we need to cheer good and loud to get the most out of them.'

The four of them turned to Clifford, who sat pinching his nose, his eyes closed. 'As it is your birthday, as you wish, my lady.'

Eleanor couldn't keep it up any longer and led the raucous laughter that rang round their table. 'You are the best sport ever, Clifford, but I shan't really put you through such purgatory. Not today, anyway.'

He opened his eyes. 'That is, indeed, good news, my lady. Because I have already planned a small surprise for your birthday myself. Although it may not be to your, or the ladies, liking, as it involves neither flouting the rules of propriety or good taste.'

Eleanor laughed. 'Don't worry, I love surprises, even ones that don't outrage society's rules.' She gestured down the esplanade. 'Lead the way.'

CHAPTER 24

Only a short walk from the restaurant, Clifford stopped and turned to Eleanor.

'On the rare occasions you visited the Hall as a child, my lady, I spent most of the time trying to keep you from mischief. Unfortunately, you were only mischievous because you were bored. I remember you informing me on your thirteenth birthday that you would neither be bored, or tempted into mischief, if you could go sailing as you used to with your parents. As there was no body of water, or craft, within a reasonable journey, I was never able to indulge you.' He gestured to a smartly painted blue sailboat bobbing at the end of a long wooden jetty. 'Apologies, my lady, I'm a little late, but I am now able to put that right.'

Eleanor smiled and shook her head. 'No need to apologise, Clifford, it was worth the seventeen-year wait!'

''Tis such a pretty boat, your ladyship,' Polly whispered, her eyes wide.

'It's a lugger, Polly,' Eleanor said, admiring the vessel's fine lines and three enormous red sails. 'See how her sails are three-sided and suspended from the spar, or wooden beam, overhanging either end. A forty-two footer, I'd say. But I haven't seen anything like her since we arrived down here. There's something of the continental about her.' She looked questioningly at Clifford. 'I didn't realise you could rent a fishing boat at this time of year. Surely the fishing season has started?'

'Ah, so the lady is part sea dog, despite her fine silk scarf and fancy togs.' Laughing blue eyes embedded in a wind-weathered face that was largely hidden by a huge shaggy beard appraised her from the boat.

'You must be the captain of this beautiful craft.'

'Percy Bertram Fisher at your service.' He lifted his blue felt cap, revealing a tiny kitten curled underneath. Feeling the rustle of the gentle breeze on its fur, it stretched out its front legs and slithered down elegantly to sit on his shoulder. 'This is Tilly.' He gently put his hands over the kitten's ears. 'Thinks she's a pirate's parrot. Haven't the heart to tell her my buccaneer days are over.'

Eleanor chuckled. 'I see we are in for more than just a wonderful boat ride, Mr Fisher. I guess from your surname that your family have been in the business for several generations.'

He gave a short bow. 'Since 1690, so we might just make it out and back. Welcome aboard the *Madame Amelie*.'

The captain's strong arms easily helped each of the ladies onto the deck. Eleanor swung herself down, Clifford following with Gladstone. She ran her hand along the weather-beaten teak rail. 'Hello, *Madame Amelie*. Lovely to meet you.'

'Here's the bag you left Mr Clifford,' Percy said, holding out a carpet bag.

'My lady.' Clifford held it out to her. 'The cabin is quite appropriate. I inspected it myself previously.'

Lifting the hatch, he offered his gloved hand as she turned to walk backwards down the narrow wooden steps. Catching her breath at the bottom, her heart faltered just for a second as she looked round the cosy space that reminded her so much of the one she had shared with her parents as a child when they were at sea.

On either side, a narrow seat covered with a patchwork quilt obviously doubled as snug bunks. To her left was a charming galley area, complete with miniature sink and a tiny cooker top. A worn, but highly polished wooden table occupied the rest of the cabin. One leaf was folded, allowing access to the forward sleeping quarters, just like on her parents' boat.

A box of rolled up charts sat to one side and opposite it a small bookcase had been made to fit the space left by the offset position of the pot-bellied stove. The cabin was wonderfully bright, hung as it was with several lit paraffin lamps, which sparkled in the wide mirror hung between the many small framed prints of boats. A single photograph of an obviously younger Percy caught her eye. He had his arm hanging protectively around the shoulder of a pretty girl in a simple print dress, who was staring at him adoringly. Eleanor nodded to herself. 'Amelie.'

A few minutes later, she re-emerged dressed in her favourite sage-green trousers, matching cardigan and her rubber-soled tennis shoes that she'd found in the carpet bag. And in the short time she had been away, bunting had been strung the full length of the boat and Clifford was busy pouring champagne into a tray of tin mugs.

Percy laughed at the look on Eleanor's face as he tickled Tilly's chin. 'It seems Mr Clifford's sleeves are even longer than you knew. He gave me quite the list of instructions on how this little lot of surprises he was hiding was to go.'

Eleanor shook her head. 'I can imagine. Right down to the temperature and precise timing the champagne should be served, I'm sure.' She took the mug Clifford held out to her.

'Thank you so much, it's a wonderful birthday surprise.'

He inclined his head. 'However, I must apologise, my lady. Mr Fisher has informed me that champagne flutes are not permitted aboard. Broken glass being deemed too hazardous in turbulent waters.'

With their mugs raised, everyone chorused a rousing, 'Happy birthday, my lady.'

'Best wishes for long, happy days with the best of the catch,' Percy added. 'Can't say as *Amelie* and me have ever had a titled lady aboard, like yourself. Let's hope it's good luck.'

She tilted her head, pointing to her flame red curls. 'Well, you've averted the first potential for an ill-fated trip by greeting me before we boarded, haven't you?'

'Ah, more than part sea dog, I see. Only one who's spent a good while afloat would know 'tis bad luck for sailors to let a red-headed woman aboard without exchanging words first.'

'I grew up sailing from posting to posting abroad with my parents. I loved it,' Eleanor found herself gushing. 'The smell of the sea as the sun rose. Hanging over the bow rail in my pyjamas watching the water flow underneath us. The beauty of our boat herself. But, most of all, the magic of the wind taking us hundreds of miles around the world in nothing more than lots of lovingly crafted wooden planks.'

Percy held up a hand. 'I know Amelie'll agree with me in that case.' Handing Tilly over to a delighted Polly, he lifted the lid of a wooden trunk lashed to the transom at the rear of the boat. His voice was muffled as his top half disappeared inside. 'Ah, there it is.' Standing back up, he held out a yellow sou'wester. 'You were right enough 'bout the fishing season having started, m'lady. Last week as it happens. But I was happy to agree to Mr Clifford hiring *Amelie* seeing as my first mate is crook. Fancy filling in for him?'

'Absolutely!' She slapped the sou'wester on and saluted. 'Where are we off to today, Skipper?'

'We shall cast off, heading West. Selsey Bill will be waiting for us if we make good enough progress.'

She laughed. 'Who's he?'

He chuckled and shook his head. 'The old sea jokes are the best, aren't they?' They both knew Selsey Bill was actually a headland they'd need to navigate around. If they got that far.

The ladies were clearly as excited as Eleanor was as they cast off and *Madame Amelie* set sail. With the familiar sound of the halyards striking the masts and the sight of the sails rippling in the breeze, Eleanor was filled with childlike delight. Once they had reached a sufficient distance out from shore, Percy set their course and then, to her surprise, handed Eleanor the helm, staying close enough to leap in should his precious boat lurch into peril. She couldn't keep the grin from her face as they slid elegantly through the gently rolling white horses.

While Clifford kept everyone's mug topped up and Polly played with Tilly, the ladies admired the striking views of Brighton's long parade and then, as the scenery changed, the many formal gardens along Hove's seafront, the town's imposing Georgian facades echoing those of its more famous cousin.

'What do you think, m'lady?' Percy said. 'Turn a little more into the wind? Or are you just hoping to see me sprint down and reset the foresail every five minutes?' He winked at her and dropped down into the cabin.

They continued on past Shoreham-by-Sea, which looked like a cosy village in comparison to the grandeur of Brighton. As they neared the more heavily built-up town of Worthing, Eleanor was poring over the chart laid out on the wooden platform in front of her.

'I say, isn't that a wreck marked on the chart there?' She pointed to a small black symbol about half a mile further ahead.

Percy looked over her shoulder. 'That it is. You'd make an excellent second mate, m'lady. I might take you on permanently.'

Clifford materialised at her side and peered at the chart. 'I imagine that is the wreck of the *Aubriana*, Mr Fisher?'

'Spot on, Mr Clifford.'

Eleanor arched a questioning brow.

'The *Aubriana* was a passenger steamship built in 1873. Regrettably she was caught in a ferocious storm en route from Bilbao and swept miles off course before sinking.'

Percy nodded. 'The passengers and crew, mind, were saved in a daring rescue by the fishermen of the Brighton, Bognor and Selsey fleets. Us fisherfolk always step up when the time comes.'

As they passed the spot of the wreck Eleanor stared out, imagining the scene on the night the *Aubriana* sank. Many of the fishermen might only just have returned safely to their loved ones, before turning around and setting out once again into the teeth of the storm, this time to selflessly rescue the *Aubriana*'s passengers. She gave silent thanks that there were such people in the world.

A few minutes later they dropped anchor and Percy produced fishing rods and pails of bait.

'Mackerel, whiting and hardback crabs should be biting if we're lucky.' He nodded in approval as Clifford passed around glasses of ginger wine.

Mrs Butters shook her head in mock disapproval. 'Oh lummy, Mr Clifford. Champagne and then ginger wine? Don't go telling me off later when I'm dancing on the deck here, not a care in the world.'

'Ooh, that's a great plan for the end of the afternoon,' Mrs Trotman called over. 'Takes a bit of practice not falling down though, doesn't it, Butters?'

Mrs Butters shook her head. 'I don't know what you mean, Trotters.'

Even Clifford couldn't contain his amusement at this exchange. 'The ginger wine is to calm your stomach, Mrs Butters, not to encourage you to perform an Irish jig on the foredeck. It helps alleviate any symptoms of seasickness.'

After an hour of fishing, it seemed the mackerel, whiting and hardback crabs weren't biting, so they rounded Selsey Bill, the furthest point they had time for, and then set off back to Brighton.

The return trip seemed much quicker to Eleanor than the one out, but she put it down to the wind being more in their favour on the return leg. Although it could equally have been down to her wish to stay out at sea for as long as she could. But Percy had much to do to prepare *Amelie* for her return to serious fishing in the morning and needed the rest of the day free.

Eleanor ran her hand along the boat's bow rail for the last time as she went to step ashore. 'Thank you, *Amelie*. Keep Percy safe, he's a good man.'

The creak of the hull in reply made her smile. She jumped lithely onto the jetty. Clifford held out a hand for Polly, who was struggling to leave Tilly.

'Maybe we should get a kitten at the Hall?' Eleanor said quietly to Clifford. 'Not just for Polly, but it might be good company for Gladstone too.'

Clifford snorted. 'I'm not sure a living creature is safe in Polly's... uncoordinated hands. Perhaps we could, however, obtain for her a stuffed cat? Or it could be a good hobby for you, my lady? Home taxidermy is all the rage at the moment, I believe.'

She gave him a pointed look. 'Polly is getting much better, she hasn't broken anything... well, nothing valuable, for weeks. And I'm not going to spend my evenings stuffing dead animals with whatever we happen to have lying around the Hall, thank you!'

Their goodbyes and grateful waves to Percy over, she turned to Clifford as he fell into step beside her. 'I don't know how to thank you enough, Clifford. That was the best birthday treat I've ever had.'

'Nothing but a pleasure, my lady. I suggest, if it is amenable to you, we leave the ladies at this juncture so they can misbehave without my censure and retire to the Winter Gardens?'

She nodded and tried to keep a straight face. 'Good idea. I'd hate to witness them flouting the rules of propriety or good taste, that just wouldn't do.'

CHAPTER 25

'Oh, but I say, this is glorious,' Eleanor whispered as she stepped into the elegant dome of the Winter Gardens. The size of an intimate concert hall and rising three floors, the entire building was bathed in sunlight. Made of glass, its vaulted supports appeared almost too fragile to bear the weight. Tall potted palms mingled with the multitude of hanging baskets cascading greenery down every column. Over sixty tables and chairs, arranged around the central carved fountain, told how bustling this would be at the height of the tourist season.

Eleanor pointed to the enticing staircase halfway along one side, which swirled up to a galleried area offering a commanding view of the entire ground floor. 'Let's get a table up there.'

Once installed and their order placed, Eleanor took a deep breath and pulled out the two halves of the wedding photograph.

Clifford scanned her face. 'Are you sure this won't spoil your birthday, my lady?'

'No, but I appreciate your solicitude. It seems Hilary has given me the opportunity to find out the truth and then... move on. Undoubtedly the best thirtieth birthday present he could have given me, although I'm unconvinced that was his intention.'

'Then, may I offer my compliments for your idea of asking Detective Chief Inspector Seldon to assist in retrieving the other half of the photograph? He is an excellent ally to have.'

She grimaced. 'Yes but it will be a fleeting alliance once he learns all the ugly facts I kept from him, like the attempted kidnap.' She groaned. 'Then there'll be no more "Call me Hugh" after that.'

She caught the twinkle in Clifford's eye and shook her head wearily. 'No, Clifford, that ship has definitely sailed. He made it clear he didn't want to spend any time with me today, despite the fact he will be driving back down to return the photograph late this afternoon.'

Clifford adjusted his perfectly aligned tie but said nothing.

She tapped her head. 'However, I just remembered he did confirm that Franklin, Longley, Blunt, Summers and de Meyer all came across on the same ship as Hilary, so at least I got some useful information out of him while he's still talking to me.'

Clifford nodded. 'As we suspected.'

'Yes. But now we have a simply enormous pot of tea and a full stand of divine looking finger cakes—'

'Petits fours, my lady.'

'Yes, those too. I simply haven't room after that sumptuous lunch, but as it's my birthday I feel honour bound to at least try and eat one or two.' She looked around. 'And besides, they obviously need the business, the place is deserted. Except, that is, for that unhelpfully love-struck young couple over there.' She pulled the two halves of the photograph from her pocket and placed them together. For a moment she just stared at the image. Finally, she let out a long breath. 'It was a fairy-tale day. Much like today has been. At least I can hang on to that memory.' She caught Clifford's eye. 'But we aren't here to stare at a picture of happy newlyweds, I know.'

'My lady, take your time.'

She shook her head. 'No, let's get this over with.' Turning each half over, she pushed them back together. As she read the first line, she felt her chest constrict.

'What is it, my lady?'

'Oh, Clifford!' She closed her eyes and tried to control her thumping heart. He topped up her tea and waited patiently. Wishing the ink inscription would somehow disappear, she reluctantly opened her eyes and accepted the handkerchief Clifford offered. She took a deep breath and looked again at the words.

Lady Eleanor   Letitia Swift
Captain Hilary   Montague Eden
Married on   June 3rd 1914
At the Hotel   Royal Pilgrim's Rest
Something old   something new
Something borrowed   something blue
And a sixpence   in her hand

Till death do   us part

She shook her head bitterly. 'What husband doesn't remember his wife's middle name? Especially one as unusual as mine? It should be "Lettice".'

'And the other lines, my lady?' Clifford asked gently.

She looked again and shook her head. 'He's got his middle name wrong as well! It should say "Captain Hilary Montgomery Eden".' She bit her lip. 'Although, I'm not even sure he was a captain now. Or if Montgomery was his real middle name. Oh, Clifford, it seems that he had so many aliases he couldn't even remember which one he married me under!'

She sat back in her seat, fiddling with the edge of the handkerchief. 'Isn't hindsight a wonderful thing? Hilary would sit with me under the stars of an evening and tell me how he was going to pan for gold and become rich so he could give me the world. It was always so romantic.' She shook her head again. 'I never thought to question how he intended to succeed, nor how we would even live the way he described on a captain's salary in the meantime. Obviously, he never intended to work, or pan, for his riches.'

'We are still short of a lot of facts, my lady.' Clifford's tone was neutral, but his brow was furrowed.

'Maybe, although I'm growing more doubtful with every new revelation about him. Maybe my marriage to him was just his attempt to use me to further his get-rich plans? There, I said it.' She ran her hands down her arms.

Clifford cleared his throat. 'I think the only thing we can be certain of is Mr Eden's anxiety that you should receive the photograph. And it strikes me that the last line of the verse is also wr—'

'Clifford!' She forced a smile. 'I realise I was wrong now. When you asked if looking at the photograph would spoil my birthday, I was adamant it wouldn't. Well, I was mistaken.' She took the two halves and shoved them into her jacket pocket. 'So I say that's enough of anything to do with Hilary for today.'

Clifford gave his customary half bow, but straightened up quickly. 'In that case, my lady, would you like me to intercept your visitor who has just appeared at the top of the stairs?'

'Gracious, Clifford, look who it is!'

CHAPTER 26

Eleanor looked up at the owner of the outstretched hand.

'Lady Swift, allow me to present myself. Willem de Meyer.' The clipped accent sounded so familiar, each letter 'a' shortened into an 'eh' sound.

He's not Dutch, Ellie, he's South African!

The man gestured to the table. 'May I join you and your companion?'

She folded her arms. 'So long as you don't deny knowing my husband like everyone else.'

De Meyer deftly undid the bottom two buttons of his Savile Row jacket and pinched each leg of his tailored suit trousers as he sat down. He gave her a steely look, which was disconcerting given that it was teemed with a wide smile. 'On the contrary, I knew your husband very well even though I never actually met him until he was dead.' At her startled look he shrugged. 'My sources are very detailed. And usually very accurate. I believe I know more about your husband than, perhaps, you do.' He leaned back and crossed one leg over the other. 'You and I could help each other a great deal.'

She let out a scoff. 'You're not the first to take that tack. And why should I trust you?'

'No reason at all,' he said, steepling his fingers. 'But tell me, how well did you really know your husband, Lady Swift?'

As Clifford stiffened at the directness of the man's question, she took a sip of her tea. 'The real question is, Mr de Meyer, how much do we ever know another person? Surely everyone has a few surprises up their sleeve? You look as though you certainly do.'

This drew a snorted laugh from him as he turned back each of his silk shirt cuffs like a magician, revealing a pair of oval, gold cufflinks. 'Oh no. I have no reason to hide anything. I prefer the transparent approach.'

She put down her tea. 'As do I. So, to answer your question transparently, I may have a few… puzzles regarding Hilary that I haven't been able to solve yet.'

'Then I repeat, we really could help each other.' There was that wide smile again, which emphasised his muscular jaw. He leaned forward. 'I will tell you what I know if you tell me something in return.'

'Hardly an irresistible offer.' She busied herself choosing another petit four. At his silence, she looked over at him but then felt her chest tighten. She swallowed hard. 'Alright. I admit I'm curious to hear what you have to say.'

'Of course you are,' he replied smoothly, leaning back in his chair. 'I always think the best way to tell a story is to start at the very beginning. Let's see then. According to my sources your husband was born in Brighton. And—'

'Brighton?' She shook her head. 'He told me Sydenham in South East London.'

He shrugged. 'My sources tell me Brighton and, as I said, they are rarely wrong. His father died when he was young. His mother wasn't able to provide much for them, and poor little Hilary spent many hungry days.' He brushed the sleeve of his jacket. 'Tragic beginning. Tragic ending.' He held her gaze. 'Predictably clichéd.'

Before Eleanor could utter the sharp retort that came to her lips, Clifford leaned forward, anger in his eyes. 'The facts, Mr de Meyer. If you truly have any, are all that are required.'

De Meyer looked at him mockingly. 'Facts are such a moot topic though, aren't they? But as you wish.' He turned his attention back to Eleanor. 'To stick to the "facts", Hilary was young and desperate, a fatal combination. He decided there was more to life than poverty and obscurity and, more pertinently, that he would do anything to get it. It started with amateur confidence tricks, but you know what a quick learner he was. Bold, if not brilliant, he soon turned to bigger and bigger things, which got him noticed.'

'By whom?' Eleanor said.

'The boss of the gang on whose territory he foolishly believed he could operate without giving him a cut. Luckily for Hilary, when the boss sent round a couple of gang members to teach him what happened to upstarts who thought they could operate on his gang's patch, Hilary managed to give them the slip. Unfortunately though, he had underestimated the gang's reach and soon realised that the only way to escape their vengeance was to leave not only Brighton, but England. So he fled on the first steamer he could get a ticket for, which happened to be going to South Africa.'

'And what did Hilary do on landing in South Africa?' she said, keeping a wobble from her voice with difficulty.

'What do you think?' He spread his hands. 'He fell back into his old ways. To be fair, I am not sure he would have had much choice arriving on her shores penniless and friendless. South Africa is far wilder and more dangerous than her lions and sharks.' He nodded at her. 'But you know that all too well.'

She eyed him coldly. 'I looked after myself just fine out there, thank you!'

Clifford rapped the table. 'Mr de Meyer, again I am warning you to stick to the facts or I shan't bother the management to eject you, I shall do it myself. And it will be a pleasure. Conclude your business, whatever it is, swiftly and take your leave.'

De Meyer nodded slowly, a lazy smile on his lips. 'If that is what the lady wishes. Although from what I saw in South Africa, she was more than capable of speaking up for herself. But anyway, back to

Hilary. He thought he had struck lucky when he met two other crooks who had been stealing small-time from my employers. As head of security, I wasn't happy about this. However, the thefts were not so amateurish that I could easily work out who it was. But then they got greedy and conjured up a more ambitious scheme along with your husband. But they still needed someone on the inside.'

'You?'

He nodded. 'None of the three of them had any idea that I was leading them into a trap. The night it was all set for I waited with armed guards, ready to ambush them. But it seems they didn't trust me as much as I'd hoped. They broke in earlier than they'd said they would and from another place. We caught up with them as they tried to get away. At least I gave one of them a permanent souvenir – a bullet in the leg.'

Bert Blunt, Ellie! He's got a limp. That's too much of a coincidence, which means Longley, his so-called cousin, must have been the other crook.

De Meyer was still talking. 'It seems from what I learned later that they decided to double-cross not only me, but also your husband. They didn't tell him about their change of plans, either. In fact, he wasn't even there when we had our little gunfight. However, it appears they underestimated him, and he found them later and, in revenge, stole the item they'd stolen from my employers.' He stifled a yawn. 'You see, thieves can never hold on to their ill-gotten gains for long.'

Eleanor frowned, trying to process what she had been told. 'But the two members of the gang that got away? Surely with all the resources apparently at your disposal you should have caught them?'

He shrugged. 'The war made tracking anyone practically impossible, and then the influenza outbreak compounded the difficulties.'

She shook her head. 'But why did you pursue Hilary all this time? You said yourself he wasn't even there on the night of the theft. What did you want with him?'

He nodded. 'A good point, Lady Swift. The answer is simple. When I did catch up with the other two, I realised that they weren't living the high life on their ill-gotten gains. Or even lying low. No, they themselves were pursuing someone. So, I said to myself, Willem, why do you suppose they would be doing that?'

She groaned. 'Because they no longer had whatever they allegedly stole from your employers. The person they were now pursuing had it. Or they believed he did.'

'Exactly! And I discovered that that other person they were pursuing was—'

'Hilary.' Eleanor couldn't keep the question from her lips. 'But Hilary was shot for gun running, not stealing.'

De Meyer nodded. 'That was where your husband's luck ran out. There has always been an element of gun running in that district of South Africa. Your husband stole a vehicle, I assume while trying to put some distance between himself and his former partners in crime. He was stopped at a roadblock by the military and they searched the back of the vehicle as a matter of course and found illegal guns hidden in the cargo.' He paused. 'Your husband was a thief, Lady Swift, but he never ran guns that I know of.' He held out his hands. 'There you go, a crumb of comfort for the widow.'

She found her breath coming short. *Ellie, is he just playing with you? Is any of this true?* She snapped to. 'Mr de Meyer, I am tiring of your game.'

He smiled, a broad crocodile smile. 'I have always had a soft spot for English politeness. It's so ingrained and unwavering.'

Her eyes flashed. 'Well, mine is definitely wavering to the point you might have a chance to see the most unladylike side of me in no uncertain terms. Now did you kill my husband?'

'I didn't.' At her derisive snort, he laid his hands out on the table. 'But I would have. Without hesitation. The only problem was, when I tracked him and his two former partners to England

and the Grand, Brighton, he was already dead.' He leaned back in his chair. 'His room had also been ransacked, so I assumed his two former partners had caught up with him first.'

Her hand strayed towards her pocket that held the two halves of the photograph, but she willed it back down. 'Well, Mr de Meyer, thank you for your time. It is refreshing that you own up to knowing Hilary and even to going into his room the night he died. What time was that, by the way?'

He cast his eyes upwards for a moment. 'Maybe ten minutes or so before midnight.'

So that agrees with Franklin's version of events, Ellie, if we believe either of them. But then again, they're bound to say he was already dead, aren't they? They're not going to admit to killing him!

'Mr de Meyer, just before you take your very overdue leave, you must believe Mr Eden had something very valuable to your employer?' Clifford asked. 'By your own admission, you have pursued it for the best part of six years.'

He eyed Clifford coolly. 'My employers make it a rule always to recover their property, no matter how long it takes. And always to make an example of those who steal from them, to dissuade others from being so foolish.'

Eleanor snapped. 'So you did kill him!'

He shook his head, a derisive smile on his lips. 'For a bright woman, you do go back and forth. I've just told you he was already dead when I got to him.'

'But you ransacked his room then?'

A pained look crossed his face. 'Please, I am a professional. If I had done it, I would have done it in a far more systematic and orderly fashion.'

Despite himself, Clifford nodded approvingly.

De Meyer rose, smoothing a hand down his trousers. 'Lady Swift, we are both too smart to play games with each other. I suggest you return whatever your husband foolishly gave you and I will see it gets back to its rightful owners.' he glanced at Clifford who had also risen. 'Otherwise, despite the best efforts of your loyal companion, you may very well have celebrated your last birthday.'

CHAPTER 27

Back in her suite, Eleanor lay on one of the blue velvet settees wishing she could have hung on to the second half of her wedding photograph for longer. Just a day. Or even an hour. After Seldon's earlier insistence that it was better they didn't meet again that evening, she'd sent Clifford off to return it to him.

A knock at her door interrupted her thoughts. Before she could react, the telephone on the desk rang. It was Clifford. 'My lady, it is Thomas who is knocking. It is quite safe.' His voice clicked off, leaving her staring at the handset.

'What the…?' She strode to the door and opened it. 'Hello, Thomas, you have something for me?'

'A small package, Lady Swift.'

More confused than ever, she accepted the neat, tissue-wrapped parcel, and locked the door. She frowned as her fingers felt a hard round lump in the middle of the otherwise soft parcel. Untying the green ribbon, a wide smile split her face as the tissue paper fell open.

'Oh my! It's from Seldon… I mean Hugh. Gladstone!'

Sprawled on the carpet, the snoozy bulldog raised his head wearily at the sound of his name. From the centre of the package's contents, she picked up the beautiful pink stone worn almost circular that she had found by the bench up on the cliffs. 'And he kept this from yesterday.'

The accompanying note was handwritten in short, efficient strokes.

Happy birthday, Eleanor. As your scarf requires significant cleaning after its adventures at sea, I have left it with the hotel staff to attend to.

He went back and found your scarf, Ellie!

I hope however this might suffice in the meantime.

She lifted out an emerald silk scarf with a delicate beaded fringe and let out a sigh of delight as she placed it round her neck. 'Gladstone, he bought me a present, and it's beautiful!'

Doubtlessly Gladstone was delighted for her, but the effort of supporting his head defeated him and he sank back down onto the carpet. She picked up the note and read the next line:

Carriage booked for 7 p.m.... if dinner and dancing are appropriate, of course? Hugh.

Her head shot up. *Ellie, he's changed his mind!* She stared at her watch – six thirty! – and then back at the note in horror. 'But I didn't bring anything to go dancing in!' Then she noticed the last line:

P.S. I have been told to tell you to look under your bed.

'What on earth?'

On the dot of seven, she stepped out of the hotel lift in her favourite emerald-green gown. The one that she knew she hadn't packed but which had magically appeared in her wardrobe and which miraculously matched her new scarf. Her dancing shoes sparkled as she crossed the lobby. She caught Clifford's eye where he sat in one of the wingback chairs, absorbed in a book. He nodded and rose to accompany her to the door, pretending to button his lip.

She wagged a finger at him. 'Oh no, we will definitely have words about the hand you played in this amazing surprise later.'

He bowed from the shoulders. 'I regret, it will be a tedious one-sided conversation as I have nothing to say, my lady.'

'You are a wizard, I swear,' she said in awe, gesturing down at her dress, then laughing at the wink he gave her in reply.

'You look… radiant,' Seldon said as she stepped into the ornate horse-drawn carriage waiting just down from the Grand's main entrance, away from any chance Inspector Grimsdale's men might see them together. 'Happy birthday. But perhaps that should have come first,' he added awkwardly.

She took the seat beside him, a frisson running down her spine at their closeness. 'Thank you for my beautiful present. And for scouring the beach for my scarf. That was so kind. And for dealing with Grimsdale over the photograph. And… and for this.' She waved a hand around the carriage. 'It's a wonderful, if very unexpected surprise.'

'Ah, now is that my first blunder? I believed you like to be the mistress of the unexpected.'

She blushed. 'Well, I'm usually the one who changes her mind unexpectedly, that's true. Not that I wish you hadn't changed your mind,' she added quickly. 'In fact, I'm so happy you did, but I can see I need to reprimand Clifford severely for collaborating with the police against me.'

He patted down his black evening jacket. 'Ah, blunder number two then. There's no policeman in here tonight. I left him back in

Oxford. Mostly because someone, sitting right beside me I might add, told me in no uncertain terms that he was no fun at parties.'

'Oops! I did, didn't I? Was that because you arrested my good friend at the last party we were both at?'

He groaned and rolled his eyes. 'Surely we can call a truce tonight?'

Her cheeks coloured. 'Sorry. I promise not to spoil this amazing birthday treat for anything.' She clapped her hands. 'Now, let's see just how much better Hugh is at partying than the eminent Detective Chief Inspector Seldon, shall we?'

'Driver?' he called out. 'The Old Ship Hotel and ballroom, but please take the picturesque route.'

She cocked her head at him. 'Why the sightseeing tour?'

He gestured out of the carriage window. 'Because irritatingly you can actually see The Old Ship from here. And anyway, tonight we need to save those feet for dancing, not walking.'

She blushed as his deep-brown eyes stared into hers.

Her feet were still dancing and her heart skipping as she waltzed back up the steps to the Grand just before the night porter locked the door. The gentlemanly kiss Hugh had placed on her hand by way of goodnight had finished the evening perfectly, if all too early to end the fun they'd had.

She ran her finger over the spot and grinned. It had been surprisingly easy not to squabble as they had both stayed away from mentioning anything to do with police protocols or murder. Instead, they had chatted amiably over dinner and their laughter had flowed as freely as the champagne. The rest of the evening had been a delicious series of dances, where he had held her as delicately as a butterfly princess.

She paused on the top step of the Grand, his parting words ringing round her head.

'Eleanor, in the possibly unlikely event that we are still on speaking terms on your next birthday, perhaps we could repeat this evening?'

She hugged her shoulders. *Ellie, who could ever have guessed that someone so rigidly obsessed with procedure and protocol would be such a debonair dancer! The way he twirled you was too heavenly. Oh, why did the perfect birthday evening have to end so soon?*

In the lobby there were a surprising number of staff and guests given the lateness of the hour. She bid the night porter goodnight and turned to see Clifford waiting at the bottom of the main staircase.

'Tell me you haven't waited up when you knew Hugh, I mean Seldon, was dropping me off at the door, Clifford?'

He shook his head. 'No, my lady, I had no doubt Chief Inspector Seldon would be the perfect gentleman. Unfortunately, even though I sincerely wish not to spoil your evening, I have no option but to impart some regrettable news.'

She looked around the lobby and then back at Clifford. 'Okay, now I'm intrigued. What is so important that it couldn't wait until tomorrow?'

He cleared his throat. 'Mr Blunt has… departed.'

Eleanor's eyes narrowed. 'So, he's made a run for it, has he? Botheration!!' She gasped. 'Do you think he found the item everyone is after?'

Clifford cleared his throat. 'If he did, I doubt he retained it for long. What I meant to say is he has departed this world. Mr Blunt, my lady, is dead.'

CHAPTER 28

'We absolutely need to do it now!' Eleanor hissed as she pretended to peruse the magazine racks on the far side of the lobby. 'Everyone should be in their rooms. Although' – she peered across to the activity in the bar – 'it seems the shock of Mr Blunt's death has kept quite a few of the guests and staff from retiring. Dash it!'

Clifford followed her gaze. 'Not surprisingly there has been a furore in the last few hours of your absence, my lady. The police left but twenty minutes ago.'

She groaned as the manager strode over to the lobby desk with two members of staff hurrying on his coat-tails. He disappeared into his office, then reappeared, a ring of keys jangling in his hand.

'Ridiculously,' he snapped just loud enough for Eleanor to hear, 'I have been called to the police station now! None of the staff are to talk about the incident to anyone, understand? It was a most unfortunate *accident*. The man was clearly drunk. Understood?' He held up a finger. 'And see that the guests are kept happy. Whatever it takes!'

Eleanor waited until he had stormed out of the front door the night porter held open for him and then whispered to Clifford again. 'It's now or never. Remember how quickly Hilary's things were cleared out of 204? This is our only chance to sniff round Blunt's room before housekeeping strip it bare.'

Clifford coughed.

She looked at him quizzically. 'What is it?'

'I meant to inform you earlier, my lady, but the moment never arose. I have a small confession. I—'

She looked back at the bar. 'What a stroke of luck, Thomas is there. Sorry, Clifford, you'll just have to hold that confession until later. Now, you've sweet-talked Thomas before. He'll help us if you play it right.'

Clifford's usually inscrutable expression was lost as he frowned. 'He might be your number one fan, my lady, but forgive my question, how exactly do you suggest I play it right? I must, it seems, ask him to give me the key to the room of a man who has just died by falling off his balcony while drunk?'

'Is that what happened?'

'An apparent accident with nothing suspicious or amiss was the view held by the police who attended. That is what the manager told me in strict confidence. And the version of events the staff has been told to tell the guests.'

'Well, how did you get the manager to talk to you about it if he is trying to hush it all up?'

'I couldn't say, my lady.'

She groaned. 'Let me guess. My name and "reporting the Grand Hotel's fearful lack of security and care for their guests to the newspapers" were mentioned in the same sentence?'

'Only twice before he gave in.' He adjusted his perfectly aligned tie. 'Hotel managers really need better training to deal with such awkward guests as yourself.'

Despite the gravity of the situation, his wry humour made her smile. 'You, Clifford, are a monster. How on earth did my uncle put up with you for so long?'

'With extreme fortitude and fine brandy, my lady.'

'Well, I shall need plenty of both in future. Oh quick! Go!' she whispered. 'Thomas is leaving the bar. You'll think of something, you always do.'

*

Up on the fourth floor, Thomas gestured to the last bedroom door, clutching a key in his hand.

'You will be ensuring the scene where her character discovers the body is the making of the film,' Clifford said in a low voice. 'She will be eternally grateful for the chance to experience the chilling atmosphere left behind after an actual death. Even an accidental one,' he added quickly.

Thomas looked up, wide-eyed. 'I never imagined being able to help the lady with her acting. It is an honour.'

'Good man. However' – Clifford gestured to where Eleanor had paused back along the corridor, breathing deeply through her hands held over her nose – 'the lady is a fanatical method actress. She cannot step out of character for a moment or the effect will be lost.'

Thomas wavered for a second. 'What exactly does that mean?'

'For the exercise to be successful, it is essential you leave us alone in the room.'

'Umm, I'm not so sure I can do that. If the manager found out, I'd be for it.' He stole a look at Eleanor, who now appeared to be engaged in a silent but impassioned conversation with an imaginary partner. The clerk looked back at Clifford in awe. 'The lady is such a professional, perhaps it wouldn't hurt?'

'As you have noted, the lady is the consummate artist in these matters.'

'I shall certainly be the first in the queue when the film comes to the picture palace! Ten minutes, no more, please!' As he scurried off down the staircase, Eleanor glided gracefully up to Clifford and paused dramatically in the doorway in case the clerk was somehow still watching.

Once inside, Clifford locked the door behind them.

'Perhaps you have missed your vocation, my lady. Quite the film star performance if I may offer my commendation.'

She groaned. 'No, don't. I feel terrible deceiving that poor man. And I'm panicking as I have no idea what to say if he finds out I'm not who he imagines I am!'

'Oh, I should think throwing a hysterical tantrum that he was so crass as to believe that a titled lady would deign to appear in a moving picture. That should suffice.'

She ran her hand through her curls. 'You know, I hope I'm never on the opposite side to you. You are incorrigible.'

She turned slowly in a half circle, surveying the scene, but at first glance, the room showed no sign of anything untoward having taken place. But it had. A man had died there. A wave of sadness hit her. *Here you are, once again, Ellie, standing in a room where a life has been extinguished only a short time before.*

She sensed Clifford hovering behind her. 'It's alright, at least there are no personal ghosts this time. Now, we both know what we're thinking. Blunt may, or may not, have fallen to his death drunk, but the authorities seem too keen to label it an accident without a proper investigation.'

Clifford nodded. 'I agree, my lady. I gathered when I spoke to the manager that the Grand's owners are not without considerable influence in the town—'

'And they don't want another potentially suspicious death bringing the popular press down here, claiming there's a serial killer loose at "Death Hotel" and scaring the new season's guests away?'

Clifford's brow furrowed. 'I believe I have been in dereliction of my duty, my lady. I promised your uncle I would guard your wellbeing, mental and physical. Yet I failed to burn those penny dreadful novels you have devoured for too many years.'

Eleanor folded her arms. 'Look here, Clifford, I reckon we've only solved the cases we have because I've read those books. Now, what would the amateur sleuth do in a penny dreadful?' She ignored him rolling his eyes and looked around.

Being one of the smaller rooms at the furthest end of the hotel, the room felt cramped after her luxurious suite. It did, however, have a cosy charm, albeit tempered by the muted grey-and-cream decor and high ceiling. And, she mused again, the fact that a man had just died there.

Clifford stepped to the chest of drawers and pulled two pairs of his white butler gloves from his pocket, holding one out for her. 'My lady, even though the police have discounted anything untoward, prudence would suggest we leave no trace of our visit here tonight.'

'I'll take the wardrobe.' She pulled on the oversized gloves. But her rummaging was soon done. 'I thought Hilary had been travelling light but Blunt has barely any extra clothes. So much for the holiday.' She checked the few items of clothing for hidden pockets. Finding none, she went to check the soles of the stout pair of boots at the bottom of the wardrobe. As she turned them over, a penny coin fell out of each one.

'What on earth?' She picked up the coins and showed them to Clifford. 'Placing a coin in one's shoes when not wearing them may supposedly bring good luck, but he should have tried pound notes. His luck definitely ran out today.' She gasped. 'I say, Clifford, didn't the rhyme on my wedding photograph say something about pennies in shoes?'

'Actually, it was sixpence.' He frowned. 'And Mr Eden had altered it for some reason. I suggest in this instance, however, that it is most likely a coincidence, and Mr Blunt was, like many, a superstitious gentleman.'

Eleanor placed the coins back in the shoes. 'Maybe, Clifford, but it seems a—'

She froze at the sound of a man's voice outside the door. Another man answered. And then silence, until the ding of the lift allowed them to breathe again.

'My lady, we must move fast. Thomas will be back all too quickly.'

She moved on to peering behind the wardrobe, cricking her neck. 'Ow! That doesn't say much for housekeeping, they haven't dusted behind here in weeks.'

Clifford paused in running his hand along the back of each of the four drawers. 'There is nothing of interest here either. I shall check the writing desk and under the mattress. Perhaps you might move on to the bathroom?'

She nodded. The bathroom door in her room had stained glass in the top panel, but in Blunt's it was frosted. She admired it, thinking she might like to have the same at Henley Hall. She shook her head. *Ellie, this is no time to be thinking of interior design, honestly!*

She slipped into the small, but fully equipped bathroom. Unsurprised by the limited number of toiletries on the narrow sink surround, she knelt to look under the three-quarter size bath, noting the lack of clawfoot details to the base. The much less ornate rounded ends, however, offered no hiding place. A pair of socks hung over the taps, a telltale rivulet of beige water pooled below suggesting they had been washed recently. From the doorway, Clifford grimaced.

'I am at a loss to understand why a gentleman would choose to wash his socks in the bath.'

Eleanor laughed quietly. 'There's nothing odd in Blunt washing his socks in the bath. I imagine the Grand is hellishly expensive for the likes of him and Longley. We know they just played the part of well-heeled gents, so any way they could economise, I suppose they did.' It was her turn to frown. 'Which, thinking about it, probably explains why I never saw them in the dining room.'

About to follow him back into the bedroom, a slight mark on the roll-top rim of the bath caught her eye.

'Hmm.' She traced the three faint wavy lines with her finger and then her face lit up. 'Bullseye!'

CHAPTER 29

Looks like part of a footprint, Ellie. But why would anyone need to stand on the edge of the bath unless they were hiding something? She glanced around. There was nothing within reach except the high-up cistern tank of the toilet, the lid of which she now noticed was not lined up. In a trice, she slid off her dancing shoes and stepped up nimbly on the bath, her feet carefully placed either side of the wavy lines. A cough from the door made her lunge forward in panic, leaving her at full stretch with one foot braced against the wall behind her.

'Clifford! You nearly gave me a heart attack,' she hissed.

'I was merely conscious of the time.' He held up his pocket watch. 'I must insist again that we hurry, despite your confidence in my on-the-spot creativity in thinking up plausible explanations to tell Thomas, I am not sure I could explain what a famous Hollywood star was doing dismantling the toilet in a dead man's room while standing on the bath.' He looked her up and down. 'I know you are a fierce advocate for women's rights, my lady, and I have no doubt a woman may be as good a plumber as a man. However, perhaps now is not the time to throw down the gauntlet?'

She ignored his sardonic remark. 'Footprint on the bath,' she panted, pointing to the three wavy lines. 'Bear with me.' She stretched to push the top of the ceramic cistern to one side. 'It's caught on something.' A harder shove however released it with a heart-stopping scraping sound.

Clifford held the small round shaving mirror from the side of the basin up to her.

'What can you see, my lady?'

She positioned the mirror to reflect into the cistern. 'A half-filled bottle. Maybe Blunt was just trying to avoid paying the hotel prices for alcohol? After all, he went so far as to wash his socks in the bath.'

'Surely discreetly placing it in his luggage, or the wardrobe would have sufficed? Although as your precarious, and somewhat inelegant, position highlights, my lady, he would have struggled to place it there himself, seeing as he was a good few inches shorter than you.'

'Then who…?' She glanced down at him. 'Someone else must have put it there.'

'Indeed. Might you be able to reach the bottle or would you like to exchange places?'

'Just catch me if I teeter off the edge of the bath,' she said, throwing him the mirror. Standing on tiptoe, she put her hand over the rim of the cistern and felt about in the cold water. 'One small, brown bottle coming down. Although if it is a clue, it'll be hard to hand it over to Grimsdale with any reasonable explanation as to how we came by it. "You see, Grimsdale, I just happened to be in the deceased man's room and felt the need to fish about in his cistern."' She shook her head and sighed. 'And as I haven't been straight with Hugh, I mean Seldon, we can't tell him either. Honestly, is there anyone on this holiday I haven't had to deceive? Even the ladies don't know we are embroiled in another case.'

'It will all come together in the end, my lady.'

'Yes, but I doubt Hugh will be speaking to me when it does if he finds out.'

'I am confident the opportunity to have spent an evening dancing with you will soften the blow slightly.'

'Slightly is not much of a consolation, Clifford.'

He coughed. 'Time really is against us, my lady.'

She dragged the cistern lid back into position and jumped off the bath. He hastily turned around as she tugged down on the skirt of her dress. He dried the outside of the bottle, which was half full, and slid it inside his jacket. Turning the towel's damp sides together, he folded it roughly back onto the silver painted iron rail but then hesitated, his hand hovering.

'You're itching to hang it neatly, aren't you?' she couldn't resist whispering.

'Actually, my lady, I was checking I had returned it to exactly the distressingly untidy position it was in before I touched it.'

'Of course.' She pointed through to the long narrow French windows of the bedroom. 'We'd best check the balcony.'

'We have three minutes at most.'

The warmth of the day had been replaced by a bitter night wind that snatched the French door from her hand and wrapped the curtain around her like an icy shroud. Disentangling herself, she pulled her scarf tighter against her shoulders and rubbed her hands together, grateful for the modicum of protection Clifford's butler gloves offered.

The light snapped off in the bedroom as Clifford joined her. 'Better not to advertise our presence out here on the balcony.' He scanned the marbled tiles at their feet by the light thrown from the Grand's decorative exterior lights.

Eleanor stepped to the railing and looked over. 'Ah, this room is at the rear of the hotel.'

'Hence Mr Blunt having landed on the rear terrace.'

'Hmm.' She measured the height of the railing against her body. 'I don't mean to keep highlighting that Blunt was at the very end of the queue when legs were being handed out—' She caught Clifford's pointed look but ignored it. 'But even with my slightly longer than average legs, and wearing heels, the railing comes up past my hips.'

He nodded. 'Way past the tipping point of such a gentleman as Mr Blunt, even if he were drunk and had accidentally slipped and fallen forward. An astute observation.'

'My jiu-jitsu and baritsu training. It paid to know the "tipping point", as you put it, of an attacker when cycling abroad alone.'

'And when defending yourself in a rectory against a knife-wielding attacker recently.'

She tutted. 'It's not like you to be so sensationalist, Clifford. It was only a letter opener, even if a somewhat sharp one.'

He joined her at the railing and looked down to the terrace. 'We have deduced that Mr Blunt would have found this to be a comfortable height to lean his elbows, rather than his hips on. Therefore, as there are no objects for him to have been standing on, it seems there are only two possible answers to how he fell. Either he climbed up and jumped—'

'Or he was pushed.' Her face clouded as she peered over the edge and stared at the spot below where Bert Blunt must have landed on the terrace. 'But if he was pushed, the murderer would surely have needed to entice him out here first? It's hardly warm enough for Blunt to have been sitting out. Which suggests he must have known his attacker.'

'Or his attacker forced him out onto the balcony at gunpoint.'

'Or knifepoint! Hilary's killer used a knife.' She shivered.

'The footprint on the bath!' Clifford gestured back inside. 'If it doesn't match the foot size of the boots still in the wardrobe—'

A moment later they stood looking at Blunt's diminutive footwear.

'You clever bean!' Eleanor whispered. 'That footprint on the bath definitely wasn't Blunt's. His foot is much smaller. It means that the murderer likely plied Blunt with whatever is in that bottle. Then he dragged him out here, pushed him over the balcony and hid the bottle so he wasn't caught with it.'

Clifford closed the French doors behind them. 'Something doesn't quite add up.'

'Perhaps the killer intended to return for the bottle later when everything had calmed down and the police had gon—?'

Eleanor froze halfway across the bedroom at the sight of the door handle turning.

'Thomas!' she mouthed, but Clifford shook his head and cupped his ear. Then he pulled his case of picklocks from his inside pocket and mimed breaking in. Eleanor's hand flew to her mouth as she spun round, looking for a hiding place.

Too late. The door swung open to reveal a familiar face, which creased into an instant sneer as a finger pointed at Eleanor. 'You! I should have guessed.'

CHAPTER 30

Eleanor felt Longley's glare bore into her as he closed the door behind him soundlessly. He started towards her, but stopped short as Clifford stepped back in from the balcony, where he had quickly hidden. 'I see your faithful hound's here with you. Of course he is. You're quite the inseparable pair, ain't you?'

Eleanor nodded to herself. Now he wasn't in public, Longley had dropped his previous plummy voice for, what she assumed, was his real accent. East London she guessed.

'We're only inseparable since we learned Brighton was so dashedly dangerous. Shocking that they don't include it in the tourist brochures, I say. Especially as we both know there have been two murders here in this hotel alone in the last five days.'

Longley's eyes darkened. 'I don't know what you're talking about.'

Eleanor folded her arms. 'What are you doing here?'

'Nah, sweetheart, that's my question to you. I've got the perfect excuse for being here, seeing as it was my cousin's room before he died. You two, however, you'd better come clean as to why you're here. And it had better be good,' he ended, cracking the knuckles on each hand.

'Not so fast.' Clifford put himself between Longley and Eleanor. 'Despite your protestations, picking the lock on Mr Blunt's door, especially after the suspicious circumstances in which he passed away, does considerably diminish the legitimacy of your presence, kin or not. Which, by the way, still lacks a significant degree of veracity.'

Longley leaned past him to address Eleanor. 'Is your friend always this long-winded?'

'Only when he's stalling to buy me some time, which as you found out during your kidnap attempt, he is very adept at doing.'

A quiet rap at the door caused all eyes to swivel towards the sound.

'However,' Clifford whispered, looking pointedly at Longley. 'Our time has just run out.' He held up a hand as Longley went to reply. 'Quiet! Then we can talk.' He gestured for Longley to step behind the door. Nodding to Eleanor, he waited until she had positioned herself.

'Here goes,' he muttered before opening the door a crack. 'Ah, there you are.' He smiled at the flustered desk clerk. Lowering his voice to a conspiratorial whisper, he asked, 'Care for an exclusive peep at how the lady works, Thomas?' He eased the door open a little more. The desk clerk's jaw slackened as he watched Eleanor unroll her body and let out a halting wail before crumpling in a heap on the floor.

'Goodness, she'll exhaust herself!'

'It is the price she chooses to pay for her art. She is so close to cresting the emotional wave needed for her character. Five more minutes? Thank you.'

As the clerk retreated muttering to himself, Clifford closed the door and Eleanor sprang up, flicking out her ruffled red curls.

Longley shook his head. 'You two are a pair of queer birds, and no mistake.'

'But effective,' she said. 'As would be telling the hotel manager that you have broken in here.'

He offered his elbow. 'Let's go together, shall we? I'd love to hear you explain what you and Mr Stuffed Shirt were doing in my cousin's room.'

She glanced at him appraisingly. For someone whose cousin had died a few hours earlier he was remarkably composed. 'Here's an idea. I suggest we don't waste the few precious minutes we have before the desk clerk returns arguing, but that we help each other instead.'

Longley shrugged indifferently, but his eyes showed otherwise.

She continued. 'You could begin by admitting you and your cousin tried to kidnap us, because we both recognise you. Then you could move on to confessing that you lied about knowing Hilary.'

He eyed them both. 'Okay, you got me. I bundled you into the car.'

'Good start. However, I can only assume that amongst your nefarious activities, kidnapping hasn't been high on the list too often, you're really not very good at it, you know.'

'Thanks for nothing! It wasn't my idea. It was Bert's.'

'Perhaps. Although the poor chap isn't around to be able to confirm or refute that, is he? Because someone killed him, just like they killed Hilary.'

He rubbed a hand along the back of his neck. 'Don't bother wasting your precious minutes talking about your old man. I already told you, far as I'm concerned, he was just some bloke staying at the hotel.'

Eleanor pulled out her uncle's pocket watch and waved it at him. 'Time is ticking and it would pay you to know that I was born with very little patience.'

Clifford nodded. 'In essence, none.'

'So,' Eleanor continued, 'tell me why you killed Hilary.'

'You're like a stuck phonograph record! I tell you I didn't. Why would I kill a man I didn't even know?'

'Hmm, do you know, I can't decide which you should work on first, your dismal kidnapping skills or your even more atrocious lying technique.'

Longley snorted. 'Seeing as we're sharing, how about I let you know that if I had killed your husband, I wouldn't be standing here answering your stupid questions. Isn't that plainer than the nose on your face!'

She tutted. 'Now you're insulting my nose. Plain indeed! So ungallant and uncalled for.'

Peering hard at her, his brows met in a hard line. 'Stone me, how have you got this far? I mean, Hilary always said you were sharper than a box of daggers, but not from where I'm standing. I've met blunt bricks with more going on, if you know what I mean.'

She winked at him. 'So a man you don't know told you I was sharp, did he?'

'Damn it!' He scratched his head and then rolled his eyes. 'Okay, okay, sure I knew your husband. But it weren't like we were mates or nothing, not after what he did. And before you ask me again, even though I would have loved to have killed him, I never. Never got the chance. Me and Bert went to search his room around eleven twenty-five I think it was, but he was already dead. Some lucky bugger beat me to it.' At Clifford's warning look, Longley raised his hands. 'Okay, back off.' He lowered them and shrugged. 'Anyway, I needed him alive.'

She tried to remember what de Meyer had told her about Hilary's partners. 'So you were in some sort of business with Hilary?'

He shook his head. 'Not in business with him. In one business deal with him, which was one too many, as it turned out. Me and Bert are… were in the removals game. Then we hit the big one.' His tone became wistful. 'The one so big, it should have set us up for life. So big, we needed help.'

'And you asked Hilary?'

He nodded. 'We knew he could pull off his end of things, alright. He'd been in business for himself for long enough.' His lips twisted into an angry snarl. 'But your darling husband double-crossed us and scarpered with the proceeds.'

Eleanor was trying to think fast. 'Look, we've got a minute left at most. Two more questions and then it's your turn. When did all this happen and how did you guess Hilary would be here?'

'The job was set a few weeks after you got hitched to Hilary.' Longley gave her a glance, which held far too much pity for her liking. 'That's right, you were picking out a pretty dress and shoes and shopping for your honeymoon and Hilary was planning a job and planning to steal from his partners. Funny how life goes, huh?'

'Hilarious!' she snapped back, trying to blink away the instant hot tears that pricked her eyelids. 'And you knew he was here, how?'

'Because we spent the last five and a half years tracking him down, night and day. Thought he was just trying to get away from us, and the others, when we found out he was sailing for England. But when we followed him and he ended up in Brighton, well,' – he nodded slowly – 'it all made sense.'

She stared at him, needing to take control of the conversation, but a part of her brain was telling her she was missing something. Randomly, she asked, 'So, why did you kill Blunt?'

Longley's fists clenched. 'I didn't kill Bert. He was my business partner for over ten years. You think in my game you can afford to do in someone who's had your back and never double-crossed you in that long? I was with him only half an hour before he died. We'd gone over our plans for tomorrow and he said he'd a couple of things to do. He promised to meet me in the bar once he'd had a shave and changed. I went downstairs and ordered a drink. Next thing, he was lying all mangled on the ground.'

He sounded genuine this time, but she knew from bitter experience how convincing liars could be. 'Did you take the lift, or the stairs?'

His eyes looked at her mockingly. 'The stairs.'

'Strange that someone you worked with for ten years you only thought of as your partner, not your friend.'

He laughed grimly. 'It don't do to have friends in my line of work. Look, lady, I ain't taken in by your posh frock, fancy title and this suited monkey you tow with you everywhere you go. You're here to collect on the deal that I should be collecting on. I saw you on the pier the other night, talking with that other snake.

I'm beginning to think that maybe you killed your husband. And Bert.' He opened the door a crack and glanced up and down the corridor, before turning back to her. 'Make no mistake, I'll be seeing you soon.' The door closed silently behind him.

CHAPTER 31

'Ah, there you are, Thomas,' Eleanor heard Clifford say as she leaned against the wall further down the corridor. 'The lady is eternally grateful. She has, however, as you so shrewdly predicted, exhausted herself.'

The sound of the key turning in the lock was followed by a 'Delighted to have been of service to the lady. Oh, most generous, Mr Clifford.' Muffled footsteps followed, running down the carpeted stairs.

Clifford caught up with Eleanor as she waited by the lift.

'Dash it, Clifford. Now with Blunt's death, this case is galloping away from us at a horrifying rate.' She let out a frustrated huff. 'How can anyone imagine Blunt accidentally fell from a balcony guarded by a rail that was too high for him to have toppled over without standing on something?'

'On account of the powerful smell of alcohol on Mr Blunt's breath leading the manager, and police, to believe Mr Blunt was intoxicated?'

'Well, if he was, I don't think it was self-inflicted. We have to find out what is in that bottle you've got secreted in your jacket.'

'There is a further reason that Mr Blunt's death is being dealt with in such a swift manner.'

'The owners of the hotel want it hushed up again, I suppose?'

'The edict has come from higher up this time, my lady. The Mayor of Brighton himself has made it abundantly clear that there shall be no scandal surrounding recent events at the Grand.'

'Hmm. Protecting his precious tourist season.'

'But even more so, the rare visit of a most important dignitary. A royal one, to be precise. Thomas informed me that the manager told the staff that the visit will be cancelled if so much as a whiff of embarrassment for Brighton gets to the newspapers.'

'And yet two men have been killed.' She rubbed her hands over her cheeks. 'If we can find who murdered Blunt, maybe it will lead to Hilary's killer. It still seems most likely it was the same person, wouldn't you say?'

'I would, my lady. As the clues in the case of Mr Blunt's murder are fresh in our minds, perhaps we should quickly review those. And, then, Mr Eden's in the hope that something that has eluded us to this point leaps out?'

'Good plan, Clifford.'

He nodded. 'I noted from Mr Blunt's balcony that the conservatory was vacant.'

In the conservatory Eleanor pulled out her notebook. 'Right. A new timeline is needed.' She took the pen Clifford held out to her and turned to a clean page. The nib flew across the paper.

Hilary's Death (between 10.30 p.m. – 2.30 a.m. according to coroner)

9.30 p.m. – Summers seen by Longley going into Hilary's room

10.45 p.m. – Thomas wishes Hilary good night

11.00 p.m. – Main hotel door locked – night porter on duty*

11.25 p.m. – Longley and Blunt go to Hilary's room – find Hilary dead, search room – find nothing

11.35 p.m. – Franklin goes to Hilary's room – finds Hilary dead – searches room – finds nothing

11.50 p.m. – de Meyer goes to Hilary's room – finds Hilary dead – doesn't search the room as can see no point as room

obviously already searched several times – so item either never there or already found
To follow up – Clifford thinks night porter lying about no one else coming in after door locked on night of Hilary's murder.

Bert Blunt's Death
8.15 p.m. – Blunt pushed to his death

Eleanor looked up. 'It looks tragically blunt when written like that.'

'No pun intended?'

'Of course not.' She turned back to the page and wrote out a list.

Suspects
Rex Franklin
Noel Longley
Bert Blunt
Grace Summers
Willem de Meyer

She sighed. 'It's a small step forward but I think we can eliminate Blunt as we agree whoever killed Hilary probably also killed him.' She crossed his name through. 'Right. Let's start in reverse order with the remaining suspects for a change.'

'Mr de Meyer first then, my lady.'

Eleanor gathered her thoughts. 'Right. First off, he openly told us his employers give no quarter when someone wrongs them.'

'Clemency certainly did not seem to be included in Mr de Meyer's job description.'

'Precisely! Which means they probably blamed de Meyer for Longley's gang getting away with the stolen item as he was in charge of security. So de Meyer was tasked with returning it and "punishing" whoever stole it. So we can assume he would have been only too happy to kill Hilary.'

'I recall he said as much, my lady.'

'Yes, and after Hilary, his next step would naturally be to kill Blunt since the two of them were in the gang that committed the theft. Allegedly,' she added pointedly.

'So, Mr de Meyer has a motive for both murders. But why has he therefore not killed Mr Longley who was also in the gang? Allegedly.'

Eleanor tapped the pen against her chin as she pondered this. 'Maybe he just hasn't found the right time. Longley would be a harder proposition than Blunt to kill.'

'Because, my lady?'

She held his gaze. 'Because of that thing you chide me as being unladylike for mentioning. Blunt was a tiny chap. Longley's height alone would make him much more of a match as an adversary.'

'Agreed. Shall we then move on to Miss Summers?'

Eleanor frowned. 'Maybe she was Hilary's sidekick. Or lover.' She felt the now familiar knot in her stomach tighten. 'Maybe Hilary double-crossed her too. Or deserted her' – she bit her lip – 'like he did me.'

Clifford cleared his throat gently. 'Perhaps she was in Mr Eden's room purely for the same reason as the other suspects, to obtain the stolen item.'

She smiled at him. 'I do appreciate your delicacy, Clifford.'

'Thank you, my lady. We do, however, know of a piece of evidence that might put her in the clear if our supposition about how Mr Blunt died is correct.'

She looked up sharply. 'What?'

'The footprint on Mr Blunt's bath. The print was from the sole of a heavy man's boot and was too big for a woman. I have in fact noted she has rather dainty feet.' He coughed. 'If you will forgive the observation.'

'Clifford, I am well aware that every male in this building will have appraised her physical characteristics from head to toe.' She held up a hand as he went to speak. 'But there's something else that also discounts her.'

'Which is, my lady?'

'If the bottle we took from Blunt's bathroom was planted by the murderer, it can't have been Summers because she's a good few inches shorter than me. Like Blunt, she would never have been able to reach.'

'Even with the inelegant gymnastics you performed,' he replied drily. 'Ah! A moment.' He glanced out the door of the conservatory. Convinced no one else was around, he closed it again before sliding the bottle they'd found in Blunt's room from his jacket.

Eleanor leaned in as he took off the stopper and sniffed the contents.

'As I suspected. Chloroform,' said Clifford.

Eleanor nodded slowly. 'So Blunt's death was definitely murder. The alcohol would have disguised the chloroform.'

'Exactly. The killer either rendered Mr Blunt unconscious with the chloroform, poured alcohol down his throat and then threw him off the balcony. Or fooled or forced him to drink chloroform and alcohol. Ingesting a small quantity of chloroform has much the same effect as dosing a rag and holding it over someone's nose and mouth. You become dizzy and disorientated.'

'Basically making it easy for the victim to fall off a balcony with a little help?'

'Exactly, my lady. I assume that the killer thought it too risky to leave with the bottle of chloroform about his person, so he hid it, meaning to return later and take it when things had calmed down after Mr Blunt's fall.'

She nodded. 'But we have beaten the killer to it.'

'Indeed. So we are agreed to eliminate Miss Summers as a suspect at the moment given the oversized footprint and difficulty she would have had hiding the chloroform?'

'Agreed.' *We're still going to find out the truth about her and Hilary though, Ellie. You'll never rest until you know for sure.*

Clifford coughed gently to bring her back to the present. 'Mr Longley then, my lady.'

'Ah, yes. He was part of the gang with Blunt, and briefly also with Hilary. Apparently Hilary double-crossed the pair of them and took the item they'd stolen from de Meyer's employer, so they tracked Hilary here and Longley killed Hilary.'

'Might I ask why you think it would have been Mr Longley acting on his own when he and Mr Blunt were partners?'

'Just a hunch. Longley was obviously the leader. Blunt seemed to me to be too nervous to actually kill anyone.'

'I agree again. I doubt Mr Longley's assertion that kidnapping you and I was Mr Blunt's idea. And moving on to Mr Blunt's death?'

'Longley's alibi doesn't hold water. They were apparently together in Blunt's room. Then Longley went down to the bar alone. I hoped he'd slip up and say he took the lift—'

'So the attendant could confirm this, or not?'

'Exactly, but he was too wily and said he took the stairs, even though the lift is right outside Blunt's door. Anyway, then he goes to the manager when Blunt's body is discovered acting all upset that his cousin is dead.'

'And whilst I cannot confirm it, I believe Mr Longley's foot to be similar in size to the footprint on the bath. He is also certainly tall enough to have easily deposited the bottle in the cistern tank.'

'Of course! So maybe we are right and he and Blunt did find the item, and he killed Blunt so he wouldn't have to split the proceeds? He's callous enough. Remember he said it doesn't do to have friends in his business.' She frowned. 'But then, having killed Blunt, why is he still here?'

'I can only conjecture because even though Mr Blunt's demise is being treated as an accident, Mr Eden's is not. Anyone who leaves until Inspector Grimsdale releases us all will automatically become the chief suspect, as we've said. Or Mr Longley and Mr Blunt never found the item and there was another reason he killed Blunt.'

'True. So, we're down to Franklin. Hilary promised him something for saving his life from the firing squad, but double-crossed him, apparently.' She faltered at the image that always came to her mind at those words.

Clifford cleared his throat gently. 'I am heartily sorry your birthday evening ended this way, my lady.'

His concern brought a smile of comfort to her face. 'Thank you, Clifford. I'm fine and like you, despite the late hour, determined to finish our list. So back to Franklin. If he really did save Hilary from the firing squad, I can see he might have then killed Hilary out of revenge for double-crossing him. Franklin would have faced a court marshal and possibly the firing squad himself for what he did to help Hilary. But his motive for killing Blunt I don't know. Unless, of course, he somehow learned that Longley and Blunt had found the item he was originally promised and confronted Blunt in his room?'

'All very plausible, my lady, but again we find ourselves in the realms of speculation.'

Eleanor sighed. With two people now dead in a matter of days, the killer was running rings around them and the police. They needed to act fast and find out who killed Blunt and why, and what the connection was with Hilary's death before the trail went cold. She let out a quiet groan.

'Please tell me you have something more tangible we can pursue.'

He nodded. 'I do, my lady. I believe in the next five minutes, with your assistance, I can prove if Mr Franklin killed Mr Blunt or not.'

CHAPTER 32

As Eleanor and Clifford emerged from the lift, she looked around the lobby. All the other guests seemed to have gone to bed. Someone had switched the overhead chandelier lighting for the more subdued green and gold lamps dotted about the opulent space. Disappointed that the only sign of life was the night porter's shoes sticking out from his canopied red leather chair, she glanced at the time: eleven twenty-seven.

At the sound of a quiet rap on the front door, the night porter pulled himself from his chair and drew back the bolts. Eleanor instinctively tucked in behind one of the enormous Grecian urns, out of view. Clifford did the same. A portly man in his early sixties, dressed head to toe in green tweed, squeezed through the door. He ran a hand over his grey moustache and nodded awkwardly. 'Game ran over terribly at the club, don't you know.' He slapped a note into the porter's hand, which deftly disappeared into an inside pocket in a flash. The man then hurried over to the lift as fast as his stick would carry him and disappeared inside.

Clifford motioned for Eleanor to stay where she was and strode over to the night porter, who jumped in surprise. Clifford exchanged a few words with the man and then strode to the bar.

Eleanor joined him and cocked her head questioningly.

Clifford kept his voice low. 'It seems we have solved the mystery of why Johnson, the night porter, misled us, and the police, about letting in late guests on the night of Mr Eden's murder. It is because he has received a generous tip for many months for allowing the man you just saw enter after hours without mentioning it to anyone. He is a retired colonel and apparently his "game" runs late at least once a week. A very elegant game she is too, according to Johnson.'

Eleanor smiled at Clifford's joke. 'And how long has the colonel been staying here?'

'It seems he is one of the Grand's permanent residents. The two old ladies you have observed in the dining room, among other places, are permanent residents too. Interestingly, Johnson also told me the colonel invariably leaves for his "game" on the dot of nine.'

Eleanor looked thoughtful. 'It seems unlikely given the colonel's gammy leg and advanced years that he could have killed Hilary and pushed Blunt off the balcony. He certainly would have struggled to stand on the bath and hide the chloroform. And what possible motive could he have? I propose, until we learn any new information, that we don't treat him as a suspect.' She looked around the darkened bar. 'It looks like the staff are trying to encourage the last of the guests to go to bed, however. I hope we are not the only ones left up?'

A motion caught Clifford's eye. 'Ah, just the man!' The clerk hurried over as Clifford gestured to him. 'Two small things, Thomas.'

The young man nodded to Clifford, his eyes willing themselves not to stare at Eleanor.

'Were you on duty in the bar when Mr Blunt had his unfortunate fall?'

'No, I was called to work in the dining room this evening and then to help Chef prepare for breakfast. We are short-staffed at the moment, as you know.'

'At least you were spared the unpleasantness of witnessing Mr Blunt's distressing fall in that case?'

'Sadly not.' Thomas shuddered. 'The hotel manager, Mr Hargreaves, insisted I go to the terrace the minute he heard it had happened.'

'That must have been rather gruesome for you,' Eleanor said gently in as American an accent as she could manage.

Thomas stared at his shoes, his voice quiet and tremulous. 'It was a little too much like some of the horrors of the war. That poor gentleman. What a terrible way to go.' He snapped to and peered round the lobby area. 'But, erm, apologies, we're not supposed to talk about it. Mr Hargreaves is in quite a temper this evening.'

'I should say.' Eleanor nodded. 'He didn't seem in the best of moods and that was before he went off to be grilled at the police station. Well, we have no wish to get you into trouble, Thomas. Perhaps you could help me with the second thing then?'

The clerk straightened his shoulders. 'Of course. Anything, Miss Swan— I mean Lady Swift.'

'Did anyone mention when Mr Longley arrived in the bar this evening? Assuming he did, of course?' she added hastily. 'It's just that someone mentioned he was there at the time of the event which we aren't mentioning, and yet I was sure I saw him strolling along the promenade. You see, I'm worried I'm losing my memory. I had another birthday yesterday. It's most troubling.'

'Oh, belated returns of the day, Lady Swift.'

Clifford whispered behind his hand. 'The real reason for Lady Swift's question, Thomas, is that she does not enjoy being wrong.'

She threw her arms out. 'Well, who does!'

Thomas let out a chuckle but stopped himself abruptly. 'My apologies, I may have forgotten myself for a moment. To answer your question, Mr Longley was already there when I went out to the terrace. But quite when he arrived, in all the confusion, I'm not sure I could say for certain. But let me think.' Thomas drummed his fingers on his chin as he frowned. 'Mr Longley can't have been at the bar for long, if at all, before Mr Blunt fell. I'm sure, because I had been there just before to collect a post-dinner brandy ordered by the last diner.'

Eleanor nodded thoughtfully. 'I see. Do you know the where-abouts of Mr Franklin at this moment?'

Thomas looked surprised. 'Mr Franklin? The gentleman is reading in the private sitting room just through there.'

'You see, Clifford, at least I was right about something. I thought it was him I saw with, er… that book I was interested in borrow-ing. I shall go and find out if he has finished with it. Thank you, Thomas, that will be all.'

The luxurious long sitting room was decorated in pale blue and silver, which reflected the minimal light of the single lit lamp. Two plush velvet settees faced each other across a deep pile rug. A mahogany bookcase filled with leather-bound books that Eleanor wondered if anyone had ever read occupied one wall, while a selection of framed oil paintings of Brighton's sights filled another. An enormous scrollwork mirror hung above the low marble man-telpiece which was flanked by two grey leather wingback chairs, their backs to the door, one occupied by a man seemingly reading a large hardback book.

'Good evening, Mr Franklin. Couldn't you sleep either?' Eleanor stepped over and pulled back one of the long silver curtains to reveal the sharp white of the reclining crescent moon. 'Isn't it marvellous?'

'Could be better.' Franklin continued to stare at the open page.

'Oh really, how so?'

He snapped the book in his lap shut. 'You could stop wasting my time and hand over what belongs to me.'

'Now that is disappointing.' She dropped elegantly into the chair opposite him. 'Because I haven't even started wasting your time yet.'

Franklin shrugged but ran a hand down one of his cheeks, which appeared more hollow than ever in the dim glow of the fire.

'And now Mr Blunt is dead too,' Eleanor said. 'This place really needs to improve its security, wouldn't you say? Although' – she looked pointedly at Franklin – 'seeing as the man who murdered both men is posing as a guest, that probably wouldn't help.'

He scrutinised her face. 'Who says the man who fell was murdered? That idiot Inspector Grimsdale?'

She ignored the question. 'It might be selfish to say but I am glad I wasn't here when poor Mr Blunt was pushed over his balcony though. I can only imagine the awful image that would have been through those long glass windows in the bar.' She shuddered. 'I wonder if he screamed on the way down?'

'He did.'

She stiffened. 'Oh, I hadn't realised you were outside when it happened.'

'I wasn't. I was in my room with the window open. My room is on the floor below his.'

'Gracious, you might have seen him flying past.'

'I was too busy planning how to get what is rightfully mine back from you to be staring out the window.'

She shook her head. 'What an awful business. I'm amazed that the manager has managed to keep it so quiet. I thought the place would be flooded with press hounds.'

'There was no crowd in there. When I ran down to see what had happened, there were just a handful of people. Only three from the hotel and one of them was the barman.'

She gasped. 'Oh but poor Miss Summers. She must have been in shock, having seen Mr Blunt fall?'

Franklin leaned forward, the firelight picking up the golden strands in his fair hair. 'I never said she was in the bar.'

Eleanor smiled. 'So you know who I'm talking about? An acquaintance of yours, is she?'

He leaned back in his chair and shook his head. 'No, Lady Swift, not of mine, of your husband's.'

She started. 'Whatever makes you think that, Mr Franklin?'

He leaned forward again. 'It's just that I've never met a woman who argues with a man she doesn't know in his own hotel room.'

Eleanor gasped theatrically. 'Now this doesn't sound good at all.' She held his stare. 'For you, I mean. Because unless you were peering through the keyhole, how could you possibly know she was in Hilary's room?'

'Because I happened to be passing your husband's door about quarter to ten the night he was murdered. I distinctly heard two voices. Your husband said, "Oh why can't you drop it, Grace. It doesn't concern you!" Her name is Grace Summers, isn't it?'

'Ah, I've always liked the name Grace. A pretty name for a pretty girl. Most apt.' She rose to leave, but Franklin put his arm out lazily, blocking her exit. 'As you insist Mr Blunt's death wasn't accidental, aren't you going to ask me if I killed him? That's what you came for, isn't it?'

She smiled sweetly. 'No, I came to see if you were done with that book. Not that you are actually reading it at the moment. You're using it to disguise the fact that you are watching the comings and goings in the lobby in the mirror, so, actually, I imagine you'll require it a good while longer.' She winked. 'Don't worry, I shan't let on if you answer one last question. When you heard Mr Blunt scream, what exactly were you doing in your room?'

Franklin's eyes narrowed. 'Why would you want to know that?'

She shrugged. 'Oh, you know, curiosity and the cat and all that, although I'm more a dog person myself.'

He drummed his fingers on the arm of his chair for a moment before replying. 'If you really must pry, I returned to my room to collect this book.' He held it up.

Eleanor read out the title. '*A Complete Guide to Brighton's Points of Interest and Landmarks*.' She glanced at Clifford, who nodded almost imperceptibly. 'Well, thank you for letting me waste your time, after all, Mr Franklin.' She started towards the door, Clifford following.

From the corner of her eye she saw Franklin half rise and then sink back into his chair. Thumping the arm, he scowled and muttered, 'What the devil was that all about?'

CHAPTER 33

After a few snatched hours of sleep, the next morning Eleanor hailed Clifford as he waited for her by the door to the garden, pocket watch in hand. 'Clifford. I say, breakfast was marvellous! The lobster scrambled eggs were absolutely sublime. Not to mention the mini caviar cups and those pastry twist fellows filled with bacon and tomato, I had heaps of those. Oh, and the mushroom pancakes were too irresistible for words.'

'No sausages?' he asked drily.

She frowned. 'Have I ever turned down a sausage!? Don't be silly. Besides, sausages are implicit in the word "breakfast". And the chef here is a marvel. He twirled them into a spiral and surrounded them in the lightest, fluffiest eggy bread I have ever eaten, except for Mrs Trotman's, of course.'

He scanned her face. 'And yet, perhaps breakfast is not the real cause of your increased animation this morning, my lady?'

She motioned for them to step out into the hotel garden where they wouldn't be heard. The sun was valiantly trying to warm the morning air, but the cold wind from the night before was still blowing and the previously scattered clouds were gathering ominously on the horizon. 'Dash it, Clifford, you're right. I was trying to fool myself more than you. I don't feel at all bright about what I need to do next. And I confess, I may have had a third round of breakfast purely as a means of putting it off for just a few more minutes.'

'At least you found an enjoyable and fortifying diversion over which to procrastinate.' He paused. 'However, delaying tactics are not your usual modus operandi.'

She groaned. 'I know, but I feel rather… witless about interrogating Miss Summers again.'

His tone softened. 'Might apprehension over the answer you fear Miss Summers will give be getting the better of you, my lady?'

'Only completely. It's such a hideous place to be. I desperately want to know if she knew Hilary while I was married to him and if they…' She tailed off.

Clifford took a moment to straighten each of his perfectly aligned cufflinks. 'Perhaps I can offer you one more moment's distraction. It would be prudent to retrieve Master Gladstone from your suite and walk round the garden.'

She laughed. 'In case we bump into the killer and need to pretend he's a ferocious guard dog instead of a lazy, lumbering loafer who only attacks sausages, you mean?'

He gave her his best dispassionate look.

'Oh, not that,' she said. 'I see. Well, it's kind of you to think of him, but he is all sorted and cosy in his bed. I couldn't sleep, you see. I was so frustrated by all the thoughts running around my head. So I rose early and took a dawn stroll with Gladstone to make sure we at least both had a suitably large breakfast appetite.' She frowned. 'I'm not sure he appreciated me getting him out of his bed at such an early hour, mind you. It did take a little… coaxing. Hence him making a dash for his bed the minute we returned.'

Clifford pursed his lips. 'My lady, forgive the directness of my observation but it is hardly safe for you to wander around alone. Particularly in the early hours and especially in light of last night's events regarding Mr Blunt.'

'Oh, but I wasn't alone. I joined the elderly sisters for their morning constitutional turn around this garden.'

He covered his eyes. 'And what protection did you feel two frail ladies in their seventies might be able to offer you in the face of an armed attacker?'

'Who knows? I haven't heard their story. One day I'll be in my seventies and yet inside I'll still be the girl who cycled around the world. And then defeated several dastardly murderers, with my eminently adept butler, I admit. Yet I shall be dismissed by everyone who meets me as just a little old lady!' At his silence, she added lamely, 'Oh, alright, it was a bish on my part, although remember'– she patted the top of her head – 'I'm thirty now.'

'But still going on the nine-year-old who refused to listen to caution and fell from the tallest tree in his lordship's orchard, perhaps? My lady, I greatly appreciate that you navigated much of the world alone and managed to make it home safely. But' – he fixed her with a steely look – 'that was not on my watch.'

'Oh, Clifford, I am sorry,' she said, genuinely contrite. 'I never mean to worry you. You know how much I appreciate your dedication to your promise to Uncle Byron to watch over me. Maybe my impulsiveness will diminish now I'm in my fourth decade?'

He ran his hand down his tie. '*Praemonitus praemunitus.*'

She stared at him blankly.

'"Forewarned is forearmed". By which I mean I am resigned to the worst.' He gestured towards the stone steps leading to the conservatory.

Halfway down, however, Eleanor stopped so abruptly, Clifford almost knocked into her. She turned and held up an accusing finger. 'Wait a minute! Before we go any further, it's your turn to confess.'

'Might I enquire in regard to which matter, my lady?'

'No, you may not, because you know perfectly well I mean a full disclosure on what you were doing while I was out with Hugh… Seldon. You fobbed me off instead of telling me last night, saying we were both too tired. How on earth did you know Rex Franklin would be reading *A Complete Guide to Brighton's Points of Interest and Landmarks*? And how did that strange fact prove his innocence of Blunt's death? In eighty words or less, please, as I have an interview to get to.'

For a moment she thought Clifford would rise to the bait, but instead he merely gave her a pointed look and cleared his throat. 'If you remember you mentioned my, as you were kind enough to call it, "impeccable organisation" and "meticulous attention to detail" might over time insidiously work their way into your psyche?'

She laughed. 'Yes. And you suggested in horror that if influence transfers one way, it would surely also do so the other and you would end up operating with my less structured way of working.'

He nodded. 'I'm afraid my worst fears were realised last night while you were out dancing with Chief Inspector Seldon. I noted one of our suspects, Mr Franklin, was otherwise engaged downstairs. It entered my head that we really should search each suspect's room when the opportunity arose.'

Eleanor gasped. 'Clifford, you didn't?'

He nodded and then shook his head in disbelief. 'On the spur of the moment I found myself entering Mr Franklin's room. However, my lack of planning was soon exposed. While I was searching the bathroom a man entered the bedroom. Fortunately he failed to enter the bathroom where I would have undoubtedly been discovered. Unfortunately, however, the opaque nature of the glass door obscured the man's identity. A moment later a scream pierced the evening air, and the figure left hurriedly. I emerged to also find out who had screamed. On my way to the door, I noted that only one thing had changed since I'd entered. A book on the side table had been taken.'

'*A Complete Guide to Brighton's Points of Interest and Landmarks* by any chance?'

He nodded.

'So you figured if Franklin had the book when I questioned him last night, he had to be the person in his room? I don't know if it would stand up in a court of law, but it's good enough for me.' She paused. 'Which means if we're sticking to our hunch that whoever killed Hilary also killed Blunt then—'

'Mr Franklin is off our suspect list.'

CHAPTER 34

Five minutes later Eleanor was still trying to rub some warmth into her hands as they rounded the last corner of the twisty herringbone path to the conservatory. Suddenly she jumped back behind the cover of a clump of bay trees. 'Ooh, look, there she is! It's Miss Summers.' She noted that Clifford didn't follow her gaze. 'You knew she was here, didn't you, and that's the real reason you suggested the walk through the garden?'

'I really couldn't say, my lady.'

Eleanor peeped round again. 'I say, that's the first time I've seen her wear even a dash of colour. What a pretty blue scarf.'

'Ah! Then it seems she has accepted your apology, my lady. I shall leave you to work your magic.' He turned to go the way they had come.

'Wait!' she hissed. 'What apology? Clifford, what did you do?'

'Aside from overhearing Miss Summers' exasperated and angry soliloquy at the end of your last meeting together?'

'Mmm.' She rubbed her forehead. 'I may have gone in a teensy bit hard.'

'Thus, it struck me last night that a sweetener would likely ease this morning's meeting.'

'In that case, thank you. And a splendid choice, well done.' She gave him a glowing smile.

She watched Clifford's coat-tails disappear round an imposing statue on the corner of the path.

Alright, Ellie, let's try a different tack this time.

Pre-empting her, Miss Summers crossed to the door and pulled it open, the magazine she had been leafing through held against the navy cardigan of her twinset. 'Morning. Coming in?'

'Well, I was, until… I realised you were reading' – Eleanor gestured to the magazine – 'and thought it rather rude to disturb you.'

A confused frown coupled with an awkward smile crossed Grace's face. 'You… thought it rude…' She tailed off. 'Thank you, by the way. It's beautiful. The scarf, I mean.' She ran her fingers along the edge of the baby-blue silk, which intensified her eyes so much Eleanor found it hard to tear hers away.

'My pleasure. A small apology for my demeanour at our last meeting. I fear I may have been swept up in recent events more than I had realised.'

Miss Summers turned away, but Eleanor was sure she caught a muttered, 'Haven't we all.' She watched the young woman fold her curves into the seat of an ornate fan-backed wicker chair and was surprised when she indicated for Eleanor to join her in the opposite one.

'I find it very restful in here,' Miss Summers said, gesturing round at the myriad potted palms and baskets of flowering succulents.

'A brief respite from your job hunting?'

This drew an exaggerated sigh. 'I haven't the heart for selling myself just at the moment. I have a little time on my side.'

'Unlike poor Mr Blunt,' Eleanor said, carefully observing the woman's face, which betrayed a flash of horror. 'Oh gracious! I am sorry,' she added quickly. 'I forgot you were in the bar when it happened.'

'So, I see this isn't a friendly chat either,' Miss Summers said sharply. 'I don't know what you want from me, Lady Swift.' She rose. 'But I am suddenly heartened to resume my search for employment. If you will excuse me.'

'Wait! Just tell me what you were doing in Hilary's room? *Please.*'

Miss Summers scowled. 'That again? We have had that conversation. I told you, I wasn't acquainted with your husband.'

'I know. But at that point, only one of the guests had seen you sliding into his room on the night he was murdered. But now I've been told so much more.'

The woman's tone was scornful. 'More lies then, clearly. Really, I expected you to be more shrewd than to listen to malicious tattle.'

'Perhaps. Although I'm confident that you are the only Grace here at the hotel. So when Hilary shouted, "Oh why can't you drop it, Grace. It doesn't concern you!" it seems likely that it was you he was talking to. Strange behaviour for two people who had supposedly never met.'

She paused as Miss Summers' hand flew to her mouth. 'I think you'd best sit down again, don't you, Grace? Especially as at this moment that information would draw Inspector Grimsdale to the same conclusion I have drawn.'

'Which is?' Miss Summers asked tentatively.

'That you may have been one of the last people to see my husband alive.'

'I didn't kill Hilary,' the woman said quietly as she sunk back into her chair. 'I would never…' A large tear tipped over the edge of each eyelid and trickled down her cheeks.

So it's Hilary now, is it? Eleanor pursed her lips. 'How did you know him? And in the spirit of decency, please spare me any more lies. I'm not actually as rhinoceros-skinned as I seem to appear. Hilary was my husband, and you were in his room.'

'But it's not what you are imagining, which I'm guessing—'

'Is the worst? Yes, it's precisely that. It was around ten o'clock at night and you were there alone with him.'

Miss Summers shook her head, causing a fresh set of tears to tumble down her cheeks. 'It isn't what you think.'

Eleanor folded her arms. 'Then what is?'

Miss Summers hesitated, then rubbed her hands over her eyes and looked up at Eleanor. 'Alright. You deserve the truth. Hilary and I were partners. Business partners. Nothing more.'

'Since when?'

'Since 1913.'

'Eight years ago. Then you were involved with Hilary when I married him?'

'Involved in his business, nothing else.'

'Why do you suppose he never mentioned you to me then?'

Miss Summers glared at her defiantly. 'Probably because he feared you would draw the wrong conclusion. Just as you have now!'

Eleanor eyed the other woman coldly. 'Stand in my shoes for a moment, Grace. In his hotel room, my husband is apparently deep in a business discussion with a partner I didn't know existed. And who just happens to have the most divine curves and the deepest blue eyes any man could ask for.'

'Any man except Hilary. He never asked for those. Ever.' The anger in Miss Summers' tone drew Eleanor up short. 'Hilary liked redheads, didn't you know?' Miss Summers said waspishly, gesturing to Eleanor's fiery curls.

Eleanor shrugged. 'Did you see Hilary at all after that?'

'No, I left because he was in no mood to continue our conversation. I went to my room. He said he was going for a walk for half an hour to clear his head.'

And to post you the photograph, Ellie! 'Was your conversation about the object that Hilary allegedly stole and got him killed?'

The other woman scoffed. 'What object? I don't know anything about an object. And I have no idea why he was murdered.' Her voice trembled. 'I… I went back to Hilary's room around midnight to try one last time to…' She sighed and shook her head. 'Anyway, when I got there, he was sitting at his writing desk... dead. I ran back to my room and stayed there all night. I didn't sleep at all.'

Eleanor wished again she was better at knowing when someone was telling the truth. Miss Summers seemed so genuine. *But...*

'Did you travel over from South Africa with Hilary?'

'Lady Swift—'

'Maybe you'd feel easier about being more honest if you called me Eleanor?'

'I have been telling the truth, Lady Swift. And I think I have answered enough of your questions.' She stood up and smoothed down her smart navy skirt.

Eleanor waited until she had finished. 'I suppose then our only common ground is that we both know that Bert Blunt's death wasn't an accident.' It was a shot in the dark, but the other woman's reaction showed it had hit its target. Miss Summers' face drained of colour so quickly Eleanor instinctively reached out, thinking the woman would faint. Regaining her composure, Miss Summers stared at Eleanor, the look in her eyes pulling Eleanor up short.

'Thank you again for the scarf, Lady Swift. However, please do not attempt to further our association so much as an inch.'

She snatched her magazine from the chair and stormed out, the door slamming loudly behind her.

Eleanor put her head in her hands and breathed deeply through her nose, trying to gather her thoughts. She was so preoccupied she failed to notice the door reopen.

'My lady?'

'Clifford!' She grasped the arm of the chair. 'Gracious, you frightened the wits out of me.'

'It is heartening to hear they have returned. How did your interview go?' He let the door close behind him.

She shrugged. 'I'm not sure I got anything of use out of her.'

'And I fear no amount of gift-wrapped scarves would smooth the ruffles this time.'

'No? More angry grumblings all the way to the lift then?'

'To my brief observation, I drew the less fortunate conclusion that it was fear and upset which propelled Miss Summers to the lift at such a turn of speed.' He coughed. 'Very impressive given the height of her heels.'

Eleanor stared moodily out into the garden. 'Oh, Clifford, I'm more confused than ever about Grace Summers and Hilary and any hand she might have had in his murder. She did admit to being in his room. So it seems Franklin and Longley may have been telling the truth about that, if nothing else.'

'Even liars sometimes tell the truth, my lady.'

She nodded, something pricking at her brain, but she felt too gloomy to pursue it. 'She seems like a certain suspect for Hilary's murder, but after speaking to her, if I'm honest, I… oh, I'm not sure, but I don't believe she did kill him.'

Clifford arched a brow. 'Why, my lady?'

She sighed deeply. 'Because… because I believe she loved him.' Clifford opened his mouth, but Eleanor raised her hand. 'And before you tell me more people have died at the hands of one they loved than anyone else, I still don't think she killed him. I also don't believe she killed Blunt given the evidence we've found against that theory. *And* there was genuine fear in her eyes just now when I said she and I both knew Blunt was murdered. She may not have killed him, but I'm pretty sure she knows, or thinks she knows, who did.'

'I wholeheartedly concur that she had the air of a woman overcome by fear when she passed me. Fear for her own safety.'

Eleanor nodded. 'Exactly. I think she believes whoever killed Blunt may try to kill her. And she may be right. After all, if she was Hilary's partner as she claims, why wouldn't he have passed her the item he stole? Why does everyone think he passed it to me?'

He nodded. 'A good point. Well, it seems, along with Mr Franklin, we can remove Miss Summers off our suspect list. However, I really feel it would be prudent to continue this discussion in a more discreet place. I have delivered Master Gladstone to the ladies' boarding house and we have an hour and a half before we need to meet up with them for our planned lunch. I know the perfect spot.'

Eleanor rose. 'Thank goodness. Let's go!'

But as they rounded the corner into the lobby, Eleanor was knocked roughly to one side. 'What on earth!' Her jaw fell slack as the hotel manager held up his hands in hurried apology, then spread his arms to block her path. Before she could object, Inspector Grimsdale emerged from the manager's office, tightening his grip on the man he had handcuffed to his wrist. Four uniformed policemen flanked the inspector, who obviously hadn't spotted Eleanor as he warned the prisoner.

'Come quietly, Franklin, or it will be worse for you. You're already under arrest for the murder of Mr Painshill, or Eden, depending what his real name was.'

At that moment, Grimsdale noticed Eleanor. Without a word, he marched his prisoner past her. As he did so, Rex Franklin caught Eleanor's eye. The murderous look he gave her made it clear he held her entirely responsible for his arrest.

Clifford stepped to her side as they watched Franklin being led away. 'Rather a serious setback, my lady, as we had only just discounted Mr Franklin from our suspect list.'

Eleanor shivered. 'I know, but we only have evidence, and loose evidence at that, that he didn't kill Blunt. We don't have any evidence that he didn't kill Hilary, except our belief that the same person killed both men. That's not going to cut it with Grimsdale, who doesn't believe a word I've said up to now, anyway.'

Clifford nodded. 'Agreed. If we are right, however, it also means the murderer is still at large in the hotel and no longer under suspicion.'

It was Eleanor's turn to nod.

'Which means he's free to kill again.'

CHAPTER 35

'What is this place?' Eleanor asked Clifford ten minutes later as she unwound her scarf from her neck and stared at the rich-burgundy painted door in front of her.

'Principally, it is somewhere safe to talk, my lady. But if you will forgive my presumption, I also thought you deserved a few tranquil moments of birthday, and holiday, decadence before we meet the ladies.'

The door swung open, held by a man in a uniform so heavily decorated with gold braid he could have been mistaken for an army hero. He tipped his top hat. 'Welcome to Postlethwaites. A waiter will be with you presently, sir, madam.'

She stepped inside. 'This is a surprise. I thought we were going to the Metropole Hotel bar as usual.'

'As the doorman said, this is Postlethwaites, my lady. The oyster and champagne bar famed throughout London.'

She frowned. 'But we are in Brighton.'

'Precisely the reason Mr Postlethwaite wrote to the editor of *The Times* in 1919 to instigate the infamous feud, now known as "The Great Oyster Schism".'

She chuckled. 'Oh, this sounds like a good tale. Go on.'

But at that moment, a waiter in a pristine burgundy uniform appeared, and at Clifford's behest, led them to an upstairs table.

Once seated, Eleanor leaned back in her chair. 'Come on, finish the story. I'm intrigued.'

'Well, my lady, Mr Postlethwaite spent a year in France where, among other things, he indulged in his delectation for oysters in Paris' famous restaurants. Having returned to England, he was forced to suffer the two-hour train journey to London every time he wished to partake of similarly excellent seafood. The reason was the lack of fine oyster establishments in his native Brighton, something he at first resigned himself to. But in 1919 the gentleman took particular exception when the railway company reduced the price of the third-class tickets.'

She laughed. 'Because the station was teeming with the lower classes?'

'More that their raucous singing penetrated to first class on his return trips when his head was rather delicate on account of over-indulgence at the capital's champagne and oyster bars. Thus he set up his own bar here in Brighton. He then wrote to *The Times* challenging the crème of London Society to travel down and find it lacking in any single regard in comparison to the capital's most renowned equivalent.'

'What a clever business move!'

'Indeed. The gentleman was so successful that the newspapers ran the story throughout 1919 and well into the following year. They dubbed it "The Great Oyster Schism" and listed the number of patrons at each establishment on a weekly basis. It became something of a trophy to visit one's favourite of the two restaurants and be able to boast that one was included in the total of the winning side.'

'Ingenious. I can't wait to see if it lives up to its reputation, although, I confess, I'm not exactly an expert on oysters. If they are half as amazing as the decor though, I'll be happy. Just look at the way the chandeliers sparkle in those simply enormous gilded mirrors running along three sides of this palatial room! And these carved velvet upholstered chairs. I feel like Louis the Fourteenth is about to stride over and ask what the devil I think I'm doing intruding in his dining room.'

'We also have a bird's-eye view over the promenade where the ladies will no doubt be.'

'You mean, where they will no doubt be engaged in something reprehensible.' She stood up. 'Please can we swap seats?'

'As you wish, my lady.'

'There.' She smiled as he waited for her to get comfortable before he settled into the opposite seat. 'Now I can enjoy whatever naughty shenanigans they are up to, and you can't see, so will be none the wiser.'

He sniffed. 'Playing spoilsport is not something I had planned on my list of holiday activities.'

She laughed and shook her head ruefully. 'Have you actually done anything you intended to? Or I, come to that? I don't think either of us has.'

'Regrettably, we have not had the opportunity, my lady, given the unforeseen events that have unfolded. Perhaps your evening spent dancing might be something of a salve for the week, however?'

Her cheeks coloured. 'Delicately put, Clifford. That, and the utterly delightful voyage you arranged were in fact the highlights of the year so far. Although I'm sure I should be sending you back to butler school for a reminder of what is and isn't appropriate. On this occasion, I am, however, grateful for your furtive colluding with a certain policeman behind my back.'

He raised one eyebrow. 'Furtive, my lady? Is that perhaps not a description more fitting to a ferret?'

She shook her head. 'Not at all. It's way more apt for mischievous butlers. And your mischievousness was artfully engineered, as always. Bravo.'

'Speaking of policemen, my lady, Inspector Grimsdale has thrown down quite the gauntlet to our investigation in arresting Mr Franklin.'

'Hasn't he just! I can't believe we are here again, trying to solve a double murder. I'm sure, however, you've been my organisation magician and brought my notebook and a pen?'

'Abracadabra!' He produced both with a flourish. 'All included in the ticket price.'

She flapped a hand at him, almost knocking over the filled crystal champagne flute the waiter had just placed in front of her. 'Now, we have a most important matter to solve. Oh, but look at those oysters!'

He busied himself with his napkin.

'Not your thing?'

'It is my humble opinion that they cannot really be anyone's "thing", my lady. Food is to be chewed, not glissando'd down one's digestive tract like a, I believe our American cousin's call it, a "garbage chute".' He failed to cover up a shudder.

'Then I shall selflessly devour the lot. Maybe it'll fortify me to wade through the muddle of information from all of our suspects. Honestly, Clifford, I'm not at all sure who is telling the truth.'

'Perhaps they all are. Or none of them. But if I might make an alternative suggestion, my lady?'

She nodded, reaching for another oyster.

'We could turn our attention again to Mr Eden's inscription on the photograph. If that is not as equally unpalatable to you as the oysters are to me?'

She paused and sighed. 'I suppose I can't wriggle out of it forever.' She swallowed and turned the pages of her notebook until she found where she'd written out the words from the back of both halves of the photograph.

Lady Eleanor Letitia Swift
Captain Hilary Montague Eden
Married on June 3rd 1914
At the Hotel Royal Pilgrim's Rest
'Something old something new
Something borrowed something blue

And a sixpence in her hand'
Till death do us part

She stared at the page. 'You know, I'm coming to terms with Hilary having got my middle name wrong. And his. I never liked mine, and, as we know, it possibly wasn't even his real middle name.' She shrugged. 'So, what does it matter?'

'I believe it matters a lot, my lady.'

She examined his face for a moment. Then her eyes widened. 'Clifford! You think the errors are clues?'

He nodded. 'Perhaps only some of them. I'm of the mind that Mr Eden spelt your, and his, middle name wrong on purpose to alert you to the fact that the other errors are, as you stated, clues.'

She gasped. 'Of course, Clifford, you clever bean! Dash it though, Longley might be right. I can be quite the blunt brick sometimes.'

'Only when your thoughts are understandably overcome with emotional distress.'

She smiled. 'Thank you. Although do feel free to refute the brick reference.'

He pursed his lips. 'If we could get back to the matter in hand, my lady? So, excluding the first two lines, which of the others has an error?'

She looked at the page again and frowned. 'None. The hotel and date are correct.' She choked. 'And, it seems the last line.'

He coughed gently. 'And the rhyme?'

She frowned. 'Do you think it's just the rhyme he meant me to focus on?'

'I do, my lady. Whilst it has been associated with weddings since the reign of Queen Victoria, there is a subtle error in it too.'

'There is?' She ran through the rhyme in her head. 'Ah, of course. It should be "and a sixpence in your shoe", yes?'

'Correct. A symbol of good luck. Pennies in general, as we know Mr Blunt believed, are a symbol of good luck when placed in your shoes, but it has long been a sixpence for brides.'

'Then why would Hilary have changed it to "hand"?' She mimed holding a sixpence in her palm.

Clifford pretended to toss one onto the back of his hand and reveal which side was showing. '*Navia aut caput*, as the Romans would say. "Heads or tails" to us.'

She took a sip of champagne and frowned even harder. 'Blast it, Clifford. I'm beginning to feel like poor old Mr Postlethwaite. My head's splitting. Why couldn't Hilary just have kept it simple?'

'I believe, my lady, that Mr Eden was trying to tell you something he wanted only *you* to know. At the same time, he was also trying to keep you safe. I believe that is why he used code and cut the photograph in half. It seems likely, as I postulated earlier, that he was interrupted in the middle of executing his plan.'

She sighed. 'Well, we'll probably never know unless Hilary finds a way to come back from the grave a second time. And I think arranging that sort of magic is beyond even a wizard like yourself, Clifford.'

His silence told her how much he wished he could.

She shook herself. 'Right, enough of that! Now, what would I do with a sixpence in my hand? Ah, spend it, of course.'

Clifford nodded. 'But it is hardly a princely sum. Certainly not sufficient to buy this mysterious item everyone seems to be seeking. If it were so, it would not be necessary to kill to possess it.'

'Yes, but remember what de Meyer said? That "to the right person it is valuable"?'

'Indeed, but I rather think that the sixpence does not refer to the item itself, but that the clue, or clues, will lead to it. Perhaps each line of the rhyme is a clue in itself? Why otherwise include it?'

She shrugged. 'You could be right, but let's concentrate on "sixpence in the hand" first.' She took another sip of champagne.

'Mmm, lovely. Now, I can only think of mundane things you can buy with sixpence, like a bag of buns or half a pound of sausages. What about you?'

'A bus ticket? Candle wax? Paraffin? Clothes pegs. Pr—'

Eleanor held up a hand. 'Okay, so you can buy lots of everyday items for sixpence.'

Clifford looked at his pocket watch. 'I believe we need to defer this line of thought and meet the ladies.'

Eleanor glanced past him out the window and laughed. 'I think they may require a minute or two to, er, make themselves presentable. No turning round!'

He rose with her, keeping his eyes averted. 'Kindly reassure me, my lady, that it is not as bad as I am imagining?'

'Of course not, silly.' She feigned horror. 'It's far worse. Let's go.'

CHAPTER 36

Out in the street, Eleanor was bowled over by the ladies', and Gladstone's, enthusiastic greeting.

'My lady,' Mrs Trotman said. ''Tis too kind of you to take us to lunch again. I'm sure you've far better things to be doing than spending it with the likes of us.'

Eleanor shook her head. 'Categorically not. I have been missing our catch-up sessions in the kitchen at Henley Hall.'

Mrs Butters scrutinised Eleanor's face. 'You look a little pale, my lady, if you'll forgive me saying?'

'No, just… never mind. Let us see if this delightful eatery can impress us once again.'

The homely atmosphere of the restaurant where they'd had Eleanor's birthday lunch had proved too good not to return to. The owner greeted them warmly, possibly remembering how much they'd eaten and drunk at their last visit.

'Ladies, and gentleman, good to see you again. Ah, and your handsome and well-behaved bulldog.'

Mrs Trotman chuckled. 'Well behaved? Good job you don't have sausages on the menu otherwise you'd see the real Master Gladstone!'

Clifford caught her eye. 'I am beginning to wonder from where some of his naughtier tendencies might have come.'

The ladies looked at each other in horror.

'It's alright,' Eleanor said. 'Clifford was facing the other way when you were outside Postlethwaithes. Besides, he is teasing you. You have my full permission to misbehave on your holiday, you know that.'

'Oh my stars!' Mrs Butters' hand flew to her mouth. 'We were only having a bit of fun, my lady.'

'I know. And I'm only sorry I wasn't able to join in. It looked hilarious.'

Polly looked confused and then horrified. 'Oh lummy, you saw us, your ladyship?' she whispered.

'It's fine, really.' Eleanor leaned in and whispered back, 'Mr Clifford had mischievous fun when he was your age too.'

'Never!' Polly breathed, staring at him, her mouth hanging open.

Clifford cleared his throat. 'Propriety was not made to be flouted.' He threw Eleanor a look, but she knew him well enough now to know he was enjoying the exchange far more than he was letting on.

The restaurant owner was listening with amusement. He bent and ruffled the bulldog's ears. 'Master Gladstone is your name, is it, fine sir? Well, whatever the mischief your chaperones have all been up to, I hope it has given them a hearty appetite. We've a great treat on the menu today.'

'What is it?' Eleanor asked as her stomach gave an unladylike rumble, which drew a sharp sniff from Clifford.

'It is our chef's speciality, madam. Care for a surprise?'

'Absolutely!'

The ladies nodded enthusiastically. Clifford held up five fingers by way of ordering and a waiter led them to their table.

The arrival of the food interrupted what Eleanor suspected was a substantially truncated version of what the ladies had been doing since they last met up.

'That looks and smells amazing!' she said, inhaling deeply.

'It is layered turbot and shrimp savoury crumble,' the waiter said proudly. 'The chef only makes this once a month. Served with parsnips and carrots in rosemary sauce with homemade bread and butter.'

Polly and Eleanor both clapped their hands, their eyes bright.

Mrs Butters poked Mrs Trotman in the side. 'Looks like you've got summat else you need to add to your menu, Trotters.'

Mrs Trotman waited until all the food was on the table, and the waiter gone before replying, 'Should be parsley and dill sauce, but I'll consider it if you wish it so, of course, my lady.'

Eleanor savoured a mouthful. The soft, slightly sweet turbot flakes mixed delightfully with the creaminess of the shrimps and the sharp salty tang of the cheese in the breadcrumb topping. She nodded.

'On the menu 'twill be then, my lady. And a pleasure 'twill be.'

'Excellent! Now do carry on telling me what you have all been up to. The bits you can tell me, that is,' Eleanor said with a wink.

'Oh, I think we've just about covered it all,' Mrs Butters replied hurriedly.

'What 'bout the museum and the gallery, though?' Polly said quietly. 'We've done those too. The orniwhatsitthingamey was my favourite.'

'Orni what?' Eleanor said.

'Sorry, your ladyship, 'tis a complicated word. I meant the paintings of the birds were my favourite.'

'Lots of seagulls?'

'Everything, your ladyship. Some of them looked like fairy-tale creatures, so colourful and beautiful.'

Clifford nodded as the waiter went to refill their glasses. 'There is an ornithological painting exhibition at the Town Hall, my lady.'

Mrs Trotman nodded. 'And only thruppence entrance fee as it's still out of season.'

Eleanor bit her lip. 'Ladies, that reminds me. I'm sorry, but Clifford and I won't be able to join you for our planned sightseeing trip this afternoon. There's something we must attend to.'

'Fancy the lady of the house apologising to us. 'Tis no matter at all,' Mrs Butters said. 'Although we would have enjoyed it enormously, my lady.'

'Oh, I'm sure we'll find a way to keep ourselves occupied,' Mrs Trotman said, avoiding Clifford's eye.

'I have no doubt about that,' he muttered.

The group's easy chatter continued over a delicious dessert of baked apples and prunes with ice cream as they imagined what it might be like to actually live at the seaside. During this, the waiter returned with a small bowl.

'For Master Gladstone. With the chef's compliments, madam.'

'Now, that is service that we haven't seen before, even at the Grand. Please thank him and the owner most profusely. Gladstone, a sausage, and a dash of gravy, all to yourself, old chum.'

Having watched him snuffle up the contents and lick the bowl clean, Eleanor asked if the ladies had decided how they were going to occupy themselves that afternoon.

'Yes, thank you, my lady,' Mrs Trotman said. 'We're off to the Royal Pavilion.'

Mrs Butters nodded. 'They say it's still like a palace inside.'

Polly gasped. 'A palace? But it must be a fearful price to be allowed in then?'

Eleanor half listened to their plans as she slid into her coat, which Clifford held for her, her mind endlessly running over the conundrum of the rhyme on her wedding photograph.

Mrs Butters patted Polly's head. 'Don't you worry, my girl. That's why I'm in charge of making our pocket money go so far. 'Tis only sixpence.'

'Sixpence!' Eleanor and Clifford chorused, exchanging a look.

Mrs Trotman looked from one to the other in surprise. 'Yes, my lady. Apparently it's been sixpence since it opened to the public in 1851.'

'And they've never put the price up since so anyone can afford to go and see it,' Mrs Butters said.

Eleanor glanced at Clifford, who nodded. 'Ladies. I do believe Clifford and I will be free to join you this afternoon after all!'

CHAPTER 37

The Royal Pavilion was less than half a mile away, yet Eleanor felt the walk to it was taking forever.

'The sea air seems to suit you, my lady.' Mrs Butters puffed by her side. 'It's like trying to keep up with Polly when Trotters tells her we're going for ice cream or that she can watch the Punch and Judy man again.'

Eleanor smiled at her housekeeper but failed to slacken her stride. 'I find the only way to stay warm in this weather is to walk faster! And that wonderful lunch has fuelled my legs.' She tried to hide the eagerness in her voice. 'And I've been meaning to look around the Pavilion since I arrived. It was kind of your friend at the boarding house to take Gladstone for the afternoon, by the way.'

'It's no bother, my lady. She's delighted to have Master Gladstone all to herself for a few hours. He's worked his doggie charm on her and no mistake.'

Clifford nodded. 'They were indeed her exact words, although, we need to purchase the lady a new pair of slippers.'

Eleanor stifled a laugh. 'Oh, he didn't?'

'True to form, he did, in fact. While I was thanking the lady on your behalf for her kind agreement to watch over him for the afternoon, he managed to steal her only pair from underneath her armchair. The lady was, however, most gracious about having lost them to Master Gladstone's rather soggy collection.'

Mrs Butters chuckled. 'He is such a terror. I don't know why we all love him so much.'

'Neither do I,' Clifford agreed. 'Anyway, we will purchase the new slippers, although the cost should rightly come out of Master Gladstone's allowance, were he to have one, right after—'

'Right after we have seen the Pavilion,' Eleanor said.

Clifford nodded again. 'Which we intend to visit every inch of, do we not, my lady?'

Mrs Butters laughed. 'Ever the one to get value for money for the household accounts is Mr Clifford.'

''Tis like the most beautiful fairy-tale palace you told us about from your travels, your ladyship,' Polly said in hushed tones a few minutes later as they stood looking at the exterior of the Royal Pavilion.

Despite the increasingly bitter wind, Eleanor paused to take in the full majesty of the exquisite Indian and Mughal design. The intricate filigree porticos running the length of the seemingly mile-long frontage were interrupted at regular intervals by semi-circular pagodas, each topped by an onion-domed cupola of varying size and grandeur. Myriad minarets rose from ornate plinths along the roofline, while the glazed cream tiles that decorated the exterior reflected the weak afternoon sunshine, making the whole edifice glow.

With their tickets purchased and Polly's once again preserved intact, they hurried into the Pavilion grounds where the young girl ran her hands down the smooth pillars and stared in delight at the patterns cast by the shafts of sun filtering through the portico above.

'Perhaps this is why Franklin was reading *A Complete Guide to Brighton's Points of Interest and Landmarks*, Clifford?' Eleanor whispered.

'Possibly, my lady, although without his having seen the photograph and read the clue relating to sixpence, I cannot fathom why? How could he have drawn the same conclusion as we have that Mr Eden may have been pointing to the Royal Pavilion? And how so without seeing your wedding photograph?'

'He probably hasn't. I imagine he was pouring over all the sites listed, looking for one that looked as if Hilary might have hidden the item everyone wants so obsessively. If so, maybe he's given up the idea that Hilary gave it to me?'

Clifford's brows drew together. 'Hopefully. But what did Mr Franklin discover amongst Mr Eden's belongings that makes him think the item may have been secreted at one of those sites, anyway?'

She thought for a moment. 'Well, the morning after Hilary booked into the Grand, he went out for the day, and didn't return until the evening. So if everyone has searched his room to no avail, and my continued insistence that I don't have the wretched thing finally convinced them, it's true—'

'They may have come to the conclusion that Mr Eden hid the item while he was away from the hotel?'

'Exactly, which is what we are assuming.' She slapped her forehead. 'Of course! Hilary had a bundle of tourist brochures on the desk where he was murdered as well.'

'Indeed, that might explain it. As to the Royal Pavilion, however, the reference to sixpence might still be a coincidence.'

She nodded. 'And even if we are right and he did hide it here, it's simply enormous.' She gestured along the length of the building. 'Someone could have hidden a herd of elephants in here and we wouldn't find them.'

'I believe something of their unmentionable habits might give them away.'

'Clifford!' She stifled a smile at his uncharacteristically crude humour.

'My lady, my quip, albeit a rather hasty and inappropriate one, I admit, was intended only to lighten your mood. I noted Mrs Butters is becoming suspicious that something is wrong. If you sincerely wish to keep the events surrounding Mr Eden's death hidden from the ladies, might I suggest we need to avoid our faces being a reflection of our thoughts?'

'You're right, of course. But I am terrible at that, aren't I?'

'I really couldn't say, my lady, but perhaps a broad-brimmed hat and your new sunglasses might have been a better choice this afternoon?'

That made her smile, which she was relieved to see Mrs Butters noticed as she was walking back over to join them.

''Tis a treat to see you are enjoying your afternoon as much as we are, my lady. Isn't this the most beautiful building ever?'

'It is even more remarkable on the inside I imagine, Mrs Butters. Shall we chivvy the others and make the most of our time here?'

A few minutes later, the five of them shuffled down the Long Gallery with a gaggle of other tourists. The collection of exotic art pieces and furnishings was brightly lit by ornate lanterns set below the central painted-glass ceiling. At the end, their bespectacled guide ushered them into the Banqueting Room.

Despite occasionally being entertained by princes, sultans and maharajas during her travels, this was one of the most extravagant and opulent rooms Eleanor had been in. Every inch seemed to be decorated with the finest velvet, impeccably detailed wallpaper, gold paint or cut-crystal glass. The delicately vaulted ceiling rose to a giddying height, the enormous chandelier threatening to bring the beautiful craftsmanship crashing down. Sloped inlays of ebony and gold nestled on golden carved rails, which also ran down the corner of each wall. Floor-to-ceiling portraits hung everywhere, except for one wall of full-length arched windows. On the long central mahogany table sat seven gold candelabra, each taller than Eleanor in her dancing heels.

She tried to marshal her thoughts and tune into the tour guide at the same time.

'King George the Fourth hosted a great many prestigious banquets for royalty and nobility from around the world in this very room even before he acceded to the throne. It is here that we can see the first example of his majesty's exuberant spending and his desire to blend innovative techniques among the more traditional architectural elements.'

'Can't he just point to whatever it is without such a long-winded preamble,' Eleanor whispered to Clifford.

'I believe the gentleman is merely trying to give the visitors exceptional value for their sixpence.'

She nodded, a little chastised, and listened to the guide again.

'Ladies and gentlemen, please regard the wallpaper between the paintings. Not only does it provide a stately backdrop to the artwork, but it is also an early example of the use of Prussian blue.'

Eleanor started. '*Blue,*' she mouthed.

Clifford nodded and gestured to the guide again.

'His majesty was so taken with the colour blue that you will see Prussian blue in many of the rooms throughout the Pavilion, along with the brighter, bolder blue verditer. Blue has become a colour synonymous with the essence of this royal palace's design.'

'Clifford!' Eleanor whispered. 'Something old, something new, something borrowed, *something blue*. It's the fourth line of the rhyme. We must be on the right track.'

'It would seem so. I assumed only the last line was a clue, or, if all the lines were, then each line would point to a different place. However, now that I think of it, I underestimated the difficulty Mr Eden faced. Not only was he rapidly running out of time' – *and life, Ellie!* – 'he had to hide his clues in text that wouldn't seem out of place on a wedding photograph.'

Polly appeared at Eleanor's side, her bottom lip trembling.

'Whatever is the matter?' Eleanor asked gently.

''Tis all too beautiful, your ladyship. Even more beautiful than Henley Hall. I want to remember every bit, but my brain is already swimming with pictures.'

Eleanor threw Clifford a discreet look, which he acknowledged with a barely perceptible nod. She put a hand on the young girl's shoulder. 'Don't worry, Polly, I think there is a way we can make sure you can remember your visit. But you'll have to wait until the last room, alright?'

'Thank you, your ladyship.' She bobbed a curtsey and went over to Mrs Butters, who gave the young girl's cheeks a squeeze before straightening her hat and tidying her scarf.

Eleanor turned to Clifford. 'Please make sure you purchase the glossiest guidebook in the gift shop at the end. Whatever the price. The household accounts will survive that one tiny extravagance, even on top of the new pair of slippers we owe the ladies' landlady.'

'It was already on my to-do list, my lady,' he said, pulling a small sheet covered in meticulous writing from his pocket.

'So thoughtful, as always. Right, now we are sure this is the right place, let's see what other clues the guide can give us.'

But almost two hours later, having passed through the dramatic music room, the opulent red drawing room and myriad gold reception rooms, Clifford and Eleanor had found no more clues. As they entered the King's Apartments, they shook their heads at each other. The guide was, to Eleanor's mind, making a meal of finishing up his over-loquacious talk for the afternoon.

'Although it is, of course, now the People's Palace. It was sold by Queen Victoria to Brighton Council in 1850 for the princely sum of fifty-three thousand pounds.' This drew a gasp from the crowd.

'Fancy that, Trotters,' Mrs Butters said, nudging the cook in the ribs.

The guide finally appeared to be winding up. 'Unfortunately, we have run out of time to explore the last snippet of the Pavilion's history as the next tour party is assembling. What was that?' The guide leaned in towards a tall angular man in tweeds standing next to Polly. He listened for a moment, replied in a similarly quiet tone and then nodded, before addressing the crowd again. 'I hope you have enjoyed your visit to the Pavilion today. Please take time to stroll around the wonderful gardens before you leave.'

As the crowd dispersed, Eleanor caught Polly's whisperings to Mrs Butters.

'That doesn't sound right at all. It can't be that the guide gentleman is wrong because he's so clever, Mrs Butters, but he and the tall gentleman said that the Pavilion was borrowed. I thought you only borrowed favours, or flour, or such like?'

Eleanor spun round, but Clifford was already heading towards the tall gentleman. He was soon in deep discussion, nodding and following the direction of the man's earnest pointing and gesticulating. Clifford shook the man's hand, who strode off in the direction of the exit.

Eleanor hurried up to Clifford.

'So?' she said eagerly.

'The gentleman has been of great assistance. He has provided further information relating to the rhyme on the photograph.'

Before he could say any more, the three ladies joined them, chattering enthusiastically.

'It was wonderful, wasn't it?' Eleanor said. 'Shall we top it off with one more treat? I suggest ice cream.' While Polly clapped in glee, Eleanor pointed through the exit to a candy-striped awning. 'Mrs Butters, would you like to secure us five seats in the ice-cream parlour over there, please? Clifford and I will join you in a moment.'

Once the ladies had gone, she rejoined Clifford, who was paying for a large, glossy guide to the Pavilion.

'For Polly,' he said.

'Perfect. Now, please tell me what you were talking to that man about before I explode with curiosity. "Something borrowed" was it? That's the third line of the rhyme!'

He nodded. 'The gentleman confirmed that the Pavilion was indeed, recently, "borrowed".'

She shook her head. 'It's a palace. Who borrows a palace for goodness' sake?'

'The army, my lady. Between 1914 and 1916, the Town Council loaned the building to be used for Indian soldiers who had been wounded on the battlefields of the Western Front. It was a suggestion of the king himself. He believed the orientally inspired architecture would make them feel at home and therefore convalesce more quickly.' He glanced back at the mishmash of domes and towers. 'I'm not sure it didn't just confuse them, but you cannot disparage his majesty's generous sentiment.'

She frowned. 'So what has that got to do with anything we've discovered so far? What was Hilary trying to tell me?'

Clifford slipped the guide into his jacket pocket. 'Hopefully, the answer will come to you as you devour, what was it, "scandalous amounts" of ice cream?'

She laughed. 'Hilary obviously didn't know me as well as I imagined. There isn't a single mention of food in any of his clues.'

CHAPTER 38

After having waved off the ladies, they both turned up their collars against the now raw March wind that yanked spitefully at Eleanor's red curls like a petulant sibling.

'At least it makes you feel alive,' she said. 'Unlike poor Hilary and Bert Blunt.' She shook her head. 'Anyway, I need the restorative of a long walk, Clifford. And before you say anything, it is not on account of the amount of ice cream I've just eaten.'

'Of course not, my lady,' he said, falling in step slightly behind her. 'Perhaps it was the three rounds of breakfast? Or the oysters and champagne? Or the hearty lunch and extra-large dessert? However, perhaps a hike across the South Downs might just counter the effects of all three? They are not as high as the Himalayas, but could suffice for a digestion soothing constitutional?'

She tried to give him a withering look, but ruined the effect by laughing at the same time. 'Shall we concentrate on our recent discoveries, rather than my overeating?'

He coughed. 'Apologies, my lady. Where shall we start?'

'At the beginning. "Something old, something new"?'

He shook his head. 'Still a mystery.'

'"Something borrowed, something blue"?'

He nodded. 'Easier. The Pavilion.'

'"And sixpence in her hand"?'

He nodded again. 'Easier still. The price of admission to the Pavilion.'

'Right. So all the clues we've deciphered so far point to the Pavilion.' She frowned. 'Which means?'

'Assuming the clues are designed to lead us to the item everyone seeks, the Pavilion is undoubtedly *not* where Mr Eden hid it.' He gave his customary half bow, leaving Eleanor frowning furiously. He then opened the scrollwork iron gate in front of them. 'Victoria Gardens, my lady. The trees will provide a substantial windbreak.' He gestured forwards along the wide, hard-formed path, neatly edged with low wire fencing to preserve the abundant beds and immaculate swathes of lawn beyond.

They walked on in silence for a few minutes, Eleanor desperate to ask how he had come to the conclusion about the Pavilion, but equally desperate to work it out for herself. She therefore missed the gardens artistically shaped beds of early-flowering sea pinks, planted along low clipped box and cotoneaster hedges. She also missed the long lines of soft pink and purple hellebores woven between snake-thin maple saplings. At the expansive rockery covered in clusters of yellow cinquefoil and pale-green euphorbia, she stopped and turned to him.

'Okay, I give up.'

He coughed. 'I cannot be certain, obviously, my lady, but it seems Mr Eden risked, and regrettably, lost his life for something we cannot as yet fathom. The clues on your wedding photograph must lead to the answer or Mr Eden, if you will forgive me for saying so, had a very inappropriate sense of humour.'

Despite herself, she smiled. 'Gallows humour, I'd call it.'

'Exactly, my lady.'

Understanding dawned in Eleanor's eyes. 'Ah! You're right, of course. Hilary wouldn't have risked it being that easy to figure out. The Pavilion is, what, a blind?'

Clifford shook his head slowly. 'I believe not, my lady. If a single clue pointed to it, perhaps. I guess, and it is a guess, that it is no more than one link, if an important one, in the chain of clues that will lead to… ' He spread his hands and shrugged.

Eleanor resumed walking. 'Well, the only way to find out is to get to the next "link". So let's tackle the first part we don't know.

"Something old."' She glanced around. 'That could be anything. Almost all the buildings along the promenade, or… or a church? There must be heaps of old churches.'

He nodded. 'Heaps, as you put it, my lady.'

'Let's hope it's not that then. That would take weeks, and we've got what feels like a rapidly shortening candle's worth of time before the killer escapes with the item.'

'Or kills again?'

'Exactly.' Her brow creased. 'Have I got something on my face, Clifford? You are looking at me most oddly.'

'No, my lady. I am merely trying to imagine what Mr Eden might have thought you would most likely think of in relation to the clues he provided.'

She winced. 'I thought we'd established he didn't have the chance to get to know me very well, hence the lack of food references. We were only together for a matter of months in truth.'

'It is not always a matter of time, my lady,' he said gently. 'Some people are more… transparent than others, if you will forgive my observation.' He aligned the perfectly straight seam of his leather gloves. 'Actually, I meant honest. And open.'

She cocked her head. 'You mean we've been looking at the rhyme the wrong way?'

'Possibly.' He cleared his throat. 'From the day you arrived at Henley Hall, my lady, it has been fairly simple to glean a reasonable insight into your thoughts.'

'Worrying as that fact is, good shout, Clifford. Let's change tack and try to think like Hilary would have thought I would think.' She shook her head. 'Confusing as that is.'

'Possibly doubly confusing as Mr Eden must have been under a lot of stress, likely knowing he did not have much time, or indeed leeway, to put together his coded message on the photograph.'

The rest of the gardens passed in a blur as Eleanor tramped along, rattling off everything that sprung to mind that could be the 'something old'. And then when they'd tired of that line of thought, anything that could be the 'something new'.

As they neared a low iron gate, Clifford stopped and looked around. 'It seems we have both been distracted and have criss-crossed the park several times and arrived back at the Pavilion, albeit at a different point. One moment while I get my bearings... Ah! We are at the southern end, I believe, my lady.'

'Excuse me, please,' a man's voice said. 'I do beg your pardon for interrupting, but this is a works site.'

Eleanor turned to see a slender Indian man, dressed in a smart blue suit, topped with a protective calico jacket.

'What works, can I ask?'

'For the new gateway, miss.'

'*New*,' she repeated, staring at Clifford, 'gateway?'

The man nodded and smiled broadly. 'To honour the Indian soldiers who came to the hospitals in Brighton, including those who had the privilege of being treated in the Pavilion itself. His Highness the Maharaja of Patiala will perform the ceremony of unveiling and dedicating the new gateway and presenting it to the Corporation of Brighton for the use of its inhabitants.'

Eleanor looked round at the initial diggings and piles of beautiful hand-cut cream stone.

'When is the unveiling to be held?'

'In October, miss, seven months away. But we have much work to do. I must complete my survey, if you will be so kind as to step on past the sign.'

'Sign?'

He pointed to a green board emblazoned with large white block-printed lettering. 'The one that asks most politely if visitors to the gardens would not cross beyond this line.' He grinned at her. 'But perhaps we should have made it larger?'

'Apologies, we were somewhat distracted,' Clifford said.

'Even more so now,' Eleanor muttered as they moved away. 'Do you think this could be the "something new", Clifford?'

'Perhaps. The gateway's intended purpose is related to the "something borrowed" element of the Pavilion. As the gentleman said, it is to honour the Indian soldiers treated there, among others.'

She peered past his shoulder. 'Mind you, it's so new it's nothing but two holes in the ground and a few poles driven in as markers. I'm not convinced. The only place he could have hidden anything would be in one of those holes.'

Clifford spoke to the man again and returned. 'It seems the holes were only made this morning.'

She sighed. 'Then I think we'll treat this as a red herring for the moment and keep on looking, but I feel we're running out of options. And time.'

CHAPTER 39

Despite the cutting wind and failing light, they took one more tour of Victoria Gardens in the hope of inspiration striking, but to no avail. Back outside the Pavilion where they had started, they called it a day and headed towards the Grand.

Before they had gone twenty paces, the sound of high-pitched giggling made Eleanor wince. Walking towards them were three young ladies accompanied by an older man, obviously their chaperone. Eleanor gauged they were not yet in their twenties, and they looked as if they had all stepped from the front cover of a society magazine. Toting rolled up pink-and-cream parasols, the young women were deep in conversation.

'But I missed his visit,' the tallest of the three wailed as they came to a stop only a few steps from Eleanor and Clifford. 'How often does one have such a distinguished visitor in one's home town, not to mention a royal one? Oh, I can't believe Hubert had booked a trip for us to see Aunt Matilda over those two days. Brothers! I could scream!'

Eleanor hid a smile.

'Esme dear,' the shortest of the three said, 'you missed out "handsome, witty, charming and next in line to the throne". To say nothing of utterly delicious.' This brought on more high-pitched giggles from the other two.

The third girl spoke. 'Do you know, though, I still don't know why he was here.'

'Apparently to unveil some dreadfully dull new memorial,' Esme said. 'Something to do with the war, they always are.'

Eleanor's ears had pricked up. *There's that word 'new' again, Ellie!* She thought fast and stepped in front of them. 'Forgive my disgraceful eavesdropping, ladies, but I heard the words "handsome" and "charming" and my stomach filled with butterflies. Are you talking about who I think you are?'

'Oh yes, he was here,' the taller of the young women answered. She twirled in a circle. 'Edward, Prince of Wales, no less! And Ophelia and I managed to get into the evening ball, while Esme was stuck drinking warm milk with her aged aunt.'

'Poor thing. She'll probably never recover.' They turned to Esme, who was still pouting.

Eleanor threw the young woman her best sympathetic look. 'You must be most sore you missed the chance to dance with him.'

'Oh no more than my friends,' Esme replied, brightening. 'These two may have wheedled their way into the ball, but they were relegated to the upper balcony. Lucky no one noticed how much they were dribbling down onto the dance floor.'

The others stared at her for a split second before all three clutched each other and walked on, still shrieking and giggling. Their chaperone gave Eleanor a long-suffering look, tipped his hat, and followed them.

'His royal highness had a most honourable reason for visiting,' a familiar voice said.

Eleanor started, but then smiled at the surveyor they had spoken to earlier. 'You heard their conversation too then?'

'It is my humble estimation, miss, that most of the occupants of the park may have done so.' He bobbed his head. 'No disrespect intended.'

She laughed. 'None supposed. Well, assuming my ears can still function, would you mind telling us why exactly the Prince of Wales was in Brighton?'

'It would be my pleasure. His highness is a most honourable gentleman who wishes to continue the good relations between our countries and our citizens. As do the people of Brighton who have raised a considerable sum. Not only for the Pavilion Gate we are building but also for another new memorial called the "Chattri". It is the memorial one of the young ladies mentioned. It's English translation is "umbrella" or "canopy".'

Her heart skipped. 'And this memorial, it's built? I mean finished?'

'Yes, indeed.'

'And is it connected to the Pavilion?' Clifford asked tentatively.

'Oh very much so, sir. It is a most gratifying memorial to the brave soldiers from my country who did not recover, despite the generous medical care afforded at the Pavilion while it was a hospital.'

'That is truly wonderful,' Eleanor said genuinely. 'And is it… *really new?*'

The surveyor nodded enthusiastically. 'So new, it is not yet appearing on any maps. There has not even been time to build a proper path to it.'

You can't get much newer than that, Ellie!

'And where is it located?' Clifford asked. 'And how do we find it, if it is not on any map?'

The surveyor pointed over the town towards the South Downs. 'It is situated up on the hills, overlooking the town and sea on the spot where the soldiers were cremated. It is a beautifully, peaceful setting, five and a half miles north from this very spot. But you will have to get directions from the tourist office as there is only a footpath from the town and it is hard to find if you do not know it.'

Once out of earshot, Eleanor turned to Clifford.

'Could the Chattri be the "something new" do you think?'

Clifford thought for a moment. 'Might I ask, if it is not prying, if you ever mentioned your late uncle's military service abroad to Mr Eden?'

She shrugged. 'I didn't know that much about it before I came to live at the Hall. I told Hilary all I knew about Uncle Byron spending a lot of time in India, though. And that I had been there on my travels as well.'

Clifford nodded. 'So, I believe we can conclude that Mr Eden would have deduced you would have worked out the Indian connection among his clues. And that you would therefore have also made the link between the Pavilion and the Chattri at some point, my lady.'

She nodded. 'And Hilary was out from morning to evening the day before he was killed. He could have made it to the Chattri and back in that time.' She glanced around. 'It's probably best for us to go after dark, I'd say. It's too easy to be seen and followed during the day.'

'Indeed, but at night it is equally hard to spot someone following you. Plus the only access is by a rough track according to the gentleman's account, which at night—'

She held up a hand. 'If you mention the word "prudence", I shall scream so shrill you will wish Esme, Ophelia and whoever the other girl was were your company for the evening.'

'Very good, my lady. Although if I might caution—'

'No, Clifford. You may not. Instead, after we've nipped back to the hotel for a layer of warmer underthings, you can find us somewhere discreet where we can indulge in some much-needed fortification while we wait until night falls.'

CHAPTER 40

The Metropole's bar hummed with busy chatter. With that night's clientele being mostly male, Eleanor's arrival turned even more heads than usual. She felt the bore of several appraising looks follow her rear view all the way to the table she chose in the furthest corner. Flattered, but not in the mood, she slid into one of the low seats facing the enormous windows.

Clifford joined her, having sorted their coats and drinks order.

'Let's hope we're both feeling razor sharp,' she said as she smoothed her notebook open. 'I brought the list you wrote out on our walk back too.'

'I might be incorrect, my lady, but I believe we may not need it.'

She caught her breath. 'What? You mean you've worked out the last clue, "something old"?'

'Possibly. I'm hopeful my suggestion will strike a chord with you.'

'Well, don't dance round the bushes. Out with it. I'm on tenterhooks.'

Before he could speak, a rather over-enthusiastic waiter appeared with their drinks. She waved away the appetiser menu he offered. Then had to bite her tongue as he started to walk them through the hotel's planned entertainment for the evening.

'We shan't be staying,' Clifford cut in. 'But thank you.'

'So?' she hissed as soon as they were alone again. 'What made you think of the answer?'

'Tolstoy, my lady.'

She frowned. 'We haven't got time for riddles.'

'Agreed. Perhaps therefore if I might be allowed to answer your question?' At the flap of her hand, he continued. 'I was waiting to meet you in the lobby of the Grand while running back and forth over the ideas we had for the last clue. Then Miss Summers emerged from the lift and I was reminded of a line from *Anna Karenina*.'

Eleanor rolled her eyes. 'Clifford, really, I don't want to hear that even you have fallen for Miss Summers' curves.'

He tutted. 'My lady, nothing could be further from the thought that struck me as she passed.'

'Oops, sorry. It's still eating me up that I don't know the truth about her and Hilary.'

'Understandably. However, the point is, I was reminded of your telling me how Miss Summers had been staring so intently at you over breakfast recently. And it brought to mind the lines where Anna Karenina is appraising the looks of Liza Merkalova.'

Eleanor shrugged, not having made it past the first few chapters of the novel despite it being part of her English Literature lessons years ago at school. 'What does Anna Karenina say?'

'It is not what she says, it is what she thinks about Liza. "There was in her the glow of the real diamond among glass imitations."' He sat back in his seat.

'Dash it. Clifford. You're making me feel like a complete dunce. What am I missing?'

He stayed silent, holding her stare.

'Look, I don't want to play ga—' But then her hand flew to her mouth. 'Oh my!'

He nodded.

'Diamonds,' she whispered. 'The "something old" refers to diamonds!'

He nodded again. 'Diamonds are one of the oldest minerals on earth. And South African diamond mines control around ninety per cent of the world's production. However, I cannot be certain.'

'I can.'

He looked at her quizzically. In a trice, he produced a pristine handkerchief, then busied himself aligning his glass with the very centre of the bar mat underneath.

'Sorry,' she muttered through a large sniff.

'No, my sincerest of apologies, my lady. I had no idea that suggestion might upset you.'

'Don't be daft. Of course you couldn't possibly have known. Oh, Clifford, I've been a total dunce on that score. It's so obvious now.' She wiped her eyes and fiddled with the handkerchief. 'Actually, I know I buried the memory because it is the polar opposite of how things turned out.'

He waited as she took a large swig of her drink and then wiped her eyes again.

'Our marriage was a simple affair with two witnesses we'd talked into coming along as neither of us had any family out in South Africa.' She smiled at him apologetically. 'I didn't invite Uncle Byron because I was afraid he would disapprove, seeing as Hilary and I had only met for the first time a matter of months before. And the wedding was a spur-of-the-moment decision, anyway. He would have missed it, seeing as it took me forty-five days to travel from Cape Town to London by air! In retrospect, I'd have been better going overland.'

Clifford gave her a rare smile. 'His lordship always said your affairs of the heart would likely be the end of him. But he would have crawled all the way on his knees if it meant he could have given you away at the altar.'

'I realise that now, but as you know my relationship with Uncle Byron back then was a little… distant. And I wish you had been there too, truly. But if you had both been there, you would have heard what Hilary declared to the room just before we exchanged vows.' She took a deep breath. 'That he was the happiest man alive and wanted nothing more than to grow old with the woman before him who…' She swallowed hard. '… would still be the most beautiful diamond ever created when she was old too.'

'A wonderful sentiment, my lady. One better remembered than buried, perhaps? And not because of our investigation.'

She smiled. 'I'll let you know later.'

'I appreciate you having shared your memory, my lady. I wonder, do you have the fortitude for some more information I gleaned?'

She took a much-needed sip of her drink and nodded.

'Very good. After I had the revelation that the "something old" might be diamonds, I visited the hotel's library, which is the room we interviewed Mr Franklin in recently. Among other items, it holds copies of *The Times*, the *Guardian* and the local newspaper, the *Brighton Gazette*. They are ironed and then meticulously filed in date order.'

She laughed. 'I bet you were in neat-and-tidy heaven rifling through them, weren't you?'

He adjusted his tie. 'I did not "rifle", my lady. I was methodical in my search because I had discovered another fact about the Pavilion.'

'Which was?'

'That amongst the various uses to which the building has been put, its time as a hospital for wounded Indian soldiers was not the only occasion it was "borrowed". Shortly afterwards, between 1916 and 1920, it was used to treat British soldiers, notably those who had suffered the loss of a limb or limbs.'

'Oh goodness, those poor men.'

'Indeed. After treatment and a programme of rehabilitation, a local trust worked hard to secure employment for them. This became a great deal easier from 1917 when the philanthropist, Mr Bernard Oppenheimer, established a six-month scheme to train them in the art of… diamond cutting!'

Eleanor's mouth dropped. 'What? Here in Brighton?'

'Here, as you say, in Brighton. The Bernard Oppenheimer Diamond Works opened the following year, and all the soldiers leaving the Pavilion's temporary hospital were guaranteed employment at a good wage. The factory even houses a clinic to continue to care for the men.'

She shook her head. 'How wonderful that someone was looking out for those who fought for their country.' Her eyes widened. 'That's it! It's been nagging at my mind. When we talked to Longley, he said when he and Blunt learned that Hilary had booked a ticket to England, they thought he was just fleeing his enemies. But when they tracked him to Brighton—'

'"Then it all made sense." Well remembered, my lady.'

Something else tugged at her brain. 'And perhaps that's what de Meyer meant when he said the item was valuable to the "right person"? Most of us wouldn't know what to do with a… well, handful of rough diamonds, I suppose. But a diamond cutter! So it seems the mystery of what everyone is after and why Hilary chose Brighton out of all the towns in England is solved.'

'It seems so, my lady.'

'And you know what else? I bet de Meyer's employers own a South African diamond mine.' She shook her head again. 'Poor Hilary, killed for a bag of rocks! Such a senseless waste. I—' Her eye caught Clifford's. There was a look in them she'd only seen twice before. 'What is it, Clifford? You look uncharacteristically worried?'

He cleared his throat. 'When the revelation that the "something old" might refer to diamonds, I confess my heart sank. And, in truth, I hoped you would dismiss it out of hand as meaning nothing to you, or Mr Eden.'

'Because?'

'Because ruthless people have killed to possess diamonds for hundreds, if not thousands, of years. I said several days ago that if we were to possess the mysterious item, the murderer would come to us for sure, hence my heightened concerns for your safety.'

She folded her arms. 'We're still going out there.'

'I knew that would be your response. But, my lady—'

'But nothing. You'd have to lock me in the trunk of the Rolls to stop me going to the Chattri tonight.'

'I confess that idea did occur,' he said without humour.

'As always your solicitude is greatly appreciated. However, we can't tell the police because Grimsdale will just arrest us on the spot for withholding evidence. And consorting with known criminals and goodness' knows what else. Besides, he's cocksure he has Hilary's murderer under lock and key. He wouldn't listen to a word we said.' She rose, downing the last of her drink. 'But enough fortitude. Let's go and get ready.'

For once, Clifford failed to follow suit and remained sitting. Slowly, she sat back down and nodded to him to continue. He cleared his throat again.

'My lady, I'm not sure you realise that if there is a single diamond, let alone a handful, hidden at the Chattri, it will bring out every cutthroat from here to Cape Town. We have faced some dangerous adversaries in the past, but I have always been confident that we could defeat them as we usually have an idea of who we were dealing with. And' – he looked at her pointedly – 'a plan.'

She nodded. 'I understand what you're saying and I'm not suggesting that we don't take precautions. I may be a little… headstrong now and then, but I'm not suicidal. I'll take your advice and—' A commotion a few tables away interrupted her. Two men were greeting each other like long-lost relatives. Once they'd quietened down and wandered over to the bar, arms around each other's shoulders, she turned back to Clifford, a glint in her eyes.

'Actually, Clifford, you are wrong on two counts.'

He cocked his head and waited for her to continue.

'Firstly, we know exactly who we're dealing with.'

The look of surprise on the face of her normally inscrutable butler made her smile, despite the gravity of their conversation.

'You mean, my lady, you've worked out—?'

She nodded and rose again. This time he did the same.

As they walked out into the gathering gloom, he coughed. 'And the second point I was wrong about?'

'The plan.'

'Ah! So we have a plan, my lady?'

'Not yet,' she called over her shoulder, 'but we will have.'

CHAPTER 41

In the dark, the car swept round the last bend, before slowing down to walking pace and pulling off the road through a gap in the bushes. It bumped along for a few feet, its headlights illuminating the wildly swaying gorse. Then the engine stopped, and the headlights cut out. Darkness returned.

Through the windscreen, Eleanor could just make out black clouds scudding across the dark sky. As the clouds passed in front of the waning moon, they were briefly illuminated, like a fox caught in a car's headlights, before once more fading into the inky background.

'The Rolls should be reasonably hidden from the road here, my lady,' Clifford said. 'From now on, we are on foot.'

Eleanor nodded and took a deep breath. *Come on, Ellie, one way or another, you'll have the answer before the night's out.*

They walked along the road in silence, buffeted by the wind. After a couple of minutes, they picked out the beginning of the path to the Chattri. Clifford clicked on his torch, but kept it pointing downwards.

'The height and thickness of the gorse should largely obscure the torchlight from a distance. It is a risk, but one I feel we need to make.'

As they set off up the rough track Eleanor wanted to believe it was the glacial wind that was making her shiver. But she knew it was Clifford's words in the Metropole bar. Her thoughts were interrupted by a gust so strong, it pushed her into him.

'I'm sorry, my lady,' he said, keeping his voice low.

'Not your fault, Clifford. I didn't come prepared for a pitched battle with nature either.'

He cleared his throat quietly. 'Hopefully, my lady, you didn't come prepared for a pitched battle with anything or anyone. I do not remember it being in our plan?'

Her determined smile was lost in the darkness. 'Don't worry, Clifford, I don't intend to fight—' She stifled a cry of pain as sharp gorse whipped against her face like the vicious lash of a hunting crop. 'Anything except this wretched stuff! Let's get going.'

The surveyor had been right. The path was nothing more than a rutted track. Clinging to the side of a vast chalk hill of the South Downs, it was barely wide enough for the two of them to stumble along. To their left, the ground fell away steeply as they wound their way uphill. Sharp flints tripped them up, while water-filled potholes soaked their feet.

'How much further do you think it is?' she said as Clifford paused beside her.

He examined the compass he was carrying by the torchlight. The pale-orange light lit his face with a ghostly glow. He turned a few degrees left then right before pointing off to one side.

'This is where the track seems to turn briefly away from due north. I believe the Chattri is probably another ten minutes ahead.' He took a deep breath and aimed the torch at the ground again. 'I am still greatly perturbed, my lady.'

She squared her shoulders. 'Come on, Clifford. We've been over this a dozen times this afternoon. I told you your influence would eventually rub off, and it has. You searched Franklin's room without a plan, and I've come here *with* a plan. You see, role reversal. I even adopted your belt and braces approach.'

'Most commendable, my lady, but I fear belts and braces may be poor defences against bullets.'

'Well, let's hope it doesn't come to that. Now, we'd better get moving.'

As they continued, their intention to turn off their torches while they were still a way from the Chattri proved impossible. Apart from a few fleeting moments, the cloud had thickened and now obscured the moon. The hairs on Eleanor's arms stood up. What was that noise? Just the wind? Or…? She shook her head. The night was dark enough, the undergrowth thick enough and the wind loud enough to hide an army of assassins following them. She grumbled under her breath as she almost turned her ankle for the umpteenth time.

Keep it together, Ellie. We must be nearly there.

At that moment, Clifford pointed up to the right. The clouds had parted and a white dome was visible a few hundred feet further up the hill. The Chattri. She imagined the Indian soldiers who had been cremated on that very spot and their ashes scattered in the English Channel. On a less inclement day, it would be a beautiful place. Lowering her head against the gale, she concentrated on where she was treading and soon covered the distance to the Chattri without twisting an ankle.

As she reached the levelled ground, the enormity of the task hit her. She joined Clifford at the bottom of the twenty wide stone steps that ran up to the memorial itself and looked around in dismay. All the while her thoughts ran over and over the rhyme Hilary had inscribed on their wedding photograph. She closed her eyes. *Well, I'm here, Hilary. Talk to me.* But only the whistling of the wind around the Chattri's pillars answered her.

With no immediate inspiration, she sighed and turned to Clifford. 'I'll take the left side of the memorial, you take the right.'

She started up the steps, keeping her torch close to the ground. Clifford materialised next to her, making her clutch her chest.

'Forgive my contrary view, my lady, but time is likely not on our side. Perhaps the dome of the memorial itself is too obvious a place to begin looking. Would not Mr Eden have been more discreet after the lengths he took to hide the location of the object? Perhaps under the steps first?'

She shook her head. 'No, I don't believe so. However reprehensible some of Hilary's actions may turn out to have been, he understood the suffering endured by the men this memorial is dedicated to. Their cremations would probably have taken place on the three stone terraces, or ghats, either side of the steps. I simply can't believe he was such a scoundrel as to disrespect that.'

'Most heartening to hear you feel that way, my lady.'

Under the small hollow dome itself, shining her torch judiciously, Eleanor stared round at the closely spaced marble pillars, each no further apart than the width of a broad man's shoulders. Sleek and simple in its design, the structure suggested no immediate places to search. No architectural recesses or corners, just elegant columns supporting a simple dome.

Eleanor pulled off her gloves and ran a hand over the small section of raised carving at the base of one of the pillars. She looked up to where Clifford's torch beam was sweeping back and forth across the inside of the dome's roof and shook her head. *We're missing something, Ellie.* She called Clifford to her side with a low whistle.

'My lady?'

'Listen. Hilary would have known that when I got here, I would likely be in a great hurry and possibly danger.'

'Absolutely.'

'So he wouldn't have expected me to scour every inch in the hope of stumbling across his hiding place. He's told me already where it is, I know it. I just haven't heard him.'

Clifford stood silently waiting, constantly watching every shadow. Eleanor closed her eyes again. *Come on Captain Hilary Montgomery Eden, tell me where to look!* Only the wind replied again, mockingly whipping her curls around her face so she couldn't concentrate. She sighed in frustration.

'Clifford, what's the one thing that Hilary could be certain about me knowing if I deciphered his clues and got this far?'

His brow furrowed and then cleared. He coughed gently. 'The one thing that Mr Eden could be certain about is that you would know... he was dead, my lady.'

She nodded sadly. 'Yes, you're right. We're only here because he's dead. Wait!' Something pricked at her brain. Something about Hilary's death... *That's it, Ellie! When Grimsdale took you to room 204. You saw the desk where Hilary died and then he asked you about Hilary's watch!*

She scanned the memorial. The eight pillars that supported the roof ran down to a low wall that formed the base of the monument.

'Clifford, check the inside of the wall. You're looking for a leather strap. The sort Hilary hung his watch from.'

She climbed between two pillars and jumped down beside the memorial itself. Dropping to her haunches, she ran her hand along the capping of the platform's base. She caught her breath as it closed around a weighty velvet bag, held by a leather strap jammed in a crack. As she pulled the bag free, a square of folded paper fell into her palm. Clifford stepped down beside her.

'Well done, my lady.' He shone the torch on her hands, looking over each shoulder as he held the light still.

With trembling fingers, Eleanor unfolded the paper.

Ellie, my darling wife,

If you are reading this, I am no more of this world. And my only sadness is that I will never have had a chance to say in person what has burned in my heart all these years.

I have done some bad things in my time. That they were borne of necessity before habit is no excuse and deserves no forgiveness. But I came to Brighton in the hope I could put right my biggest wrong, which was to you. And if I can give you nothing else, please leave knowing that my intention was never to do wrong by you, never to desert you, nor break your heart.

Ellie, you were my only world from the day we met. So bright, so bold, adventure should have been your middle name (You know 'Lettice' always made me smile).

Her hand went to her lips as she let out a silent sob.

Even before I read about your travels, I knew if our story ever came to such a sad ending, our spiritual connection would remain and you would work out the trail I would be forced to leave you.

In trying to make things right between us, however, I've made the situation worse. And I've placed you in peril. But when I heard that you had inherited your uncle's estate, I thought all was lost unless I could truly provide for you. Like the husband I should have been all along. The contents of the bag were to be my offering for a new start. My all-consuming apology.

Sorry, is not enough.
Ellie, I will love you forever.

Hilary xxx

'It's more than enough,' she whispered as she kissed the note before placing it carefully into her coat pocket. Wiping the tears from her cheeks, her mind whirled as her fingers fumbled with the knotted drawstring of the velvet bag. Clifford shone the torch for her.

'Is it a bag of uncut diamonds as we suspected, my lady?'

But before she could reply, a voice cut through the darkness. 'I think you will find the answer is no.'

CHAPTER 42

They both slowly turned around. A man's dark shape stood on the second to top step with, what Eleanor took to be, a pistol in his hand. He walked up until he was level with her and Clifford.

'As I said, I think you will find there aren't diamonds in that bag. However, I must congratulate you, Lady Swift. You are quite the detective, aren't you?' His civilised tone was incongruous with the gun he held. 'As I mentioned before, Hilary was right about you.'

She nodded. 'Yes, I have discovered that he was. And I was right about him. But Clifford was right all along, too. He said if I had this' – she held up the velvet bag – 'the murderer would come to me, Mr de Meyer.'

De Meyer eyed the bag. 'An astute observation.'

She swallowed hard. Talking in the warm and civilised Metropole bar about how they would lure the killer to the Chattri and then deal with him was one thing. It was quite another to actually do so on a freezing March night on the wild coastal hills high above the town. She glanced down at the twinkling lights of Brighton far below, briefly dreaming of this all being over and her and Clifford sharing a celebratory drink.

De Meyer's voice brought her back to the present with a jolt. 'So, Lady Swift, it's up to you how this ends.'

She nodded slowly. 'Yes, I suppose it is.' She took a deep breath. 'Well, Mr de Meyer, as we know you are *not* the murderer, let's see if the real murderer is here, shall we?' She looked past de Meyer out into the darkness. Raising her voice against the wind she called out. 'Why are you still skulking in the shadows?' She held the velvet bag aloft again. 'Here it is. This is what you've killed for. Twice.'

Behind de Meyer, a shadowy figure appeared silently on the steps. This one, however, carried a longer, darker shape. A shotgun or rifle, Eleanor judged.

She leaned towards de Meyer. 'I suggest you don't turn around. I believe our killer has come forearmed, as it were.'

A voice rang out around the Chattri. 'That's right. I've got a rifle pointed at your back, de Meyer. Drop your pistol.'

The barrel of de Meyer's gun swung round his index finger as he spread his hands wide. He placed the gun carefully on the stone floor.

'Now join the others,' the voice said.

As de Meyer moved across to stand next to Eleanor, she shook her head discreetly at Clifford. He hesitated, but then dropped his hand from his inside pocket.

The shadowy figure stepped up level with the dome itself, with the rifle trained on Eleanor. 'Good evening, Lady Swift. Or should I call you Miss Swanson?'

She smiled coldly. 'Lady Swift will do fine, Thomas.'

The clerk shrugged. 'Whatever you like. Now we've dispensed with the pleasantries, open that bag.'

'Of course.' She balanced the bag in one outstretched palm and slid the other hand inside. A frisson ran down her spine, her fingers tingling. She held it up. The item looked like a lump of grey rock about the size of the paperweight on her desk back at the Hall. But even in its rough form, in the torchlight it sparkled like no paperweight she'd seen.

For a moment everyone was spellbound.

Beside her, de Meyer smiled. 'You see, it wasn't a bag of diamonds. It was *one* diamond. A magnificent, uncut specimen of unimaginable exquisiteness. One of the biggest to ever come from my employer's mines, in fact.'

She arched a brow at him. 'Why didn't you say so yesterday afternoon when we talked?'

'What?' Thomas frowned in confusion, pointing the rifle at de Meyer and then back at her.

Ignoring him, de Meyer winked at Eleanor. 'I never trust anyone completely, Lady Swift. But now you understand why my employers are so determined to have it returned.'

Clifford cleared his throat, his eyes not moving from Thomas and the rifle he still held squarely in Eleanor's direction. 'Mr de Meyer, that diamond must be worth a king's ransom.'

He nodded.

Eleanor shook her head. 'Maybe. But it wasn't worth a man's life. Let alone two.'

Thomas took a step forward and jammed the rifle against one hip, his hand held fast to the trigger. With the other, he reached out, making her shudder when his fingers brushed hers as he lifted the diamond from her palm. 'Now, that is where you're wrong. This *was* worth two. Mr Eden's and Mr Blunt's.' He shrugged. 'Small sacrifices, I think.' With the deftness of an illusionist, the diamond disappeared into his coat pocket.

De Meyer smiled laconically. 'Don't become attached to that, Thomas, you won't be keeping it for long.'

Thomas laughed. 'I'm the one with the gun. And the diamond.'

De Meyer shrugged, the smile still playing on his lips.

'There is one thing I'd like to know, Thomas,' Eleanor said calmly. 'If, of course, that is your real name.' She looked at de Meyer, who shrugged again. She sighed. 'Honestly, are Clifford and I the only people at the Grand who aren't using false names?'

Thomas waved the rifle at the three of them. 'Stop talking!'

Eleanor stepped forward. 'As you failed to reply, I'll answer the question for you. No, it isn't your real name.'

Thomas' tone was shrill. 'Move another step and I'll shoot you dead where you stand, do you hear?'

Eleanor's voice was colder than the wind whistling around the Chattri. 'At least you'll have the decency to look me in the face when you kill me. I thought you normally stabbed people in the back or got them drunk on chloroform and alcohol and pushed them off balconies.'

Thomas shook his head slowly. 'Oh, no, I'm not that stupid. What do you think I'm going to do? Confess to killing Eden and Blunt? This isn't one of those ridiculous detective novels.'

'Shame. I'm rather fond of them, as Clifford will vouch. Won't you, Clifford?'

'Indeed, my lady.'

A rifle shot rang around the Chattri.

Thomas smirked. 'There, that got your attention! The next one won't be aimed at the sky, but at—'

'You, Mr *Eden*.'

The look on Thomas' face would have made Eleanor laugh at any other time, but she wasn't in a laughing mood.

De Meyer stood behind Thomas, holding a pistol in his back. He nodded to Eleanor. 'Thank you for the diversion, Lady Swift.'

She nodded and smiled grimly. 'No problem, Mr de Meyer, it's included in the ticket price.' She turned back to Thomas. 'That is your real surname, isn't it? *Eden?*'

'Shut up!' Thomas' voice shook with barely controlled rage. He hesitated for a split second, then raised his gun and fired at Eleanor. In that instant, somehow Clifford materialised between her and the rifle.

As the sound of the shot died away, she reached out to him in horror.

He coughed. 'Apologies, my lady. Force of habit. Just in case.'

She smiled. 'Thank you, Clifford.'

At the sound of the second shot, another shape had appeared out of the dark. The man ran up the steps and stopped in front of Eleanor.

'Thank God!' DCI Seldon turned and in one fluid movement disarmed Thomas, knocking him to the ground.

'Impressive,' de Meyer said. 'I didn't realise English policemen were so well trained.'

'I fought in the war like everyone else,' Seldon said curtly. He bent down and pulled Thomas to his feet. The clerk looked at Eleanor in disbelief.

De Meyer smiled. 'You look confused, Thomas. Let me explain. Your rifle was loaded with blanks. I broke into your room this evening before you came here, found your secret store and replaced the bullets with blanks myself. A suggestion from Lady Swift. Apparently, the same trick saved her husband's life once. Unfortunately for him, only once.'

As Seldon took the diamond out of Thomas' pocket, Thomas moved to stop him. A sharp dig in the back from de Meyer's pistol dissuaded him. Seldon held up the diamond and looked at de Meyer.

'As Mr Eden had this at the time of his death, this belongs to his wife until proved otherwise.' He passed it over to Eleanor. Thomas and de Meyer's eyes never left it.

She cupped it in her hands. *Hilary died for this, Ellie. And Blunt.*

She held it out. 'Mr de Meyer I believe this belongs to your employers. Legally, that is. Morally I feel it belongs to whichever poor soul was forced to risk his life to dig it out.'

He took the rock and slipped it into his pocket. 'Thank you, Lady Swift. I will see that it is returned to my employers on the terms we agreed earlier.'

Eleanor turned to Thomas, whose eyes were fixed on the pocket where de Meyer had placed the diamond.

'You know, Thomas, I didn't come to Brighton in March to lounge on the beach. But neither did I come to bury my husband. You see, however briefly, Hilary *was* my husband... I loved him. I always loved him.' She paused and swallowed hard. She had to know. 'But now I am going to bury him, I need to know something, Thomas *Eden*. Why did you kill your own brother?'

CHAPTER 43

A flicker of something Eleanor couldn't place crossed Thomas' features. He looked up at her.

'Hilary was my brother, *once.* But he made his choice.' His face twisted with anger. 'And that choice didn't include me!'

She shook her head. 'Was it just greed? You wanted the diamond all to yourself?'

Thomas laughed bitterly. 'You really didn't know much about Hilary before you married him, did you?'

'I didn't know about you,' she replied quietly. 'Maybe if I had I could have prevented all this but—'

'But he never mentioned his kid brother, did he?' Thomas ran a hand through his hair. 'Ironic, isn't it? We stole together as kids. And now, here we are, what could have been my biggest moment, but my big brother isn't here to see it.'

She failed to stop her words tumbling out. 'Only because you murdered him.'

He glared at her. 'You have no right to judge me. You don't understand. We grew up here in Brighton, but back then two gangs ran everything. Split Brighton and all the nearby towns in two, they did. Hilary and I used to pickpocket for one of them when we were still nippers. Course we had to hand over what we'd stolen and take what they handed back, which was just enough to make sure we had to keep stealing to survive.' He shrugged. 'We didn't have any choice once Dad died. We had nothing. Mum tried, but she couldn't even make enough for us to eat.'

Verity Bright

De Meyer glanced at his watch but kept the pistol trained on Thomas.

Eleanor shook her head. 'I wasn't judging what you had to do to survive. But' – she held out her hands – 'how did it lead to this?'

He shrugged. 'After years of trying to live off the pittance the gang let us keep, Hilary thought he was old enough and smart enough to outwit them. So he set up on his own.'

'But you were too scared to join him?'

He laughed harshly. 'No! I was too bright, for all the good that did me. Stupid idiot, the police caught him doing a job and told the gang leader. Yeah, that's right.' He looked scornfully at Seldon. 'Most coppers were on the make in them days. Anyway, one night they came for Hilary, only he saw them coming and got away and fled the country.' His eyes darkened. 'But they found me and told me I'd have to take my big brother's punishment.' He paused and swallowed. He looked as if after all these years he was still reliving the memory in his mind. 'They gave me the beating of my life.'

Eleanor's breath shortened. 'I don't believe Hilary knew that would happen.'

His eyes flashed. 'Who cares? He ran out on me just as he ran out on you. I was in hospital for three months. When I finally got out, I had to flee Brighton. I swore Hilary would pay one day. Then the war came along, but in between dodging bullets and praying the trenches wouldn't collapse and bury me alive, I never forgot my big brother. After the war I drifted from town to town, petty thieving. Then I met a man who told me he'd gone from picking pockets on the street to stealing from the guests in the hotel where he worked. Much easier and richer pickings. I knew the gangs in Brighton had been wiped out by the war, so I returned and got myself a job in the first hotel that would take me. And then I worked my way up to the most expensive.'

'The Grand,' Eleanor said.

'Yeah, the Grand. It was easy pickings. So long as I kept the amounts small and infrequent, the manager just compensated the guests in exchange for not making a fuss. All plush hotels do the same. They know some of their staff steal, but what with the roaming pickpockets and con artists who target guests as well, it's too much trouble, and potential scandal, to root it out. Let sleeping dogs lie, is their motto.'

Eleanor's mind was churning all this over. 'But it wasn't coincidence Hilary came to stay at the Grand, was it? You told him to come, didn't you?'

Thomas nodded. 'Four letters in fifteen years. That's all I got from him. And the fourth was to tell me he was coming to England to put right his biggest wrong. Which was to his wife he'd only known for five minutes, not me, his only brother. Evidently the mess he left me in didn't qualify as a "wrong". That's when I decided it was my chance to settle the score. So I told him to come stay at the Grand.'

De Meyer's voice made Eleanor jump. 'Did you know he had the diamond with him?'

He shook his head. 'I offered to fiddle his bill because he said after he'd paid for the liner ticket he was skint. He told me, though, it wouldn't be for long. He had something of massive value. I didn't care about that at first, I just wanted to pay him back for the beating I took for him. I didn't even mean to kill him in the beginning, but then I found out what he'd brought with him.' Thomas' eyes clouded over. 'I'd be rich for life. All those posh guests who thought they were so much better than me. I would be richer than any of them. Then I'd look down on them and order them around!'

She eyed him, half of her angry and half sad. 'So you killed him and ransacked his room. But you didn't find the diamond, did you? He'd already hidden it.'

He nodded, bitterness written over his face. 'When I couldn't find it in his room, I found out from the other clerk he'd sent a letter to you, so I figured he must have told you. Then you turned up at the hotel and I knew it couldn't be coincidence. You'd come to get the diamond.'

She opened her mouth to correct him, but then closed it. What was the point? He'd never believe her. 'And when you realised he hadn't, Thomas, you pretended you recognised me as an American film star you adored. And you used that as cover to feed Clifford and I false information as well as to find out what we were doing. Bravo! But I think we've probably heard enough.'

She nodded to Seldon, who produced a pair of handcuffs. Thomas shook his head.

'Oh, no. You can't arrest me? On what grounds? I didn't kill anyone. You've no evidence.'

Seldon's lip curled. 'How about how you just confessed to murdering Mr Eden and Mr Blunt in front of us all?'

Thomas looked at him mockingly. 'You mean just now? When I was forced to make a false confession under duress with a gun in my back?' He pointed at de Meyer's pistol. 'You think any court's going to convict me on that?'

Eleanor waved her hand at the rifle Seldon had wrestled off him. 'So what exactly were you doing up here with this?'

Thomas shrugged. 'My brother was murdered by Rex Franklin and him.' He pointed to de Meyer. 'I followed him up here to capture him and hand him over to the police.' He grinned and winked at Seldon.

De Meyer smiled lazily at Thomas, but his eyes were deadly. 'So, you were going to frame me for murder as you'd done with Mr Franklin?'

'And what about Blunt?' Eleanor said. 'Why did you kill him? Did he discover you were Hilary's brother and put two and two together?'

He didn't reply, but she could see from the look in his eyes that she'd hit the mark.

She shook her head sadly. 'You're right, you know, Thomas. There probably isn't enough evidence to convict you of either murder.'

She looked questioningly at Seldon, who shook his head.

Thomas grinned smugly.

She turned to de Meyer. 'Mr de Meyer, we had an agreement. I believe I've fulfilled my side?'

He patted his pocket. 'Agreed, Lady Swift.'

'Then you're happy to fulfil yours?'

He nodded, eyeing Thomas like a snake eyes a rabbit.

Thomas' smug grin faded. He looked from one to the other in confusion. 'What's going on? What agreement?'

Eleanor eyed him dispassionately. What little sympathy she'd had for him had been eroded by his callous attitude. 'You see, Thomas, I'm usually really rather impetuous. I try not to be, however...' She shrugged. 'But this time I decided to think ahead. Earlier today I took Clifford's advice and made a plan before coming here.' She glanced at Clifford, who inclined his head. 'I told Mr de Meyer that I would guarantee he'd have his employer's property in his possession this evening, if he also guaranteed that my husband's killer would be handed over. To justice.'

She glanced at Seldon this time, who nodded briefly. In the last few minutes the wind had finally abated and they no longer needed to raise their voices to be heard. Suddenly all she wanted was to be back home at Henley Hall with her staff. No, her family, because that's what they'd become.

'So, Thomas,' she said quietly, fixing him with a tired look. 'It's your choice.'

Thomas was still looking wildly from one to the other, but the confusion in his eyes had been replaced by fear. 'Wha-what choice?'

'You can confess to Detective Inspector Seldon here and take your chance with British justice. Or…'

'Or what?'

'Or you can stay here with the man you just confessed you were going to frame for murder. And take your chance with his kind of justice. I'm no expert, but I'd say a mercenary like him is going to do far worse things to you than that gang ever did.'

De Meyer said nothing, but the look in his eyes was chilling.

Thomas seemed close to hysteria. 'I'm… I'm not afraid of him.'

She shrugged. 'Well, you should be. I think he's even more ruthless, and merciless, than the people he works for.'

Thomas pointed at Seldon with a shaky finger. 'But you're a policeman. You… you can't leave me here with him!'

Seldon shook his head. 'Actually I'm on holiday and way out of my jurisdiction. If you confess to me now, I'd have the devil of paperwork and explaining to do. I'd rather you went with Mr de Meyer. At least then, I'll still get some of my holiday.'

Eleanor spread her hands. 'Your choice, Thomas.'

CHAPTER 44

'I wasn't sure you'd speak to me. Not after, well, everything.'

'Likewise, Grace.' Eleanor smiled and ordered two of the rather over-decorative cocktails Grace Summers had been drinking at their first meeting.

Settled in a quiet corner, the women stared at each other. Eleanor broke the silence. 'Did you know it was the desk clerk, Thomas, who killed Hilary and Blunt?'

'No, not at all,' Grace replied wide-eyed. 'I thought it was de Meyer. I knew he'd been sent by the mine owners and of course I knew of his ruthless reputation.' She hesitated. 'Lady Swift, I—'

'Eleanor, please.'

'Eleanor, Hilary and I, we…' Grace bit her lip. Eleanor's throat clammed up. 'Forgive my frankness, but I loved Hilary. I loved him from the day I met him all those years ago.'

Eleanor felt her heart twist. 'I see.'

Grace rushed on. 'But he… he never cared for me.' Her eyes filled up. 'He broke off our business partnership a few weeks after he met you because he feared you would jump to the wrong conclusion. That he and I were together as… lovers. The truth is… he only loved you.'

Eleanor shook her head to keep back the hot prickle that threatened to herald a rush of her own tears. Tears of relief. 'You must have hated me before you even met me.'

Grace nodded, and they both laughed.

'I'm not proud to admit it, Eleanor, but I knew Hilary came to England to try and win you back. And… and yet I followed him to try and finally turn his head before it was too late. That's what we were arguing about in his room that night.' Her cheeks coloured. 'He was horrified when he realised I'd followed him. He told me in no uncertain terms once and for all that he was not, and never had been, interested in me. I was so humiliated, I only went back to his room later that night to apologise. But he was dead. Oh, it was so awful.'

That's why none of the others pursued Grace for the diamond, Ellie, because they knew Hilary would never have given it to her.

She squeezed Grace's hand. 'What are you going to do now?'

Grace shook her head. 'I don't know. I think I really will stay in England and look for a job. There's nothing for me back in South Africa.'

Eleanor raised her glass. 'Here's to a new start.'

'Lady Swift?' a voice called from across the room. Rex Franklin, suitcase in hand, strode up to them. 'I owe you an enormous debt.'

He put the suitcase down and she shook his hand warmly.

'As I do you for saving Hilary's life six years ago.'

He smiled. 'Well, I saved your husband from the firing squad and you've saved me from the hangman. I'd say Hilary's debt is repaid. How about that?'

'Sounds perfect. So what's next for you, Mr Franklin?'

'I'm taking de Meyer up on his offer of a job.'

She tried to hide her surprise. 'Then I sincerely hope it works out for you. Do you know if Mr Longley has checked out yet?'

He nodded. 'He left about half an hour ago. Said there was nothing for him back in South Africa, so he was going to head to East London. Apparently, he's still got family there.'

See, Ellie, he was from East London, I thought so all along!

Franklin picked up his suitcase. 'See you around, Lady Swift. And you, Miss Summers.'

Eleanor watched him stride off, whistling. She turned back to Grace, but caught sight of Grimsdale beckoning to her, pointing towards the manager's office.

Grace laughed. 'It seems there's no rest for the wicked.'

Inside the office, Grimsdale took the chair behind the desk and waved Eleanor into the other. Clearing his throat, he scanned the pages of his notebook.

'Please excuse me imposing on you again, Lady Swift, but there are some elements relating to the events of this case which are not clear from your statement.' She blinked at his polite tone. 'First of all, how did you realise Thomas Williams killed Mr Eden?'

So that was Thomas' supposed surname? She gathered her thoughts. 'Almost to the end, I had assumed all, or at least most, of the people Clifford and I had identified as suspects were lying. However, having reached a dead end in our investigation, I remembered something Clifford said in passing. That even liars sometimes tell the truth. So I started again with the premise that all the suspects had indeed been telling the truth.'

Grimsdale laughed mirthlessly. 'That would be a first. Go on.'

'Well, Miss Summers said she left Hilary's room around nine forty-five in the evening on the night he died and he was still alive. Longley, Franklin and de Meyer, however, all stated that Hilary was dead when they went to his room. And Miss Summers also insisted he was dead when she returned to his room around midnight. So, if they were all telling the truth, it meant that Hilary actually died between nine forty-five and eleven twenty-five. That was the time Longley told me he and Blunt had found Hilary dead.'

Grimsdale grunted. 'So how did you narrow Mr Eden's time of death to...' He consulted his notebook. 'Between ten twenty and ten thirty?'

'Again I assumed all the suspects were telling the truth. Franklin told me he'd heard Hilary and Miss Summers arguing in Hilary's room around nine forty-five, something Miss Summers later confessed.'

'No to me,' Grimsdale muttered.

Eleanor ignored the interruption. 'Hilary had a row with Miss Summers and told her when she left his room at nine forty-five that he was going for a walk for half an hour to clear his head. That meant he would have been back somewhere around ten fifteen or thereabouts, certainly well before ten forty-five. Which meant that if all of our suspects were telling the truth, who could be lying?'

Grimsdale nodded. 'Thomas. Very impressive.'

She hid a smile at the unexpected compliment. 'Thank you, but what was less impressive was when we looked back over the other information Thomas had given us. It was only a theory that it might be Thomas at this stage, but we soon realised a lot of the information we'd amassed had been second-hand. We'd simply taken Thomas' word for it, rather than gone to the actual source. He was the one who asked the staff on our behalf each time. Anyway, from all this, we concluded if Thomas *was* the most likely suspect, then Hilary had probably returned to the Grand around ten fifteen and gone to his room. Thomas must have noted that no one saw Hilary return and decided it was his opportunity to act. So he went to Hilary's room and killed him around ten twenty—'

'The statement he gave to Chief Inspector Seldon agrees with that.'

'Good. Then Thomas made sure he was on reception duty at ten thirty and waited until no one was in the lobby, which happened to be ten forty-five. The night porter was in the hotel by then, but he was in the kitchen for a few minutes getting a Thermos for the evening. Anyway, Thomas then told you that was the time when Hilary had returned.'

'When, in fact, he was already dead.' Grimsdale scribbled something in his notebook.

She nodded sadly. 'Yes, but I was really only sure it was Thomas once Clifford and I had worked through all this last night before we traipsed up to the Chattri.'

Grimsdale stopped writing and looked up. 'And when did you realise Thomas was your husband's brother?'

'Ah, well, that was when my suspicions in the Metropole bar were confirmed. You see, Clifford and I realised we'd been jumping to other false conclusions.'

'Such as?'

'After Longley said it all made sense when he knew Hilary was going to Brighton, we seized on the notion it was because of Brighton's diamond connections. But then I thought, suppose it wasn't? Why else would he come to Brighton? De Meyer had already told me Hilary was brought up here, not London as I'd thought. So why would he go back to his home town?' She looked at Grimsdale.

'Because he had someone here who would help him,' Grimsdale replied thoughtfully.

'Exactly. When you're in trouble, it's not a case of *where* do you go, but *who* do you go to.'

Grimsdale nodded. 'Family, of course. If you have any.'

Eleanor nodded. 'And then I saw two men greeting each other like long-lost brothers in the Metropole bar last night and it struck me that Thomas might be Hilary's brother. But I wasn't sure until I remembered something Clifford had said, this time about a dye that some chap had created while actually trying to make a synthetic form of quinine.'

Grimsdale's eyebrows rose. 'And the relevance to Thomas being Hilary's brother?'

She shook her head. 'You have to understand, I was under immense stress. I really wasn't noticing things I'd normally notice.'

'Of course.' Grimsdale fiddled with the top of his pen. 'Lady Swift, I... I am sorry for the way I... I questioned you about your husband's death. You must also understand it did look very incriminating, you turning up here as you did. However, it was... insensitive of me.'

Eleanor blinked in surprise. Not only at his apology, but at how much it meant to her.

'I do understand, Inspector. And thank you. Now, where was I?'

'This dye?'

'Oh, yes. Clifford told me that it has since been used for many things, including hair dye. And that's when it hit me after seeing those two men in the Metropole. Thomas dyed his hair. Black. Once I'd pictured him with Hilary's much fairer colouring and added six or seven years, I could see the resemblance. As I said, I might have noticed it earlier, but I was not myself. Also Hilary never said he had a sibling.'

'Naturally.' Grimsdale scribbled a few more notes and closed his notebook. 'Thank you, once again, Lady Swift. I shall ensure all of Mr Eden's effects are packaged in line with the instructions given by Mr Cliff—'

She held up a hand. 'Actually, if you will note my new instructions regarding Hilary's effects? Please donate any you can to a good cause and do as you will with the others.'

'As you wish.' He coughed. 'I will, however, need—'

'My half of the wedding photograph,' she said quietly. 'Of course you do.' She pulled it out of her pocket and placed it on the desk.

Grimsdale put it in a folder. 'I do understand that the item is of sentimental value to you, Lady Swift. I will make sure both halves are returned immediately the trial is over, if possible.'

She shook her head. 'I do not need it returned, thank you, Inspector.' Her hand went to her other pocket, where the note she'd found at the Chattri was safely stowed. 'I have all I need.'

Grimsdale nodded. 'As you wish. The coroner's office has released the body, I mean Mr Eden. You might wish to make the funeral arrangements before you leave Brighton?'

'Oh gracious. Yes. Thank you.'

As she left the manager's office, Clifford gestured her towards one of the private sitting rooms leading off the lobby.

'Perhaps a moment to gather your thoughts, my lady?'

She sunk into a deeply upholstered wingback chair as the waiter appeared with two glasses of brandy. Clifford nodded and took the tray. 'A little fortification?'

She took the drink gladly. 'A glass of warm comfort, thank you. I'm pleased to see you're going to join me too. It's been a rough ride of a week for you as well.'

'Actually, my lady, if you feel sufficiently composed, I will take my leave for a moment?' Without further explanation, he left, closing the door behind him.

She was staring into her glass, distractedly swirling the amber liquid round when she heard the door open. Without looking up, she sighed. 'I'd like to make the funeral arrangements swiftly. Hilary deserves to be allowed to rest in peace as soon as possible, Clifford.'

'Most understandable, of course.'

She jerked her head up. 'Hugh!' The sight of his familiar blue wool overcoat and the matching scarf made her wish she could curl up in his arms, just for a moment. Her cheeks coloured. 'I mean, Chief Inspector Seldon. You probably only meant for it to be first-name terms while you were on holiday.'

He smiled warmly, turning his bowler hat in his hand. 'I'm not sure I did, actually. Besides, "Hugh" still has two more days' leave.'

She gestured for him to take the other chair.

'Thank you, Hugh. For everything you've done.' She bit her lip. 'But I don't want you to waste the rest of your holiday listening to me gushing on. Really, you've done enough.'

He smiled. 'Perhaps I will take you up on your offer to borrow Clifford's meticulous planning and organisation skills.'

She laughed. 'Just know that he is fiendish and more dogged about a schedule than a Jack Russell with a rat.'

He chuckled, a deep rich rumble that woke the butterflies in her stomach. She pointed to the other glass.

'Oh gracious, how rude of me. Clifford left one for you.'

'As Dutch courage? He is very perceptive.' He lifted the brandy, took a large sip and put it back down. She caught her breath as he reached out and took both of her hands. 'Please forgive me if it is wholly inappropriate, but would you permit me to attend Hilary's funeral? I just want to be there for you. In spirit, of course.'

'Only in spirit?'

He nodded. 'Just that. Until… until the time is right.'

'Oh, Hugh! That would mean the world.'

CHAPTER 45

As Clifford set the first of their cases down in the entrance, Eleanor closed her eyes and took a deep breath. She savoured the familiar smell of Henley Hall, beeswax polish mixed with delicious aromas wafting from the kitchen. She sighed. It was wonderful to go on holiday. But sometimes it was equally wonderful to come home.

She was brought out of her reverie by the postman at the open door. 'Good morning, Lady Swift. Sorry I'm so late this morning, had to stop and help Mrs Atwood.'

Eleanor opened her eyes. 'Oh dear, the pigs got out again, did they? I've had my share of trying to snare the ringleader amongst them myself.'

He looked shocked but tipped his hat and passed the post to Clifford, who had returned with another round of cases. Clifford held out two envelopes and a letter opener to her. She took them and rummaged in her handbag. 'I've still got two in here I didn't manage to open before we left for Brighton.'

As Clifford returned to the Rolls to collect yet more cases, she opened the first letter she'd been carrying around. *Ah, a lunch invitation from Lord and Lady Langham. That will be a treat, Ellie.* She smiled at the thought that she would ever have found such an aristocratic, older couple so delightful. The writing on the next envelope however made her shake her head.

Clifford materialised by her side. 'Nothing untoward, I hope, my lady?'

'No, thank you. I don't even need to open it. I know it is my old employer, Mr Walker, asking me for the fifth time to return to South Africa and resume setting up new tourist routes for him.'

'And, my lady?' There was an edge to his voice.

'And I shall write back this very afternoon to say I am happily settled here. At least for the moment.' She ended with a wink.

'Most heartening to hear. The ladies would have been very disappointed. Myself also.'

'Speaking of the ladies?'

'They will be with you presently. They have been caught up in trying to rescue one of Joseph's boots from Master Gladstone. Unfortunately, he made it all the way to the orchard before they realised.'

She laughed and opened the first of the new letters, wondering about its City of York postmark. 'Oh, Clifford.' She handed it to him. Scanning it, he nodded in approval. 'They have given your finder's fee for retrieving the diamond to the British Miners Charity as you instructed Mr de Meyer. Most gratifying.' He passed her the letter back.

She read it again. 'I'm so relieved. At least something good will come out of the whole affair.'

'Let us hope that this missive is equally positive,' he said, pointing to the last letter, clearly concerned by the Brighton postmark the envelope bore.

She ran the letter opener along the top and peeped inside. Biting her lip, she slipped it in her bag and turned to him. 'Erm… is that the last of the cases?'

'Just one more set, my lady,' he replied, scanning her face anxiously.

Before he could pry further, the sound of panting interrupted them.

'Welcome home, my lady,' Mrs Butters said as she bustled in, followed by Mrs Trotman and Polly. 'So sorry we weren't here to greet you. 'Twas Master Gladstone's naughtiness again.' She scanned Eleanor's face, just as Clifford had. 'We are so sorry about Mr Eden, my lady.'

Polly gave a loud sniff and wiped her eyes with the flap of her apron.

Eleanor shook her head. 'Ladies, I am fine, really. It might take a little time to process everything but I've made peace with Hilary and it's a great comfort knowing he's at peace now too. I can't tell you how much it meant to have you there at the funeral. I'm only sorry Clifford and I kept it all from you. It's just that I really wished for you to enjoy your holiday, which I hope you still did?'

'Rather too much, perhaps?' Clifford said. 'Certainly if any of the "Wanted" posters adorning every street lamp in Brighton as we left are anything to go by.'

Realising he was joking, Mrs Trotman chuckled. 'Long as them posters don't have photographs of us on the beach, we'll be alright, Mr Clifford.'

Mrs Butters and Polly stared at her in horror as she blushed, realising what she'd said.

'I think you're safe, Mrs Butters. I didn't notice any photographs of Henley Hall staff parading around in public in *homemade bathing suits*.' He winked as the three of them gasped.

'It's alright, ladies,' Eleanor said, crossing her fingers behind her back. 'I'm the only one who saw you. And frankly, next time, I hope you'll let me in on the bet. I would have loved to have joined you.'

Mrs Butters and Mrs Trotman nudged each other at Clifford's horrified sniff.

Polly giggled and then clapped her hand over her mouth. 'Paddling with the mistress must surely be against the rules?' she whispered.

'Definitely,' he replied.

Eleanor laughed. 'Well, let's see next time we're on holiday. Although, frankly, at the moment, I can't think of leaving Henley Hall for a long while. It's so very good to be home.'

'And 'tis our greatest treat to have you here, my lady,' Mrs Trotman said. 'I have your uncle's, his lordship's, favourite end-of-holiday dinner prepared in case you wanted to continue the tradition? But anything can be conjured up to suit, just as you wish.'

Eleanor sighed with delight. 'That sounds absolutely perfect, thank you. What is it?'

'Piddington Pudding, my lady. 'Tis tender beef with kidney and mushrooms in onion gravy, topped with rosemary dumplings, baked in suet pastry. Most important, though, 'tis in the shape of Piddington Hill, steeper on the left side as you look at her.'

Eleanor laughed. 'Uncle Byron's traditions never disappoint. And neither does your wonderful home cooking. I can't wait.'

Mrs Butters grinned at Eleanor. 'Not to mention, the more than generous slop of Mrs Trotman's famous homemade walnut whisky she always adds to the gravy.'

Mrs Trotman tutted. 'I don't slop it, thank you! 'Tis a precise and careful drenching.'

They left, chattering, Mrs Butters turning back to throw Eleanor a motherly smile. Soon Clifford reappeared with the last of the cases.

'Oh, Clifford, it is marvellous to be back.' She stared at the portrait of her uncle, Lord Byron Henley, that hung in the entrance hall. 'I have to marvel for the thousandth time what a wonderful mix of English eccentric and daring adventurer he was.' She bent down to ruffle Gladstone's ears and reluctantly accept the muddy boot he'd brought in from the orchard.

'It is greatly heartening to see how his legacy lives on, my lady.' He broke into a rare smile. 'In yourself.'

'Me! Eccentric, no?'

'Perhaps unorthodox is a more gracious description.' He shook his head. 'Solving murders? Rounding up pigs? Betting with one's staff? The suggestion one might visit the beach in' – he ran a finger round his collar – 'less than appropriate dress? I rest my case.'

'Ah, but you missed out staying up with them until all hours savouring Mrs Trotman's parsnip perry and cherry brandy as I fully intend to do tonight.'

His eyes twinkled. 'We are looking forward to it most heartily, my lady.'

Later that evening in the kitchen, with the delicious Piddington Pudding devoured and the five of them contentedly full, they were all enjoying reliving the fun the ladies had had in Brighton. Gladstone was snoring in his bed by the range, dreaming of his revenge on that pesky seagull, with the photograph of them all posing with him on the beach hanging above his bed in a silver frame.

'Clifford,' Eleanor said airily. 'I think we need a toast to the end of the holiday.'

'It was to be my next task, my lady. If I am able to move at all after Mrs Trotman's all too fine feast.' He rose and disappeared out towards the butler's pantry.

'Ladies, you are in for one last treat before we need to toe the line,' Eleanor whispered. 'Ready?'

As Clifford returned with a decanter of port and a small glass of cordial for Polly, he pulled up short in the kitchen doorway, wincing at their shrieks of laughter.

'Do come and join us, Clifford,' Eleanor said mischievously, waving him over.

'I am trying, my lady, but with my hands full, I am unable to protect my ears.' This set the rest of them off again. 'Perhaps the port should be foregone, my lady? I can only assume the ladies have shamefully attacked the wine cellar in my momentary absence.'

Eleanor wiped the tears from her eyes. 'They haven't had so much as a snifter.'

He set the tray down. 'What then is the cause of this outbreak of hilarity?'

As Eleanor reached under the tablecloth, the ladies held their breath. She passed him the envelope she'd slipped into her bag earlier.

'Ah,' he said quietly on turning it over and seeing the Brighton postmark. He pulled out the photograph inside. It was of him on the beach, soaked from the waist down. Trousers rolled to different heights and covered in sand, in his arms, a soggy Gladstone who was licking his face in gratitude for being rescued.

'Sand is a terror, my lady. It gets absolutely everywhere. In all the cracks.'

Like the ladies, Eleanor threw her head back and roared. 'Oh, Clifford, you are such a good sport.' She smiled fondly round the table. 'It's amazing, but despite what I said earlier, I'm already starting to feel restored enough to let you plan our next holiday. Besides, as Tolstoy helped us solve the final riddle of "something old", I flicked through your book of his quotes on the way back in the Rolls. And one struck quite a chord: "Happiness consists of living each day as if it were the first day of your honeymoon"' – she paused and then hurried on – 'and the last day of your vacation." Perfect, wouldn't you say?'

He nodded. 'Almost, my lady. However, for once I feel I must allow our American cousins precedence. I am minded to paraphrase the words of the writer and philosopher, Elbert Hubbard. "No woman needs a vacation so much as the woman who has just had one."' He dropped his hand to where Gladstone had pottered over. 'I sincerely hope your next holiday is less incident packed!'

'No, Mr Clifford! Master Gladstone's stolen the photograph of you on the beach!' Mrs Trotman jumped up as the bulldog disappeared out through the back door into the garden. 'He'll have hidden it to bury later afore any of us can get to him.'

'Mr Clifford, quick. You've the longest legs,' Mrs Butters cried, rushing round the table.

Eleanor clamped her hand to her mouth as her butler sat motionless, his legs blocking the way out to the garden. 'Regrettably, Mrs Butters,' Clifford said, 'I have mysteriously become welded to my chair. I fear it is the effect of too much Piddington Pudding!'

A LETTER FROM VERITY

Dear reader,

I want to say a huge thank you for choosing to read *Mystery by the Sea*. If you did enjoy it, and want to keep up to date with all my latest releases, just sign up at the following link. Your email address will never be shared and you can unsubscribe at any time.

www.bookouture.com/verity-bright

I hope you loved *Mystery by the Sea* and if you did I would be very grateful if you could write a review. I'd love to hear what you think, and it makes such a difference helping new readers to discover one of my books for the first time.

I love hearing from my readers – you can get in touch on my Facebook page, through Twitter, Goodreads or my website.

Thanks,
Verity

@BrightVerity

veritybrightauthor

veritybright.com

HISTORICAL NOTES

Brighton

There have been signs of habitation in and around Brighton for 250,000 years. By 1780 it was a small fishing village of 2000 people. Then, Doctor Richard Russell, a famous doctor from the nearby Lewes (the ladies take a day trip to the town) declared a dip in its seawater to be a cure for many ills and the rich and titled soon flocked there, including royalty. The population had reached around 150,000 by the time Eleanor, Clifford and the ladies visited and it was firmly established as the poshest seaside resort in the South of England.

The Grand

Built in 1864, the Grand was soon the most prestigious place to stay in Brighton and nothing had changed by the time Eleanor and Clifford arrive. Unfortunately, most people know the Grand nowadays as the hotel the IRA bombed in 1984 during the Conservative Party Conference.

'Something Blue', 'Something Borrowed', 'Sixpence in the hand'

In the mid 1780s George, Prince of Wales, was advised by his physicians to benefit from Brighton's fortunate climate and to try out the seawater treatments. He rented a small lodging house in Brighton. In 1815, he became the Prince Regent because his father, George III, had been deemed incapable of acting as monarch. Immediately he commissioned John Nash to transform his modest residence into a magnificent oriental palace, which became known as the **Royal Pavilion.** Nash made sure George's love of the colour blue was evident in the decor.

In 1837 Queen Victoria took the throne. She found the Pavilion too small and inconvenient for her family and sold it for £50,000 to Brighton council in 1850. The Pavilion was converted and opened to the public in 1851 as a venue for many different events and functions from fetes, bazaars and shows, to balls, exhibitions and conferences.

From 1851 to the 1920s the admission fee to the Royal Pavilion was sixpence. During World War I the Royal Pavilion was 'borrowed' as a hospital for Indian soldiers injured fighting in the British Army and later to treat wounded British soldiers.

'Something New' – a red herring

Royal Pavilion Gateway. To honour Indian soldiers who came to Brighton hospitals, including the Pavilion, Brighton erected a new Pavilion gateway. On Wednesday 26 October, 1921, His Highness the Maharaja of Patiala accepted an invitation to perform the ceremony of unveiling and dedicating the new gateway and presenting it to the Corporation of Brighton for the use of its inhabitants.

'Something New' – the correct clue

To honour those Indian soldiers who died at the hospitals in Brighton, including the Pavilion, a memorial, **the Chattri,** was erected in 1921. It was built on the spot where the Hindu and Sikh soldiers were cremated. It was officially opened by Edward, Prince of Wales, in February 1921, which made it only a few weeks old when Hilary would have hidden the diamond there. The only historical licence taken was to move the date the Prince of Wales visited forward a few weeks.

'Something Old'

Diamonds are one of the oldest minerals on earth. The oldest diamonds ever found were hidden in zircon grains and ranged from 3 – 4 billion years old. Normal diamonds can be as much as 1 billion years old. And for purists, Eleanor isn't quite right when she says, 'Poor Hilary, killed for a bunch of rocks' as diamonds aren't actually rocks.

Brighton and the Diamond Connection

Sir Bernard Oppenheimer, 1st Baronet (1866 – 1921) was a British diamond merchant with links to South Africa. He established a diamond-cutting works in Brighton in 1918. Being a philanthropist, he also established a scheme to train disabled soldiers from the Brighton hospitals, including the Royal Pavilion. They received six months' training, subsidised by the government, and then were guaranteed a job at a good wage in the diamond works. Sir Bernard Oppenheimer also made sure there was a clinic at the factory for the workers, many of whom were severely disabled. Hilary actually came to Brighton because his brother, Thomas, was there. Whether he intended to try to sell the diamond he'd stolen to Sir Bernard Oppenheimer, Eleanor will never know.

The South African Military Nursing Service (SAMNS)

In August 1914, South Africa formed a military nursing service to treat South African soldiers injured in the fighting. However, there was no fighting in South Africa itself, so the nurses were sent abroad, mostly to a military hospital in Abbeville, France, and another in Richmond, England. Eleanor ended up in Abbeville before returning to South Africa, but that's a story for another time...

ACKNOWLEDGEMENTS

To Maisie, our wonderful editor, and the rest of the team at Bookouture who made writing *Mystery by the Sea* such fun.